FALLING FOR THE ACCUSED

TRUE NORTH SECURITY BOOK 1

KRISTY MALLORY

HARBOURVIEW PUBLISHING

This book is a work of fiction. Names, characters, places and events are the product of the author's imagination or are used fictitiously. Any resemblance to actual events, locales or persons, living or dead, is coincidental.

Copyright © 2025 by Harbourview Publishing

Cover Design by Avery Kingston

All rights reserved.

No part of this book may be reproduced in any form or by any electronic or mechanical means, including information storage and retrieval systems, without written permission from the author, except for the use of brief quotations in a book review. If you would like permission to use material from this book other than for review purposes, please contact kristy@kristymallory.com.

CONTENT NOTES

This information is provided so readers can be aware of subject matter they may find disturbing. This list is based on classifications used by other authors and/or movie classification notes. The list is very high level in an effort to prevent "spoilers".

- Book contains coarse language
- Book contains sex/nudity
- Book contains discussions/descriptions of prior drug addiction, sex work, sexual assault, and violence
- Book contains references to death of a parent off page

It is my hope that this information makes your reading experience more enjoyable.

CHAPTER 1

*S*aturday

"THAT'S RIGHT, baby, ride me good."

Gemma Milani resisted the urge to roll her eyes and rocked her hips faster, squeezing her internal muscles around the cock inside her. The sooner she got Russell off, the sooner she could scrub his touch from her skin and get the hell out of here.

He finally let out a long groan, and his hips jerked spasmodically. Gemma waited until he started to go soft before sliding off him and grabbing tissues to deal with the condom. She insisted he wear them, but that meant she also had to clean him up after their encounters. Gemma was sure her humiliation added to his enjoyment. *Prick.*

"I'm going to shower." Gemma sauntered across the hotel room, unselfconscious in her nudity. Let him look. If everything went right, tonight was the last time he would ever see her naked.

As the hot water pounded down on her, washing away Russell's touch, Gemma inspected her body for marks. Russell liked his sex a little rough, and more than once he'd left bite marks and bruises in inconvenient places. She skimmed a soapy hand over her shoulders, down her breasts and hips, all the way to her ankles, probing and testing for bruises or abrasions. Some of the knots in her stomach unclenched when she was done. He'd gone easy on her tonight. Her arm was tender where he'd squeezed too hard, but her tattoos would cover any bruises there. He'd left one bite mark on her left breast, easily concealed by clothing. Many nights had been far worse. One night early in their agreement, he'd whipped her and left her back bleeding. She'd had to find a way to bandage it and keep it hidden from her mother, which hadn't been easy. Covering bite marks and bruises with makeup was easier. Not that she'd had much choice in the matter. The money Russell was paying her gave him license to do almost anything he wanted.

That ended now. Her mother's life insurance money had finally come through, paying off the house they had shared. There had been enough left over to take care of debts left behind after her long illness. As Gemma had learned when Helen was ill, Canada's health-care system might pay for all the necessary treatments, but her mother's disability payments weren't enough to replace the lost income when her mother couldn't work. Gemma's job as a housekeeping attendant at Harbourview Casino Resort didn't come close to covering all their bills, especially since she was also going to school part-time, which meant tuition, books, and no time to pick up extra shifts.

A year ago they'd missed their third mortgage payment, and the bank had threatened to foreclose on the house. Completely desperate, Gemma had done the only thing she could think of to make some money in a hurry. She'd reached out to a man she'd never wanted to see again, Russell Molloy.

The deal she had struck with Russell had been simple: He would loan her the money to get caught up on their mortgage payments, and he'd continue providing her with a monthly allowance large enough to pay their bills. Gemma would provide him with sex.

Gemma stepped out of the shower and wrapped a towel around her long hair. After drying off, she smoothed some of Harbourview's complimentary body lotion over her skin, enjoying the subtle citrus scent, using the time to calm her nerves. Her terminating their arrangement was not going to go over well. Russell was a control freak—and a cruel one. He loved to arrange for their encounters to take place at Harbourview. The fact she worked there added to his satisfaction. He'd told her more than once he got a kick out of thinking about her cleaning up the very room she'd fucked him in the night before.

God, she hated him. In the years since she'd left the life, getting into rehab, quitting sex work, and going back to school, Russell had transitioned from being a mid-level dealer to a major player in the Vancouver underworld. He gambled regularly at Harbourview, where he was known by name and frequently given his rooms free of charge. In her role in housekeeping Gemma never had to deal with him, until she went to him last year to beg for money. She never should have done it, but she'd seen no other options. Losing the house her mother had worked so hard for, while her mother was suffering from a terminal disease, was something she would not let happen. So she'd buried her emotions and done the only thing she could think of.

Russell was sitting up on the bed, drinking a beer, when she came out of the bathroom and began pulling on her clothes. Her skin crawled as he watched her every move, the calculating way he was staring at her making her feel like a piece of meat. Gemma hurried to tug on her jeans and pull her sweater over her head. Everything about this made her feel used, and she couldn't wait to be free of him. Owing Russell anything meant he acted like he owned her, and she wanted her life back. During her mother's illness, dealing with the doctors and nurses, dealing with her own grief, she had been able to compartmentalize her actions. Since her mother had died, every minute waiting for the insurance policies to come through so she could be rid of Russell had been agony. Tonight, that would finally end.

Gemma slipped on her boots and stood near the desk, closer to the door in case she needed to make a run for it. Russell was wildly unpredictable. If he was bored with her, he wouldn't care—he'd take the money she was offering and their agreement would be over. If she pissed him off by rejecting him, there was no way to know how he would react. He was still lounging naked on the bed, so if he tried to come after her, she was ready. "There's something I wanted to talk to you about."

"I don't pay you for talk."

Unless it was dirty talk. Russell loved it when she talked dirty during their encounters. "That's what I want to talk about. My mother's life insurance paid out this week. I settled the final outstanding debts yesterday, and I have enough to pay you back too. So our arrangement is over." Gemma held her breath, waiting for his reaction. Russell laughed. He actually *laughed* at her, and she struggled to control her temper. Letting him see she was mad would give him too much power. "There's nothing funny about this."

"That's where you're wrong, little girl. The fact you think you have any say in this is hilarious. I'm extending the terms of our arrangement. I have a business partner in town who prefers his girls not be junkies. You're just his type. I want you to meet with him tomorrow night, be real nice to him. Show him a good time."

Fury rose in Gemma at his nerve. Bad enough she'd had to fuck him for money; now he wanted her to go back to having sex with strangers? There was no way she was going to let that happen. "That wasn't part of our deal."

The smirk he wore was taunting, but his eyes were what made Gemma's blood run cold. They were reptilian, deadly. "I'm changing the deal. You belong to me now. You'll do what I want, when I want . . . and who I want you to do."

White-hot anger made her want to scream at him, and she struggled to hold on to her self-control. Russell had no real power over her. Not anymore. "I won't do it. I told you, I don't need your money anymore. Our deal is over."

"Maybe this will change your mind." Russell turned on the television, and with a couple of taps on his phone, a video began playing.

Everything felt like it was in slow motion. There she was on the screen, naked, blindfolded with her hands bound behind her back. A man's hand gripped her hair while he roughly thrust the head of his penis into her mouth. Gemma's gag reflex kicked in, and she swallowed hard, fighting the memory. Even without being able to see the man's face, Gemma recognized Russell. It wasn't uncommon for him to restrain her during their meetings.

This must have been recorded during one of their "dates" a few months earlier. Anxiety clawed at her. How had she not known he was recording their encounters? And what was he planning to do with these videos?

The video continued, morphing into another scene where she was splayed out on the bed and he was whipping her. The sound of leather hitting skin made her flinch. The video quality was good, even though the camera angles were odd. Not that it mattered. Every frame was easily recognizable as her performing a wide variety of sex acts.

"You recorded us?" Gemma struggled to keep her fear and revulsion from showing. Self-loathing overwhelmed her, as well as disgust that she'd been stupid enough to believe Russell would live up to his end of their deal. Allowing Russell to see how scared she was would only make it worse. Russell fed on fear. She did not want to give Russell more power over her than he already had. Right now there might still be some way to get out of this without doing what Russell wanted.

"Every single time. You didn't think I was going to give you all that money for nothing more than a little pussy, did you? You're not that good," he jeered. "I needed an insurance policy of my own, for the day you thought you could end our arrangement. So now you have a choice."

"A choice?" Gemma echoed. A trickle of cold sweat ran down the centre of her back, her palms were clammy, and it took all her strength to not let Russell see her tremble. Being a paid companion was bad enough, but this could ruin her future. Naked photos and revenge porn were embarrassing, but this was hardcore BDSM. This video could destroy her.

Russell's smirk morphed into a grin that could only be described as evil. He was in control, and he knew it. Having power over people was his drug of choice, and Gemma's hatred of him burned white-hot, fighting the fear that she might be forced to give in to Russell's blackmail.

"Of course you have a choice. You can keep fucking me, and any other person I tell you to, or..."

Gemma swallowed again, forcing the bile back down her throat. She could not let this video out. She'd lose her job at Harbourview, and she would never land a decent nursing job if people saw this. "Or what?"

"Or I'll upload all the videos to every porn site on the internet. This is the highlights reel. I have hours of you performing for the camera. I'll make sure to keep copies to email to prospective employers once you graduate too. You've got, what, a month left to finish your nursing degree? How many hospitals do you think will want to hire the hottest new porn star on the internet?"

Gemma's legs wobbled, and she reached a shaking hand to the wall to hold herself up. Dear god, what had she gotten herself into? Russell wasn't only threatening to humiliate her; he could ruin her entire future. She didn't hide from her past, but it was one thing for people to know she used to be a sex worker and addict. It was entirely different if they were confronted with vivid images of her splashed all over the internet. Or worse, winding up in their email inboxes.

Gemma grabbed the trash can just in time to heave her dinner into it. The noise of her retching drowned out the video still playing in the background as well as any sound Russell was making. He grabbed her hair and jerked her head up from the can, and she cowered back from him, anticipating a blow from his fist. It never came, but his pleasure at her terror was unmistakable.

"I need to go clean up. You think about what your decision will be while I'm in the shower. Oh, and clean that mess up." Russell pointed at the can. "After all, we wouldn't want to leave it for some poor housekeeping attendant to find, would we?"

CHAPTER 2

Matt Foster, detective constable with the Vancouver Police Department, looked down at the victim and swore under his breath. The body had been left in the bathtub of a Harbourview hotel room with the shower running. The pruning of the skin was visible testimony for it having been there for an extended period. The running water had washed away most of the blood from the scene and had likely destroyed any trace evidence. Since the water had been warm, determining time of death via temperature was unlikely. The coroner would have to find another way. Someone had turned the water off, and he needed to determine how much of the scene had been disturbed.

"Who found the body? And who turned off the water?" His partner, Rebecca Sutton, addressed the cluster of people standing in the hallway, all employees of Harbourview. Matt stepped out of the bathroom to join her. Rebecca's boyfriend, Nate Quinn, was the assistant manager at Harbourview. Nate was a former military police officer and had done everything possible to protect the scene. Matt was thankful that Nate had the law enforcement background he did, or investigating this death would have been even harder. Hotel room crimes were always a challenge. Too many people in and out, no detailed cleaning in between.

"We found the body. I'm Tim Wilton." Matt noted that a man in his mid-twenties dressed in a Harbourview security uniform spoke. Rebecca turned her phone toward him, recording to make sure they caught everything and could go over it again later if there were any questions. The man pointed at himself and an older woman who was crying quietly and appeared to be a housekeeper. "I turned the water off, wearing gloves. Maybe I shouldn't have, but I thought if I could prevent any further evidence from being washed away, that would be a good thing."

Matt couldn't fault the man's logic. "Why were you with house-keeping? That's not standard procedure."

"The room was supposed to be empty," the housekeeping employee said. "Checkout is eleven. I knocked and opened the door at one. I heard the shower running, so I left. I came back about an hour later, and the shower was still running. That's when I called security. We're not supposed to go into a guest's room alone when it's occupied."

"We'll need your name for our report, ma'am," Rebecca said, speaking softly to the housekeeping attendant.

"This is Wanda Bailey," Nate said. "She was following a new safety policy we put in place after there was an incident last year. One of our staff was assaulted by a drunk guest. This keeps everyone safe."

Not a bad policy. Definitely helpful in this circumstance. Matt turned back to Tim. "Tell me what you saw when you walked in."

"After Wanda called me, I knocked on the door before I entered the room. I could hear the shower running, and I called out, and no one answered. I thought maybe it was a prank, a guest who left the shower running for kicks. It happens sometimes. The bathroom door was open about halfway. I did not touch the knob, I didn't have to. I pushed the door open with my hand about here. I didn't have my gloves on yet." Tim held his hand halfway up one of the doors lining the hallway. "As soon as the door swung open, I could see that the curtain was down and the person was in the bottom of the tub. Considering the condition of the body, I assumed he was dead. I didn't touch him. I pulled on my gloves to turn off the tap. I didn't touch anything in the bathroom except the tap. As soon as the water was off, I backed out of the bathroom and radioed my supervisor and surveillance. They called you. I stayed here with Wanda and made sure no one else came near the room. Then Nate arrived, and we waited for you to show up."

The rattle of wheels drew Matt's attention as three people in coveralls rounded the corner at the end of the hall, one of them pushing a gurney for the deceased. A tall, lean woman with short red hair and an angular face led the group: Lena Anders, the coroner, had arrived along with two crime scene technicians.

"I think we have everything we need for now," Rebecca told Tim. "We may have follow-up questions in the future. If so, we'll coordinate through Nate." Tim and Wanda, wearing identical looks of relief, hurried past the crime scene team down the hall.

"What am I looking at, Officers?" Lena gazed at them expectantly. Matt had worked with her more than once, and he liked her no-nonsense approach and her dedication to following the evidence.

"Our vic is a white male, early fifties. He appears to have been stabbed multiple times, and the body may have been mutilated. But you're the expert, so take a look, and tell us what you think," Matt said.

Lena raised a curious eyebrow. "Appears to have been mutilated? Want to expand on that?"

Matt sighed. "His genitals have been cut off."

His statement sobered Lena. "Well. That explains why Sex Crimes is here. Do we have an ID on the vic yet?"

"That's the other reason we're here. It's Russell Molloy. Vice was investigating him for drugs, prostitution, you name it. We were investigating him for sexual assault and sexual coercion."

"And someone stabbed him and carved him up," Lena said slowly. "Sounds like you'll have no shortage of suspects."

No kidding. The list of people who might have wanted Russell Molloy dead was a long one. "We've got a lot of work to do. You'll let us know when you're going to do the autopsy?"

"Of course. I'll make sure you get a report of everything we find." Lena ushered the forensics team into the room to start collecting evidence.

"What about surveillance video?" Rebecca directed this question at Nate.

"I already have our team pulling everything from last night. I'll take you there now to see what they found."

As Nate led them through the meandering back halls of Harbourview, Matt turned the scene he'd witnessed over in his mind. Russell Molloy was a terrible human being who preyed on anyone younger, smaller, and weaker than him. They had to hope that the resort surveillance cameras had recorded something that would help them narrow down the suspect pool. Harbourview typically had a high-quality system, even in nongaming areas, which made him cautiously optimistic that they would find something helpful when they reviewed the videos.

Nate ushered Matt and Rebecca into the surveillance viewing room, where they were greeted by Les Carpenter, Harbourview's head of surveillance, someone Matt had worked with several times before.

"It's been a long time." Les greeted Matt and Rebecca with a tired smile. "I wish we were getting together under better circumstances."

"Working on a Sunday? That's not normal for you, is it?" Rebecca asked Les.

"Finding a guest murdered in their room isn't normal either. Nate asked me to come in and make sure we found every possible camera angle." Les seated herself in front of the workstation and began pulling up cameras for them.

"Here's what I have so far. The victim checked in around nine last night. About ten minutes after he checked in, a woman knocks on the door. She has her hood up, so I don't have a good shot of her arriving. Shortly before ten, room service delivers two meals. I pulled the bill—someone ordered a steak, the other dish was a pasta dish. Several bottles of beer were delivered at the same time."

"The coroner can use that to help establish time of death. We'll need a copy of that food order," Matt said.

FALLING FOR THE ACCUSED

"You'll have it," Les said before continuing. "There's no further activity in or out until two in the morning. Here." Les slowed the video down to half speed, allowing them to see a woman exit the room. The video wasn't high enough quality to get a good look at her face, but she had long black hair hanging down her back. She also carried a bag in one hand. She walked quickly down the hall, wasting no time. Almost like she didn't want to draw attention to herself.

"No one else entered or exited the room until Wanda attempted to clean it at one this afternoon."

"Any idea what's in the bag? And are there any better shots of her before she leaves the property?"

Matt's phone buzzed while Les was pulling up the next piece of video. He glanced at the screen, not wanting to miss anything important that Les might find. He switched focus when he saw Lena's name flash on the screen.

> Lena: You need to see this. Found it on the vic's phone.

There was a video file attached to the text. Matt hit play. A woman with long dark hair was performing sex acts with an unidentified man. Excitement built as he recognized a tattoo on the arm of the man. It was Russell Molloy, and this video might be nothing, or it might be motive. He looked at the blurry image from the surveillance video and compared it to the video playing on his phone. The poor quality of the surveillance video made it hard to tell. Both figures were slim, with long dark hair. It *could* be the same person.

He tapped Rebecca's shoulder. "Lena just sent this to me. Think it's the same woman?"

Rebecca watched a short bit of the video, frowning. "Maybe. Hard to tell without a better surveillance image. The camera angle looks off. I'm thinking he was using a hidden camera. She didn't know she was being filmed."

Matt watched another minute. The video moved too fast between images for it to be one recording. It had to be clips from several different sex acts edited together. Some of the scenes were filmed close-up and with the woman directly facing the camera, while a few were taken from an odd side angle. Rebecca was right—the creator had been using a hidden camera for at least some of the recordings.

"She did a pretty good job keeping her head down as she was leaving." Matt turned his attention back to the video monitors when Les started speaking again. "Even our elevator cameras didn't get much more than the top of her head, until she went out back and tossed that bag into the dumpster. We've secured it, so you can search it at your convenience. The good news is, we've had some issues with people climbing into our dumpsters and getting injured. We installed cameras out there to deter them. Here's the best shot we have." Les pulled up a still image of a woman's face.

Matt studied the picture. She was around thirty, with long dark hair that looked wet in the surveillance photo. That made sense if she'd come from killing Russell in his shower.

It was the same woman who was in the video Lena had sent them. She looked vaguely familiar, but he couldn't put his finger on why.

An indrawn breath was followed by a whispered "Fuck."

Matt turned away from the monitor to find Rebecca looking curiously at Nate, who was staring at the image on the screen.

"You know who she is?"

Nate nodded. "I do. Her name is Gemma Milani. She works in our housekeeping department. I've known her for years and helped her get the job here. There has to be a mistake. There's no way she could kill anyone."

CHAPTER 3

Having clocked out, Gemma reached to grab her purse from her locker. She was exhausted, and all she wanted to do was go home. After leaving Russell's room last night, she had hardly slept before she had to report for work at seven. Sundays were always busy, and this weekend the resort had been fully booked. At least she had been assigned to a different part of the hotel than the suite she had shared with Russell. It had allowed her to block out the terror she felt and ignore the dread eating at her.

Movement blocked the light coming from the hallway window, and Gemma looked over to see Nate walking towards her. His mouth was turned down in a frown, and the dread that had been following her since last night hit her again. Nate made a point of connecting with the staff, but he usually did it by sitting down in the break room and sharing coffee with them. He rarely came to the locker area. Why was he here now?

"Hi, Nate." Gemma forced a smile and avoided looking directly at him, hoping this would be quick. Even the random drug tests that Harbourview required would take more energy than she had right now.

"Gemma." The heaviness and regret in his voice had her eyes

meeting his. The pain there made her suck in a breath. What was going on? He couldn't know about Russell, could he? Russell hadn't already sent out the videos, starting with her current employer?

"What's wrong?" Fear gripped her, making it hard to speak.

"I need to talk to you before you go home. Let's go to the conference room."

Gemma walked ahead of Nate towards the conference room, her stomach rolling. The conference room had to mean that this meeting would involve more people than her and Nate. Usually when he needed to talk to her privately, they met in his office. The conference room was reserved for the kinds of meetings that led to discipline, or even termination. That didn't bode well for her.

In the five years she had been at Harbourview, she had tried to be a model employee. She'd never failed a drug test, she was never late, and the only time she'd taken off had been to care for her mother and to grieve. Even her hookups with Russell weren't against the rules; employees were allowed to stay at Harbourview. This could mean only one thing: Russell had sent the video to Harbourview.

Humiliation burned in her gut, warring with the panic building inside her. Was she going to get fired? As they approached the frosted-glass doors of the conference room, Gemma could make out two shadowy figures at the table. A representative from HR and a union rep for her, probably. She clutched her purse tighter.

When the door swung open, Gemma pulled up short. Two uniformed Vancouver police constables broke off their conversation and stood up from the table, studying her as she froze in the doorway.

"These two officers have some questions for you. I'll be right outside." Nate exited and closed the door behind him.

Gemma recognized the blond female officer immediately as Nate's girlfriend Rebecca, from pictures she'd seen in his office. That tenuous connection eased a bit of her anxiety.

The other officer was a whole different matter. Memories of a life she'd left behind came rushing back as Gemma surveyed the man standing beside Rebecca. Years earlier, Matt Foster had been one of several officers involved in a raid on a drug house where she'd been. He was built like a bear, at least six four, with wide shoulders and bulging muscles. He wore his brown hair cropped close to his head, and when she'd first met him, he'd been clean shaven. Now he wore a full beard that gave him a rugged look. His eyes were blue, with laugh lines around the corners that made her think he had a sense of humour.

What she remembered most about him was that he'd treated everyone arrested that night like they were human. He'd been kind and polite, which was more than she could say for most of the other officers involved in that bust. She'd been arrested and charged, although the charges were later dropped, but she'd never forgotten him.

Her biggest question was what they were doing here. She hadn't broken any laws. Russell might have the power to get her fired, but she couldn't see how anything she had done was a police matter.

Gemma crept closer to the table where the officers sat. She'd heard there was a commotion of some kind in another part of the resort today. Since it hadn't been in the section she'd been assigned to, she'd ignored it and continued with her job. Police at the casino were a common event, especially after a busy Saturday night. Gemma had learned a long time ago to ignore them.

"Please have a seat. Miss Milani, correct? I'm Constable Rebecca Sutton. This is my partner, Constable Matt Foster."

Rebecca and Matt sat down as Gemma pulled out a chair across from them.

"What's this about?"

Rebecca set her phone on the table between them and tapped the screen. "We have some questions for you regarding an ongoing investigation. Tell us, do you know a man named Russell Molloy?"

Gemma schooled her features into a blank mask, even as her anxiety had her digging her nails deeper into the soft leather of her purse. Why were they asking her about Russell? If this had anything to do with his criminal enterprises, she had no connection with them. She knew nothing. "Yes." She'd learned a long time ago to only answer the questions the police asked and not volunteer any extra information.

"How would you describe your relationship with Mr. Molloy? Are you friends? Or is it a business relationship?" Rebecca continued.

Fuck. How best to answer this? Technically the selling of sex in Canada was legal, even if the purchase of it wasn't. If she told the police the whole truth about their relationship, and they hauled Russell in for questioning, he would be pissed. He was already threatening her. She could only imagine what he would do if the police got involved. She'd seen the aftermath of people who tried to get the law involved where Russell was concerned. Burns, broken bones, overdoses. One or two people had simply disappeared. She wasn't stupid enough to tell them the truth. "We have a personal relationship."

Rebecca raised an eyebrow. "Can you define that? Is he your uncle? Godfather? Lover?"

"Lover." Gemma managed to spit the word out without gagging on it.

"When was the last time you saw him?" Matt's voice matched his size: deep and rumbly, his tone curious, not hostile. Something about him made her want to open up and tell them everything about her problems with Russell, but that was futile. They would never believe her, and even if they did, nothing would happen. It was her word against Russell's, and too many cops were on Russell's payroll. She'd learned that the hard way before. She wasn't going to risk trusting the police again.

"Last night."

"This will go faster if you answer the questions fully." Matt was trying to sound friendly, harmless. Gemma knew it was all part of his job. She'd been arrested more than once in her younger years, and she wasn't going to fall for the "I'm just trying to help you" act. Matt was better at sounding sympathetic than some other cops she'd dealt with, which meant she needed to keep her guard up. She couldn't give in to the temptation to trust him.

"I'm answering the questions you ask." Gemma kept her own voice level, not letting any emotion creep in as she spoke. If they sensed any weakness, she'd never shake them off. It had been a long time since she'd had to talk her way out of trouble with the police. She was out of practice, and she was tired, but her safety depended on getting out of this mess without implicating Russell. These two would get nothing from her.

"What time did you see him? Did you spend all night with him? And where were you?"

Gemma swallowed a laugh. They were learning. Rather than get her to answer one question at a time, they'd ask her a bunch instead. Another way to try to trip her up. "We met up at about nine last night. Russell had booked a room right here at Harbourview. It was about two when I left. I had to work this morning and wanted to go home first," she added. Sometimes it helped to throw them a bone. She needed them to get to the point, fast. She still hadn't figured out how to handle Russell's threats. The clock was ticking, and he was not a patient man.

Matt took a page out of the file folder in front of him and slid it across the table to her. "Is this you?"

A chill made the hair on Gemma's arms stand up, and she resisted reaching for the photo in case she couldn't keep her hands from shaking. The image didn't show her face, but she recognized the jeans and sweater she'd worn the night before. "Yes, that's me. Again, what is this about? Is there a problem? Is Russell accusing me of something? Do I need a lawyer?"

Gemma hoped not. Lawyers cost money, and after she paid Russell back, that would still be in short supply. She did have the house, but the liquid cash from the life insurance policies only went so far. If Russell had done something . . . She wouldn't put it past the bastard to have planted drugs on her and then reported her to the cops. He hated cops, though. No, if he'd done that, he would have done it anonymously. Besides, if she got in trouble, he lost his plaything. Something else had to be going on.

Both officers ignored her questions. As Rebecca flipped through the folder Matt had taken the photo from, Matt was typing on his phone. Suddenly the sound of Russell telling her to suck his cock filled the room.

The wave of nausea that hit Gemma when the video started was only slightly less intense than the one from the night before, and she was grateful that she had skipped lunch today. Humiliation burned at the knowledge other people had seen these videos, and she bit the inside of her cheek to keep herself from reacting. She sat straighter in her chair, holding her head high. Gemma had worked hard to no longer feel shame about her past. She hadn't even been ashamed about her arrangement with Russell, until last night when she found out he'd recorded their sessions without her knowledge. Now, though, there was no denying that shame was her overriding emotion.

Matt gave her a sympathetic look, and somehow that made it even worse. "Can you confirm this is you in the video?"

"It's me."

"Did you know you were being recorded?" Rebecca spoke softly, and her concern sounded genuine.

When Gemma met her eyes, she almost burst into tears. She so wanted to believe that the care and concern reflected there were real, that they would believe her if she told them the truth. That would never happen, though. Police never believed sex workers when they complained about being assaulted. Her own experience told her that too often they were the ones doing the assaulting.

"If he filmed you without your permission, that's against the law. You could press charges."

Gemma snorted. "That would be a very bad idea. No, I didn't consent to being filmed, but he did it, and I found out last night. So whatever he's told you I did, just tell me."

"How did you find out about the video? You must have been angry." Rebecca's sympathy sounded so authentic, Gemma almost believed her.

Gemma sighed. There was no point in avoiding the subject any longer. They had the video, so they already knew some of it. "Russell and I had an arrangement. He paid my bills, and I provided him companionship on demand. Last night I told him I wanted to end that arrangement. He used the video to convince me to change my mind. How did you get the video?"

The only explanation that made sense was that Russell had followed through on his threats and had sent the video to Harbourview. Nate would have called VPD. And if Nate had seen it, how many other people had seen it? Fresh embarrassment rolled through her at the thought of Harbourview management seeing her fucking Russell. Even if Nate didn't fire her, if the videos were released, it could damage Harbourview's reputation.

"Was Mr. Molloy asleep when you left last night?"

The abrupt change of subject confused Gemma.

"No, he was in the shower. He showed me the video, then told me he was going to clean up and we could talk when he was done. I needed some time to think before I talked to him again, so I left."

The night before, she'd been terrified as she left Harbourview. The shock of the video combined with Russell's threats had been too much to deal with. She'd spent most of the night trying to find a way out. She still didn't have an answer, but she was not giving in to Russell's threats.

"Do you still intend to end your agreement?" Rebecca continued.

Gemma shook her head. "I haven't decided. He's threatening to post the videos on the internet. I don't want that. He also wants me to agree to have sex with a friend of his. I don't want to do that either. That's why I left. I had to think about what I could do about Russell."

Matt and Rebecca exchanged a look Gemma couldn't interpret.

"How did you feel when you found out about the recordings? You must have been angry." They were tag-teaming her again, with Matt repeating the question Gemma had ignored when Rebecca asked it.

Gemma resisted rolling her eyes at the ridiculousness of the question. Any woman would have been pissed about being recorded like this. "Of course I was angry. I'm still angry. He recorded our most intimate interactions. He gets off on humiliation, so this is simply another way for him to enjoy himself."

"What was in that bag?" Matt tapped the photo of her walking down the hall, carrying her trash bag full of vomit. Not her finest moment, but it didn't even crack the top ten of her worst either.

"When Russell showed me the video last night, I threw up. He insisted I clean it up and dispose of it. I took it with me and threw it in one of the dumpsters when I left."

"And Russell was fine when you left?"

As this question sank in, things began to fall into place. Something had happened to Russell, and he was accusing her. Had one of his business rivals assaulted him? Or maybe one of the sex workers he "managed." How typical of him to use this opportunity to add extra pressure to her. Accuse her of hurting him, then agree to drop the charges and leave her indebted to him. He might have even arranged his own beating to set her up.

"Russell was absolutely fine when I left. Whatever he says I did, it's a lie. Let me talk to him. I'm sure we can sort it all out." How she was going to get out of this without giving in to Russell, she would figure out later. For now, if he was trying to get her arrested, she needed to talk him out of it. Any arrest could lead to her parole being revoked, going back to jail, being expelled from nursing school, losing her job. It would destroy her future.

Rebecca was shaking her head. "That won't be possible."

"Please ask him. He'll talk to me."

Matt locked eyes with her, his expression grim. "He won't be talking to anyone. Russell Molloy is dead."

CHAPTER 4

As Gemma's eyes widened, Matt noticed they were brown, rich and warm, dotted with golden flecks. In Russell's videos, she'd been wearing heavy, dramatic makeup. This afternoon it was like she was a different person, wearing the housekeeping uniform of a polo shirt and black pants, with almost no makeup. Even with minimal makeup, her long dark lashes drew attention to her eyes, and her lips were a deep, lush pink. Her silky-smooth skin had a golden glow that reminded Matt of a beach at sunset. Gemma Milani was a beautiful woman.

At the news about Russell, colour drained from her face, and her body went rigid in her chair. She was either an excellent actress, or Russell's death had truly shocked her. With the evidence they had so far pointing to Gemma being the killer, Matt was leaning towards the former. He was trying to keep his emotions out of it, as the idea that she was playing them was depressing. He wanted to believe her. Her story was as sad as it was compelling.

Nate had briefly filled them in on her background after their meeting in surveillance. Once Nate told them that Gemma had been an addict and sex worker, Matt's memory had kicked in. She'd been arrested at a bust he helped with back when he was a patrol cop. It had been years ago, and she'd changed a lot since then. Her cocky exterior hid a vulnerability that reminded Matt of why he did this job. He couldn't help every woman who was being exploited, so he helped as many as he could in the memory of his mother.

Gemma wrapped her arms around herself and shrank away from the table. She lowered her head, her long hair hiding her face. "Russell is dead?"

Her voice wavered, making Matt wonder once again just how good of an actress Gemma Milani was. Survival on the streets often meant playing a role of some sort, and from what Nate had said, Gemma had spent a lot of years living on the streets of Vancouver. To have survived that long said a lot.

"Was there an accident? How did he die?"

Throughout their interview, her voice had been strong, even cocky at times. Now it was husky with emotion. She hadn't loved Molloy, had she? Nothing would surprise Matt. He'd seen too many women love the men who abused them.

"We believe he was murdered."

Rebecca delivered the news matter-of-factly, making Gemma's head snap back up to meet their eyes. She could no longer hide her fear, yet another ambiguous clue. Was she afraid because she had killed him, and was worried about being caught? Or was she afraid that whoever killed Russell might come after her too?

"His body was discovered this afternoon, here at Harbourview," Rebecca continued. "Would you like to amend your account of your activities last night?"

The look Gemma shot both of them was frosty. "Do I want to change my story? No. Am I free to go?"

Matt had been dreading this question. Under the Canadian constitution, they were allowed to detain her briefly without arrest while they investigated Molloy's murder, if they suspected she might be involved. The key word was *briefly*. If they couldn't come up with some hard evidence quickly, they would have to release her or arrest her. Arresting her too soon could hurt the case. Releasing her meant risking her destroying evidence. If she actually was innocent, charging her with murder would be all over the media, and even if she was cleared, the cloud of suspicion would follow her around forever. "Not yet. There are still things we have to look into."

Her perfect lips turned down in a tight frown. "Am I under arrest?"

"No. Right now we are detaining you until more facts come to light about any involvement you may have in the death of Mr. Molloy." Matt caught Rebecca's nod towards the door, a silent request for a private conversation. "You'll need to remain here until further notice. We're going to take custody of your phone, but we will not search it without a warrant." Matt held out his hand for Gemma's phone.

Gemma stared at his outstretched hand and cradled her purse closer to her body. "No, I don't think so. I want a lawyer."

Matt sighed. They'd pushed her a step too far. There was no way he wanted to leave her alone with her phone while he and Rebecca left the room to discuss next steps. If she'd lied to them about her arrangement with Russell, or if there was any other evidence on her phone, he couldn't risk her deleting it before they got their warrant. "You are not under arrest; a lawyer isn't necessary." *Yet.*

That got him a snort and an eye roll from her. "Like I haven't heard that before. I should have asked for a lawyer the minute I saw you two. I'm *rectifying* that mistake now." She looked over at Rebecca. "You're not the only one who knows how to sound important."

Matt bit his cheek to prevent himself from snickering. He loved Rebecca like a sister. Her battle to climb through the ranks of an old boys' club meant that she was constantly having to prove her worth to them. Sometimes she took that battle into suspect interviews, using language designed to trip up people who had less education than she did. Gemma's snarky remark made it clear that wouldn't work on her, no matter what her background was. Unfortunately, Gemma's hostility was going to make everything harder for all of them.

"I'll ask Nate to sit with her while we talk." Rebecca rose and left the room. After a moment Nate came in and sat next to Gemma.

As Matt joined Rebecca in the empty hallway, he overheard Nate asking Gemma how she was doing.

"I'd be a whole lot better if your girlfriend and her partner would get off my back."

Matt pulled the door closed, making it impossible to hear the rest of their conversation. Gemma's frustration about their questioning her was one more piece of a puzzle that wouldn't come together. She didn't sound guilty. She treated them with suspicion, but based on the sketchy bio Nate had provided, and his memory of her arrest, she'd been on the streets a long time. Long enough to have developed a distrust of all things law enforcement. He couldn't blame her. He'd seen more than one of his fellow officers abuse their power and get off with next to no penalty, if they were punished at all. Her suspicion of them was understandable.

"What do you think? Do we have enough to arrest her?" In his opinion, they couldn't make that decision until they had a few more facts around the case. Like an estimated time of death, for one thing. If Lena could prove Molloy was dead *before* Gemma left his room, the case would be a slam dunk.

Rebecca blew out a frustrated breath. "I hate this. We have a dead body, and video telling us no one else came or went from his room. Ergo, she must have killed him. Her story is something else, though. I want to believe her. Molloy was a complete bastard. Their arrangement, and his blackmail to keep her under his thumb? That's definitely something he would do. So even if she did kill him, was she justified? Was it self-defence, and she's afraid we won't believe her? Dammit, the thought of victimizing her again after what Molloy did to her makes me sick, but killing him wasn't the answer."

Matt grunted an agreement, trying to think of a scenario where Gemma wasn't the killer. If it had been self-defence, she might have some injuries of her own. He hadn't noticed any visible ones. That didn't mean there weren't any. The first thing he'd looked at were her hands, searching for any sign of cut marks from knife slippage when she stabbed Molloy. *If* she stabbed Molloy. If Molloy had even been stabbed. Until Lena did the autopsy, they were assuming cause of death was blood loss due to stabbing. He was no expert, so maybe something else had killed him, and the stab wounds and mutilation had occurred postmortem.

Matt's phone rang, Lena's name on the caller ID. *Good.* With any luck, Lena would have something for them to work with. He didn't want to get tunnel vision and assume that motive and opportunity equalled guilt when it came to Gemma Milani. He didn't want her to be guilty at all. Only because he had sympathy for her situation, though. There was no other reason he wanted her to be innocent. Nope. None. "Foster here."

"Matt, I've done as much as I can here. We've collected all the evidence possible from the tub with the body still in it, so I'm taking it back to the morgue. The rest of the team will stay behind and finish processing the room."

"Do we know anything yet? Cause of death? Time of death?"

There was mumbling in the background as Lena answered a question from one of the evidence technicians. "I can't say for sure until I do the autopsy, but it does look like cause of death was exsanguination, probably from the wound in his neck. There was no sign of the vic being restrained, so I believe the genital mutilation happened postmortem. The shower made a mess of the scene. I'll need to run a tox screen to see if he was incapacitated before the wounds were inflicted. If he was, that could change my opinion on the timing of the mutilation. There's no way that was done while he was conscious."

"So what you're saying is we don't know anything we didn't know a few hours ago. Nothing that will tell us if our prime suspect actually killed him or if we should be looking somewhere else." *Damn.* Matt had really hoped Lena would have something they could use to direct the investigation. On the surface, Gemma was still a solid suspect. The surveillance video was not going to be enough to convince the Crown prosecutor; they needed more evidence. The sex tape was motive, but pinning Russell's murder on Gemma felt wrong, if he was being honest. Russell had exploited her. Even if she'd gone into their arrangement voluntarily, recording her without her knowing was sleazy as well as illegal. He didn't want a murderer to go free, but he wouldn't be sad if they found something to exonerate Gemma.

"Sorry, nope. Autopsy will be tomorrow morning. If we find out anything between now and then, I'll let you know." Lena ended the call.

Matt pocketed his phone, considering the facts they had so far. What evidence they had made Gemma a suspect, but any good defence lawyer would poke a million holes in the case.

"I heard. No new information. So we have circumstantial evidence that Gemma was the last person to see Molloy alive, and she had motive, means, and opportunity." Rebecca ticked each point off on her fingers. "Given Molloy's line of work, his enemies list is a long one, although no one else seems to have had the opportunity. I also don't want to give our suspect any additional time to dispose of evidence, if she is guilty. We need to search her home for the clothes she was wearing last night, and for any proof of her arrangement with Molloy. We need to access her phone before she deletes anything. We have to arrest her," Rebecca said with resignation. "It's the only way to preserve potential evidence."

Everything about this felt wrong to Matt. Instinct told him they were missing something, and that moving too fast could jeopardize the case. On the other hand, he didn't want his sympathy for Gemma to affect his judgement either. "Our case is thin."

"We'll build a better one. We can't do that if we lose any more evidence. I don't want to do this any more than you do, so what other options do we have?"

Matt had been asking himself the same question and had come up empty every time. "None. Let's go arrest her."

CHAPTER 5

Gemma looked up as the door swung open, and her stomach dropped. The grim expressions worn by both officers told her everything she needed to know. The door had barely closed behind them when Rebecca began speaking.

"Gemma Milani, you're under arrest for the murder of Russell Molloy." Her tone was flat, matter of fact. The words hit Gemma like a hammer. Rebecca continued informing her of her rights, and Gemma tried to listen over the buzzing in her ears. She had done everything possible to turn her life around. Being arrested again had never crossed her mind, especially considering she was innocent. At least her mom wasn't still alive to see this happen. That relief was followed immediately by the realization that she had no one else. There was no family to call for help; she was truly on her own. The loneliness was overwhelming.

Rebecca moved to stand behind her and urged her out of the chair, securing handcuffs around her wrists with a click that rang loud in the quiet room. The sound broke the silence, and Nate reacted first.

"You've got to be kidding," Nate growled. "There's no way Gemma did this."

"Not now, Nate. This has nothing to do with you," Rebecca said firmly.

Matt grasped her elbow gently, steering her towards the door. The warmth of his fingers was a stark contrast to the chill of the room. Her skin felt tight all over, and she struggled to hide her fear. All her emotions were too close to the surface, and letting her feelings out might give the police more ammunition to use against her. She would not let them see her lose control. Nate's defence warmed her, helping her focus her attention on what needed to happen right now. "It's okay," she told him. It wasn't, but there was nothing he could do to stop the inevitable. She needed to get a grip on her emotions and start thinking about what would happen next. The booking process, the questions, hiring a lawyer. Spending the night, or many nights, in jail. The dehumanizing process that was the prison system. She needed to focus on getting through that.

"Where are you taking her?" Nate demanded.

"She'll be booked down at the station, then remanded to Alouette until court is in session tomorrow," Matt said as he nudged Gemma towards the door.

"Don't worry about me, I'll be fine." Gemma shrugged, not wanting them to see how scared she really was. "I won't be able to work for a while. Can you take care of letting people know?"

"You're worried about missing some shifts?" Nate asked incredulously. "You're being arrested for murder. Work is the least of your worries right now."

Gemma forced a grin, hoping bravado would get her through the next few hours. "I need to have a job to come back to when they figure out I didn't do it."

Nate gave her an exasperated nod. "I'll take care of it. Do you have a lawyer you can call?"

A lawyer? Not one she trusted, and definitely not one with murder experience. Her previous lawyers had all been public defenders who handled mostly drug-related crimes. "Don't worry about it. I'll figure something out." Without another word, Matt and Rebecca pushed her through the conference room door and led her out of Harbourview.

MATT OBSERVED Gemma through the two-way glass, noting how even as she projected an air of unconcern, her knee was bouncing under the table. Rebecca sat across from her, peppering her with questions, but Gemma remained stubbornly silent. At the same time, her fingers were laced together in her lap, her knuckles white from the pressure.

She was nervous, scared. Was it because she was guilty and upset about being caught? Or because she was innocent? Guilty or innocent, the prospect of going to prison for up to twenty-five years had to be terrifying.

On the ride down to the station and through the booking process, Gemma had refused to answer any of their questions. She hadn't said anything at all. If she didn't talk soon, they would have no choice except to stop questioning her and send her to the women's correctional facility for the night. Her first court appearance would be tomorrow morning, and then the lawyers would get involved. This was their best chance to get her to tell them anything.

Matt studied her, trying to sort out his own mixed-up emotions. This should be easy: investigate murder, arrest suspect, testify if required, move on. He and Rebecca mostly handled sex crimes. Even so, they'd dealt with enough murders that nothing should surprise him anymore. What was it about Gemma Milani that was getting under his skin?

He shook off his thoughts as Rebecca came out of the interview room.

"She's not talking. Says she'll get a lawyer tomorrow and won't talk before then. I'm calling for transport." Rebecca dragged her hand through her hair, a sure sign of frustration. "I hate this. Molloy was a bastard who victimized her and countless others. Nate is pissed that we arrested her, but with the evidence we've got, what choice did we have?"

None. They only had until tomorrow morning to pull together enough evidence to convince the Crown to prosecute. Considering this was a murder case, Gemma would have to request a release hearing or she would be held until trial. The court would likely detain her. Just in case the court actually considered releasing her, Matt and Rebecca needed to be prepared to demonstrate why Gemma should be kept in custody. Right now he was struggling to find a good reason to keep her locked up until her trial. They probably had a few days before any lawyer could arrange a release hearing; still, they needed to be prepared in case it happened sooner.

The entire case was bugging him. Something felt off, and he couldn't figure out what. It was almost too easy. Gemma came across as smart and savvy, and she'd straightened out her life. She was too clever to kill Russell in a time and place with lots of cameras and where she would be the only suspect. She could have done it in a fit of rage, but her surprise at finding out Russell was dead had seemed real.

Matt returned to his desk to start building their case. He pulled up Gemma's criminal history on his computer and began assembling a profile for the Crown to use in court. Despite her being charged with murder, there was always a possibility a sympathetic judge might release her until trial. After a Supreme Court ruling a few years earlier, most defendants were released before trial unless charged with extremely violent crimes. Even violent offenders often qualified for bail if they had good lawyers. None of which should matter, except the thought she was innocent nagged at him. He hated the thought of her being locked up for months until trial, all because she couldn't afford a good lawyer or post bail. Worse would be if he and Rebecca got it wrong.

Matt scanned Gemma's criminal history. Arrested for drug possession. Arrested for theft under $1,000. Arrested for solicitation. All of the arrests were for similar charges, covering a period of years. They ended abruptly more than five years prior. Matt kept digging, finding no other arrests, no mention of Gemma at all, not even as a person of interest in other cases.

After her last arrest, the judge had sentenced her to six years of probation after she had petitioned the court for leniency and proved she had completed a drug-treatment program. She still had a year left on her probation, and she'd stayed out of trouble until now.

Matt looked up from the computer as Rebecca led Nate to her desk. "What's he doing here?" Matt didn't want Nate's personal feelings compromising the investigation into Gemma. Matt was certain there was nothing romantic between Nate and Gemma; Nate was head over heels in love with Rebecca and had been since the week they met. Nate clearly felt protective of Gemma, and that could be a problem if it caused a conflict between him and Rebecca. Nate had too much integrity to keep evidence from them, but the perception of a conflict of interest could hurt the case. And he didn't want to see this case come between Nate and Rebecca—they were too good together.

"We need to start interviewing her friends and family," Rebecca said. "Nate came down to see if he could do anything to help. Since he's not family or legal counsel, he wouldn't be allowed to see her even if she was still here. Might as well get his statement. I'm taking him to interview room three."

Matt followed Rebecca and Nate into the interview room, sitting across from Nate. Matt took the lead on the questioning. Truthfully, Rebecca shouldn't be involved in questioning Nate at all, to prevent any defence attorneys from accusing them of having a conflict of interest. Matt turned on the recorder on his phone, noting the date, time, and location. Documenting the entire interview would make any evidence obtained usable in court. "What is your relationship with Gemma Milani?"

"I'm one of Gemma's managers at Harbourview Casino." Nate's posture was stiff. He kept his tone neutral and his answers short and professional. His body language signalled he wasn't happy about this, but he wasn't going to sabotage their investigation.

"How long have you known her?"

"Almost seven years."

"Did you meet her at Harbourview?"

"No."

Matt wasn't surprised by Nate's short answers. Before joining Harbourview's security department, Nate had been an army military police officer for a number of years. He understood how the game worked and wouldn't volunteer any information until asked directly. Especially if that information might hurt Gemma. The questions Matt was starting with were to document for the record the information Nate had already given them while they were at the casino. Unless Nate changed any of the answers, this would go smoothly.

"How did you meet Ms. Milani?"

Nate frowned and paused before answering, clearly choosing his words with care. "I do a lot of volunteer work with youth charities. I met her through one of them."

Matt let out a long sigh. "This would go faster if you just told us your history with her, you know."

"I could, but then I wouldn't get to watch you try to figure out what to ask me." Nate grinned, breaking the tension, and Matt relaxed. They'd been friends for almost two years; this told Matt they would still be friends when the case was over. Probably. He hoped so. He and Rebecca had been partners for a long time, and they hung out off duty. If this case damaged his friendship with Nate, that might end.

"What can you tell us about her history with Russell Molloy?"

Nate leaned back in his chair and glanced away from Matt and Rebecca before he answered. His poker face was near perfect, but Matt detected a hint of resignation when Nate began speaking.

"When I met Gemma, she'd been on the streets, working as a sex worker to support her drug habit, since she was a teenager. I met her a few times through my volunteer work. At that time, Russell was dealing, and she got a lot of her drugs from him. Sometimes she paid with sex rather than money. He was never her pimp, although I think he tried once or twice. Until today, I didn't think Gemma had seen him in at least five years." Nate scowled, his eyes reflecting a combination of anger and sadness. There was a hint of hurt too. "I know she's not using again, because she drug tests regularly as part of her employment agreement. I have no idea why she was involved with Russell again."

Matt wasn't about to share Gemma's reasons with Nate. If she'd wanted him to know, he would know, and now everything she'd told them was part of their investigation. "How did Gemma come to work at Harbourview? You said she needs to take drugs tests as part of her employment contract?" Random drug tests were against the Canadian Charter of Rights unless a company could prove a safety risk. Housekeeping at Harbourview would not qualify. Was she being violated at work as well as by Russell?

Nate leaned forward, an earnest look on his face. "The drug tests are a condition of her probation. Not violating her probation is a condition of her employment. If she failed a drug test, we'd find out. Gemma was brought on board at Harbourview through a program I helped develop. I work with a lot of people trying to overcome addictions and housing insecurity. Getting stable employment is often next to impossible for them. We launched a project where we would hire people who were coming out of rehab, or being placed on probation, and give them that employment. We place them in positions such as housekeeping, maintenance, or the kitchens, where the regulator is willing to approve us hiring people with criminal records. Gemma was one of those people." The passion in his voice echoed in every word. Nate was proud of this work.

Matt had known Nate did a lot of volunteer work. He had no idea Nate had taken his advocacy this far. Nate had never talked about this before, and Matt was curious why he hadn't. Matt would have been happy to support Nate's efforts. "How is the program working? And was Gemma a good hire?"

"It has been a big success. Most of the people we hire stay for at least eighteen months, and in this job market that's a miracle. Very few of them wind up relapsing or reoffending. Gemma has been with us for a lot longer. After she had been with us for a year, she was eligible for our education support program, and she finished high school. Then she enrolled in nursing school. Everything was going so well for her until her mom got sick."

With every word, Nate was painting a picture of someone who had turned her life around, and who was building a bright future for herself. Getting off the streets. Finishing rehab and not relapsing.

Going back to school. Any one of those things was hard, and she had done all of them. "You said her mom is sick?"

Nate shook his head. "She was. Helen Milani passed away a few months ago. Cancer. Gemma has been dealing with a lot ever since her mom was diagnosed. She seemed to be handling it okay. She never missed work, and from what little she told me, she's on track to graduate from nursing school in a couple of months. None of this makes any sense."

"She had her reasons." Even without pulling her financial records, Matt would bet he would find that Gemma and her mother had run out of money, and Gemma had gone to Russell for help.

Nate's information was filling in the blanks from Gemma's story. Gemma had approached Russell out of desperation, and Molloy had taken advantage of that. Had that been enough to make her kill him? None of this improved their case. If anything, it made Gemma a sympathetic defendant. The VPD brass was not going to be happy that they had arrested her if he and Rebecca couldn't find more evidence and the Crown refused to file charges. The brass hated that; they felt it made VPD look incompetent. The Crown hated it, because it wasted their time. Matt was starting to think they had made a mistake. Nothing in her history said she was violent. They had motive and opportunity, nothing more. Matt had seen better cases get dismissed, and the forensics testing wouldn't be finished for weeks. He needed to wrap this up and start talking to other potential witnesses. Innocent or guilty, they needed more evidence.

Nate slumped in his chair, arms crossed over his chest. "I wish she'd talked to me. Maybe I could have helped, maybe we wouldn't be here if she had. I honestly thought she'd left that part of her life behind."

Rebecca reached over to squeeze his shoulder, breaking her silence for the first time. "She's going to need all the help she can get now. She's going to need a friend."

Matt hid his smile at Rebecca's move. She was all assertive and tough with her colleagues, hiding her softer side that she let out with him and Nate. She and Nate were going to be okay.

Nate rose from his chair and grasped her hand. "I'll see you at home when you have time to take a break."

Envy rolled over Matt as Nate and Rebecca communicated wordlessly, their love strong enough to overcome the conflict between them. Nate's easy acceptance of Rebecca's long hours and erratic schedule was something most cops didn't get unless they married another cop. The last woman Matt had tried dating had broken up with him after he'd missed yet another event because of a case that needed his attention. He'd tried telling her that crime didn't recognize weekends, holidays, or plans. She'd wanted none of it. It had made him hesitant to think about dating again.

Matt turned his attention back to the task in front of him. Somehow they had to convince a judge to give them a search warrant for Gemma's house before court tomorrow morning, and if she was guilty, they needed to find some corroborating evidence inside it. There was no time to waste.

CHAPTER 6

Gemma sat on the bunk in her cell at Alouette Correctional Centre for Women, brooding over how badly her life had gone off the rails. She'd been here before, when she'd been arrested for drug-related charges. Those charges had been nonviolent, and she'd been out the next day. Now, charged with murder, she sat in the maximum-security wing of the prison, facing up to twenty-five years behind bars if she was found guilty.

Terror gripped her when she thought about that future, so instead she focussed on getting through the next couple of days. When Constables Foster and Sutton—she could no longer think of them as Matt and Rebecca; they were *not* on her side—had come back into the conference room and placed her under arrest, she'd been resigned, but Nate had been horrified. He'd honestly believed that somehow this would turn out to be a misunderstanding and she would be released. Gemma knew better. The evidence they had that pointed towards her killing Russell was bad. Besides, who was going to take the word of a sex worker and former drug addict? Especially one with a motive, which she'd given them unwittingly by telling them about Russell's blackmail.

A corrections officer banged on the door of her cell. "Milani! Your lawyer is here." Gemma froze. What lawyer? She hadn't called anyone. This had to be some kind of mistake. No one knew she was even here except the police, and Nate.

The guard unlocked the door and slid it open. "Don't just sit there. He's waiting for you."

Gemma stood and let the guard usher her down a hallway. It was almost ten at night on a Sunday. What lawyer would come all the way out to the prison that late at night? And who was he that he had the influence to bend the rules to see her this late? Her experience with lawyers had all been through Legal Aid. Considering she now owned the house she had shared with her mother, she doubted she would qualify for Legal Aid, and she had no idea who was reputable. Her plan had been to show up at her bail hearing and use the court-assigned lawyer on duty, then worry about finding her own lawyer later. She would have plenty of time for that. She was accused of murder. The court would never give her bail. She was going to be inside until they realized she was innocent and arrested someone else, or until her trial. And if her case went to trial? Well, that led back to being terrified of spending her life behind bars. Best not to think about that.

With a start, Gemma realized they were standing in front of one of the secure rooms inmates used for meeting with their lawyers. *Focus, girl.* Inattention over the next few days could be a disaster. She needed to pull herself together.

The guard pushed the door open for her. "I'll be right outside." The door was locked behind her.

Gemma had never seen the man sitting at the table. He had short, spiky blond hair and wore a suit jacket and shirt, collar unbuttoned, no tie. Gemma estimated he was close to her age, and everything about him screamed wealth. Who was he? And why was he claiming to be her lawyer?

The man looked her over, taking in the prison-issue grey sweatsuit and white sneakers. Gemma might have felt self-conscious except there was nothing sexual about it. It felt more like he was checking for injuries, that he was worried about her. He motioned for her to take a seat across the table from him.

"I'm Brent Walker. I'm sorry I wasn't here sooner."

Brent Walker? The name didn't give Gemma any more clues as to why he was here, or who hired him. Based on his clothes and fancy shoes, she couldn't afford whatever he charged.

"I think there's been a mistake. I didn't hire you. I haven't hired anyone yet." Even as she said the words, she took the chair across from him, hoping against hope this wasn't a mistake. She *did* need a lawyer.

"I'm here as a favour to a former client, whose husband is a good friend of mine. They tell me you're in a bit of trouble."

A former client? Gemma couldn't think of anyone she knew who would help her like this. "I don't understand. Who called you?"

"Leslie Carpenter. Head of surveillance at Harbourview? She told me she was a friend of a friend."

Les Carpenter? Gemma knew who she was through the grapevine at work and a few conversations with Nate. Nate was friends with Les, so maybe Nate had asked for a favour. Not that it mattered. Brent was here now, and he was prepared to help her. "I know who she is. And you could say I'm in trouble. They think I killed someone." Gemma kept her head up, refusing to give in to the shame that saying the words out loud for the first time caused. She wasn't guilty. That was what she needed to focus on.

Brent simply shrugged. "I know right now the police are recommending charges, and the Crown is looking at second-degree murder. They may try to up it to first degree because of the genital mutilation, but I'll fight that. What I need to know if I'm going to represent you is whether you intend to plead guilty?"

Genital mutilation? Gemma gripped the edge of the table. "He was mutilated?" she asked, hating how weak her voice sounded. She might have hated Russell, but mutilation?

Brent gave her an appraising look. "Pretty badly, from what I hear. I haven't seen crime scene photos yet. You didn't answer my question: How do you plan to plead? Do you want me to get you a deal?"

"I didn't do it!"

Brent's nod was slow. "I believe you, although you wouldn't be my first client to plead guilty to a lesser charge to put a problem in the rearview mirror. The trial could drag on for years. You may be denied bail because you're deemed too dangerous to release. If you're found guilty? Minimum ten years, up to twenty-five. Are you ready to spend half your life in jail?"

Fear clawed at her, and Gemma bounced up from the table and began pacing the small interview room. "I never thought I'd wind up back here." Her arms hugged her body protectively. She was grateful her mother wasn't alive to see this. Her mom had taken a second mortgage on her house to pay for private rehab. Gemma had promised to stay clean and change her life. And she'd done exactly that. Even during the worst of her mother's illness, when Gemma had wanted nothing more than to disappear into the numbness of drugs, she'd resisted. She'd attended meetings, she's gone to work and to school, and she'd done whatever was necessary to help her mom and keep her word. She was not going to go down without a fight now.

She turned and met Brent's eyes. "The longest I've ever been locked up is a few months, and that was enough. I can't plead guilty to something I didn't do, not when it will mean ten years or more, if I'm lucky. I fought too hard to straighten my life out. My mom sacrificed so much. I can't let her down."

Brent pointed at the chair she'd been using. "Then sit back down and tell me in your own words what happened between you and Russell. I need to know everything."

The next morning, sitting in court, Gemma resisted the urge to wipe her palms on her pants. Brent had met her at the courthouse this morning and handed her a garment bag, telling her that her house was still being searched, so he'd had his assistant pick her up clothes for court. The pants and matching blazer she'd pulled out had designer labels, and the accompanying blouse was probably worth one of her entire pay cheques from Harbourview. She didn't dare wipe her sweaty palms on them before she returned them. At least she looked like she could afford a fancy lawyer like Brent. It was a far cry from the last time she'd been in court. Then, her jeans had been threadbare, and her hoodie three sizes too big, hiding a body that had been emaciated by drugs.

Gemma noticed Matt Foster the minute he came into the courtroom, talking with his partner and the Crown counsel. Embarrassment heated her cheeks. She held her head high and forced herself to project confidence. When she caught him looking at her appreciatively, the warmth spreading through her had nothing to do with embarrassment. Gemma ignored her body's reaction. Something about this man, this cop, broke through her defences and made her pulse race. Which was a problem. She knew cops couldn't be trusted, so her body's inexplicable reaction to Matt was freaking her out. Gemma had had her fair share of experience with cops over the years, from being arrested to being coerced or extorted for sex in order to avoid arrest. Now Matt was the cop who had arrested her, who was trying to get her sent to prison for a crime she didn't commit. Her attraction to him was nothing but inconvenient biology, and the sooner she remembered that, the better. She broke eye contact and intentionally turned her attention back to Brent.

The bail hearing proceeded similarly to others she had been involved in, with the Crown asking for her to be remanded into custody until the trial due to the violence of the crime. Rebecca Sutton took the stand to testify about the body discovery and their subsequent search for evidence. Gemma listened intently, trying to puzzle out how someone else could have killed Russell. The who and why didn't matter. Things would not go well for her if someone couldn't figure out how another person got in the room. The Crown logged the Harbourview surveillance tapes as the primary proof that no one except Gemma had had the opportunity to kill Russell.

Then it was Brent's turn, and he needed to prove to the judge why she should be released. Gemma sat straight in her chair, trying to project confidence. After Rebecca's testimony, how could the judge let her go? Brent seemed like a good lawyer, and she trusted Nate, but her overriding emotion was terror, and it was getting harder to have any hope.

"Your Honour, my client is not a flight risk. While she does have prior convictions, they are all from years ago, and are drug related. As you can see from her probation records, she has been drug-free for over five years. She has a steady job that she never misses, she owns her own home, and she attends school several nights a week. She poses no risk to the community, and keeping her in custody until her trial would violate her charter rights. As well, I have several high-profile members of the community ready to stand as surety for her."

He did? Gemma stayed immobile to ensure her surprise did not show on her face. Who was Brent talking about? Gemma had been prepared to put up her home to guarantee her appearance in court. Now that the insurance had paid off the remaining debt, the house was worth seven figures thanks to Vancouver's ridiculous real estate market. A surety meant someone else with significant assets was willing to vouch for her. And she didn't know anyone like that.

The judge pursed her lips and stared down, her gaze raking over Gemma from head to toe before meeting her eyes. Unlike the judges from so many of her other court appearances, this judge didn't radiate condemnation or contempt for Gemma, and a small spark of hope flared inside her chest.

"I don't like releasing murder suspects, Mr. Walker, especially ones accused of violently stabbing and mutilating their victims. If I were to agree with your petition, the conditions would be onerous. Who is offering to provide surety?"

"Her employer, Harbourview Casino, will offer any financial guarantee. I have a sworn statement from the CEO, Jules Roberts, to that effect. As a personal surety, Nathan Quinn, Harbourview's assistant manager, will stand on behalf of the employer. I have a statement from him as well." Brent handed the judge several documents.

Gemma laced her fingers together to keep them from shaking. She understood Nate offering a personal surety. He knew her, and he trusted her. She'd never let him down. For him to have convinced the CEO of Harbourview to offer financial security was shocking. Jules

Roberts was engaged to the billionaire majority shareholder of Harbourview, and Gemma had never met her in person. Her throat grew tight, and she blinked furiously to keep her tears from falling. No one except her mom had stood up for her like this before.

After scanning the papers and conferring with Brent, the judge nodded. "I'm satisfied that the accused has sufficient ties to the community to not be a flight risk, and that she does not pose a threat. Now let's discuss conditions."

The judge's words made it impossible to hold back the tears that she had been fighting, and two lone tears of relief rolled down her cheeks as the tightness in her chest eased. The rest of the hearing passed in a blur as Brent and the Crown argued about the conditions they felt the judge should impose. Gemma didn't care. The sheer relief coursing through her, combined with the adrenaline from being in court, left her unable to focus on anything except the fact she would be getting out.

After a final warning to Gemma to be on her best behaviour, the hearing ended and she was free to go. When Brent led her from the courtroom, Nate was waiting. A relieved smile creased his face, and he pulled her into a brotherly hug.

Gemma wallowed in the comfort of his hug for longer than she normally would have allowed herself before pulling away from him. It had been a long twenty-four hours, and while she was happy to be free on bail, the charges still hung over her head. Proving someone else had killed Russell was going to be difficult. She didn't trust the police to clear her, which meant she would have to advocate for herself. The biggest problem was that she didn't even know where to start.

"Did you arrange this? Hiring Brent, and getting Harbourview to act as surety? Why would they agree?" Gemma could not believe that the CEO was willing to take that kind of risk, not on her.

Nate shrugged. "I called in a few favours. You've been an exemplary employee, and when I sat down and explained it to the leadership team, they agreed to support you. Les suggested Brent, and he agreed to take your case. And speaking of favours, you need to come by the casino later this afternoon. I have someone you need to meet. You should come with her." The last statement was directed at Brent.

Come by the casino? All Gemma wanted was to go home, shower, and sleep for a week. Could she even go home? Or was VPD still searching her house? Another thing to worry about. "Can it wait? I'm exhausted." She wasn't ready to face her colleagues at Harbourview yet. The last time many of them had seen her, she'd been led out in handcuffs. She was incredibly grateful that management had supported her, but her emotions were raw.

Nate was shaking his head before she finished speaking. "This can't wait. We need to find out who killed Russell before the evidence disappears and VPD builds a decent circumstantial case against you. The people I want you to meet can help do that. Come by around three and we can figure out what the next steps are."

CHAPTER 7

"I still can't believe the judge released her," Rebecca said as they walked into the squad room after returning from court. "I know Nate vouched for her, but she's charged with murder."

Matt didn't bother responding. Rebecca's frustration over the Supreme Court's position on bail was one he often shared, especially when judges released repeat offenders who were at high risk to reoffend while they waited for trial on pending charges. Their work in sex crimes had them run into this exact situation frequently, and it infuriated him when men they were certain were guilty were released to do more harm.

Gemma's release felt different. The fact her prior record was all for drugs and solicitation offences made it unlikely she was a danger to anyone else. Part of him still wanted to believe her when she claimed to be innocent—evidence to the contrary notwithstanding. There was something about her; she'd been through a lot. She made him think about his own past and wonder whether things might have been different if someone had stood up for his mother the way Nate had stood up for Gemma. He wasn't going to admit that to Rebecca, though. She didn't know about his mother; no one did.

Matt appreciated Nate defending Gemma and arranging for the

very talented, very expensive Brent Walker to be her defence lawyer. Pointing that out to Rebecca without her knowing why he felt that way would paint a target on his own back for her to direct her frustration at. The last time she'd been pissed at him for something, she'd challenged him to hand-to-hand combat training in the department gym, and kicked his ass. He'd been sore for a week afterwards.

"Hey, Foster, I hear your murder suspect got bail. What did she do, fuck the judge?"

Matt glared at Claude Morin, one of the older officers working in the Sex Crimes Unit. Morin wasn't just older, he was old school, a cop who shouldn't be working in Sex Crimes. Claude was the kind of cop who made the victim feel like they were to blame for what had happened to them. He had the highest percentage of cases labelled "unfounded," which was police speak for closing a case without investigating thoroughly. Matt had heard rumours of worse behaviour involving Morin, including exploiting vulnerable women, but had never been able to find evidence against him. Guys like Morin were the reason he'd transferred to Sex Crimes. Someone needed to look out for the victims.

"You're a pig," Rebecca growled.

"The suspect was released on bail," Matt stressed. "As the judge said, with no prior history of violence, and reliable sureties to guarantee her appearance and conditions, there was no reason to hold her." He turned away, hoping Morin would piss off and find someone else to needle.

"Is the little whore getting to you, Foster? I mean, she is a sweet piece of ass."

Morin's taunts were getting under his skin, and Matt fought to ignore him. *Don't feed the trolls.*

The sound of leather hitting skin echoed through the room, followed by Russell's voice degrading Gemma. Mocking laughter filled the room.

Matt pushed away from his desk, his hands balling into fists as he moved towards Morin's workstation. Red rage filled his vision when he found a handful of officers clustered around the computer, watching the video that Matt had entered into evidence the night before. "That's evidence. Turn. It. Off."

Rebecca grabbed his arm to calm him, snapping at Morin. "Do it."

Morin snickered and turned up the volume. "Why do you care? She was a willing participant. This video is probably all over the web by now."

The thought of Gemma's humiliation being broadcast for all to see infuriated Matt. He lunged, grabbing the shocked Morin by his shirt and shoving him up against the wall hard enough to rattle the picture frames. "Her name is Gemma Milani. Not a whore, not a piece of ass. You can refer to her as the suspect, or as the victim, because those recordings were done without her consent. Those videos are evidence, and if I catch you showing them off again, you'll regret it. Do we understand each other?" Matt towered over the much shorter man. Morin nodded sullenly.

Even as he was threatening Morin, Rebecca had shut down the video and ordered the remaining officers to return to their duties.

"Foster! My office, now." Superintendent Michelle Chan rarely raised her voice. This shout rang across the room. A cold finger of dread ran through Matt, and he released Morin's shirt.

Matt slunk past Michelle, who stood with her arms crossed. The door clicked softly as she closed it behind her. Matt's heart was racing from the adrenaline. He'd crossed a line. Morin's refusal to see Gemma as a person, as someone who'd been exploited, had pushed him too far today. Thinking about how things might have been different for his mother, knowing that guys like Morin were part of the reason things had ended the way they had . . .

"Sit down, Matt."

Matt took a chair across from her desk and met her annoyed gaze. Michelle had been a good supervisor to him for as long as he'd been in Sex Crimes. Now she was clearly irritated. He'd lost his temper, even if he had been provoked. Sure, he'd shoved Morin into a wall, but he hadn't hurt him. Other officers had gotten away with worse. "I'm sorry about Morin. It won't happen again." Next time he'd get Rebecca to go downstairs to the gym with him so he could take his frustration out on the heavy bag. And there would be a next time, as long as he and Morin were both working in Sex Crimes.

Michelle was shaking her head before he finished talking. "Not good enough. What were you thinking? You pushed him into a wall. I can't let that slide. You're on leave pending a review. Make sure Rebecca has everything related to your cases."

The words rained down on Matt like punches. He was being suspended? Because Morin was a pig? He fought to stay calm. Getting angry at Michelle wouldn't get his suspension lifted.

"You're not serious. Did you hear what Morin said? He called our suspect, who is also a victim, a whore."

Michelle's lips pressed into a thin line, and her dark eyes flashed. "I'll deal with Morin. His behaviour doesn't justify yours. Grab your stuff and head out."

Matt shoved himself out of his chair and left without another word. Anything else he said would do nothing except extend his time off. Fury burned deep in his gut, and he called on all his years of training to pretend nothing was wrong, that he hadn't just been disciplined for his actions. None of his colleagues were making eye contact, and word would get out pretty fast. He wasn't going to give them anything else to gossip about today. No one else on the force knew about his mother, so none of them understood his reaction today, and he wasn't going to explain it. His mother's history was no one else's business.

The worst part was, being suspended meant not working the case, and if Gemma was telling the truth, that meant there was a killer on the loose. He wanted to make sure the guilty party was caught.

As Michelle called Morin into her office, Matt took a seat at his desk and logged back in to his computer.

"What happened?" Rebecca came to stand beside Matt. Her voice was pitched low, to ensure no one overheard them.

"I'm suspended pending investigation. I don't know how long that will take. As soon as I finish updating the files, I'm gone." His own words came out in a whispered hiss.

Rebecca dropped into a chair beside him as he typed. "She

suspended you." Disbelief dripped from every word. "She's got Morin in there now. If she doesn't suspend him, too, I will personally make his life a living hell until they reinstate you."

Matt swivelled to face her and was met with a wicked grin. He and Rebecca had been partners for years, and her sense of fair play was well known throughout the department. Matt didn't envy Morin at that moment. "I love you for what you're thinking, but don't do anything that might get you kicked off the case."

Rebecca shook her head. "By broadcasting that video to the entire room and calling Gemma names, Morin created a hostile work environment. I'm going to file a sexual harassment complaint. Even if he's not suspended, it'll go on his record permanently."

Matt considered her words, trying to view her idea from all perspectives. "Filing a harassment complaint could derail your career. You know the brass tries to pretend we don't have problems like that. Remember what happened to the officer who filed a complaint a few years ago?"

After a training session gone horribly wrong, where officers were asked to strip naked as part of an undercover exercise, a female officer had filed a formal complaint. After an investigation, the police watchdog had censured both the trainers and the department. In the end it hadn't mattered: The officer who filed the complaint had been quietly bullied into leaving the force. No actions were ever taken against the members of the department who had done the bullying. Matt hadn't even known the officer or been at the training, and he still felt sick over the way the force had handled the incident. Rebecca loved being a cop. Matt didn't want to see her jeopardize that for him.

Rebecca gave him a withering glare. "I dare anyone around here to try to bully me. I grew up with brothers. I can handle a few disgruntled cops. Besides, if everyone keeps refusing to act, we'll never change the department. Be the change we want to see, right?"

Matt blew out a frustrated breath. He and Rebecca had both transferred to Sex Crimes after another scandal had been exposed, where officers were dismissing sexual-assault reports as unfounded without even investigating. At the time, the department had claimed it wanted to change the way it operated, and a few of the worst offenders had been terminated or transferred to other units.

Unfortunately, some days Matt felt little had changed. Guys like Morin were still pervasive, and too many victims were ignored or dismissed as liars. He and Rebecca, and a few other newer, younger officers, did their best, but it was like sticking their fingers in a leaking dike. Now he was being suspended for who knew how long. The unit couldn't afford to lose Rebecca too. The victims couldn't afford to lose another advocate. "Just be careful. I don't know how Morin has survived as long as he has, unless he has friends in high places. Don't hurt your career on my account."

"Don't worry about me. What are you going to do until this blows over?" Rebecca's blue eyes reflected concern.

Matt inhaled slowly. Sharing his plan with Rebecca was risky, but she'd been his partner for a long time, and he trusted her with his life, and she was clearly worried about him. "I'm going to do a little investigating on my own. Something about this whole thing is bugging me. Gemma Milani was too calm when we interviewed her yesterday, and her shock about Russell's murder seemed genuine. I want to dig into Russell's life and figure out who else might have wanted him dead."

Rebecca nodded slowly. "I hear you, and Nate is certain that she's innocent. Her arrest gutted him. We watched the video, though. No one else entered or exited that room. Even the Crown thinks it's an open-and-shut case. Russell was a bad guy, so it won't be hard to find others with motive. The problem is means and opportunity. If you really think she didn't do it, that's the question you have to answer."

"I can't work on answering those questions until forensics releases the hotel room. I'm suspended, which means no access to any crime scenes. If you can stay on top of them, make sure you know everything they do, I'll start looking for alternative suspects. If I find anything, you'll be my first call."

Going rogue and investigating on his own was dangerous. If he contaminated evidence, or discovered the truth without following procedure, it might blow the Crown's case. Even so, he wasn't willing to step away yet. Something about this case felt wrong. If he kept

Rebecca informed, she could use what he knew to track down his leads by the book and make a case. None of that could happen until he found some new information.

His investigation needed to start by reaching out to people who associated with Russell, and with Gemma in her former life. The addicts, sex workers, and low-level dealers on the Downtown Eastside of Vancouver.

CHAPTER 8

Gemma followed Nate into the Harbourview meeting room, her pulse pounding. Everything that had happened over the last day was surreal: Russell being murdered, being arrested for the crime, having her coworkers at Harbourview surround her with support to help her fight back. That was the part she didn't understand. The fact Nate believed in her was surprising enough, and it was his reputation on the line if it turned out she really had killed Russell. *She* knew she was innocent, but proving it was going to be incredibly difficult. Brent had shown her the evidence. Even she thought she looked good for this.

A glance at the people around the table had her swallowing past the lump in her throat, fighting to remain calm. Brent had arrived early, and as promised was there to protect her. He would make sure nothing happened that could come back to haunt her later, if they wound up going to trial. He caught her eye and gave her a nod, and some of the tension pressing against her chest eased.

Beside Brent sat Les. It was the two men sitting at the centre of the table that made her nervous. One was at least twenty years older than her, and while he was dressed in a nice suit, his silver hair was trimmed with military precision, and he had an aura of power, control, and even danger surrounding him. His blue eyes were so pale they resembled ice, and Gemma repressed a shiver. She'd have considered him a silver fox, if he wasn't so scary looking.

The other man was also clearly ex-military, his wide shoulders and muscled arms stretching the fabric of his polo shirt. There were tattoos on his forearms, and his hands were roughened with calluses. It was his eyes that caught Gemma's focus, though. They were as dark as obsidian, accenting his black hair and bronze skin.

Nate took a seat across from the two strangers, leaving her an open chair between him and Brent. Gemma sank down slowly, trying to quell the nervous churning in her stomach. Would these men be willing to help her? Would they judge her for who she used to be and write off the case as a lost cause? How much would all this cost? Even though both Brent and Nate had reassured her that Harbourview was contributing money to assist in her defence, the cost of proving her innocence was rising rapidly.

"I'd like you all to meet my ex–commanding officer, Carlton Murphy, and his right hand, Abel Devine. Murphy founded True North Security after retiring from the Canadian Forces, and his entire team has military or law enforcement backgrounds. If we want to prove Gemma's innocence, I can't think of anyone I'd rather have investigating this murder." Nate flashed Gemma a reassuring smile. "We'll find out who really killed Russell, so you can move past this."

Even as relief eased the tension in her limbs, Gemma forced herself to meet those cold blue eyes. Carlton Murphy was still an intimidating man, even if he was here to help her. She was lucky to have friends like Nate. She didn't know anyone else who would have gone out of his way to help her like this. She tried to keep her voice from wavering, not wanting to seem vulnerable or unappreciative of everything Nate had arranged. "Thank you for agreeing to help me, Mr. Murphy. Where do we start?"

The silver fox let out a quiet chuckle, and a smile transformed his face, making him much more approachable and reassuring. "Call me Murphy. No one calls me 'Mister' except bankers and people trying to sell me stuff."

Gemma nodded, relaxing as Murphy continued talking. His low pitch and calm presentation were soothing, and now she understood why Nate trusted him.

"I want to make it clear, murder is not something we normally get called in on. Our firm specializes in investigating things like corporate espionage and insurance fraud, and we offer personal protection services. Our insurance fraud investigations have included a couple of wrongful death cases, one of which we were able to prove was murder. Abel was military police, and he had to investigate a few suspicious deaths in that role, which is why I brought him along to look into your situation. I can't promise we'll find out who killed the victim, but we don't have to follow the same rules that the police do, which means sometimes we uncover information they miss. That's what I'm counting on here."

Gemma considered everything Murphy had told them. She didn't care whether the police couldn't use any evidence Murphy found to convict the real killer. As long as Murphy and Abel could prove that someone else killed Russell, the charges would be dropped and she would be cleared. That was all she wanted.

When Murphy paused to take a drink, Abel spoke: "Has the crime scene been released by the police yet?"

Nate shook his head. "Not yet. The crime scene team tells me they expect to be done by tomorrow. This isn't the first time someone has died in one of our rooms. We have a cleaning company we bring in that specializes in this sort of thing. I'm assuming you want me to give you access to the room before they clean it."

"That's exactly what we need. Les filled us in on what the video evidence shows. We'll want to see it too. If we want to prove Gemma didn't do this, we need to find out how someone else got in and out of that room without showing up on the cameras. Once we figure out how they might have done it, then we can work on the who. Which doesn't mean we'll be sitting on our hands until tomorrow." Abel directed his attention back to Gemma. "I'm going to need as much information as you can give me about Russell's life. His friends, his enemies, his business associates. Murphy and I will start tracking them down tonight to question them. The more people we eliminate as suspects, the easier it will be to convince the police when we do find the right person."

Gemma's mind raced, going over all the names from her past, and the new names she'd heard Russell mention over the past several months. After she'd gotten into treatment, her addictions counsellor had advised her to cut all ties with her past life, to reduce the temptation to relapse. She had listened, for a while. Then she had been accepted into nursing school and had started volunteering with harm-reduction organizations based in the same neighbourhoods Gemma had lived in, and she had rekindled some of her friendships within the community. Her volunteering had dwindled after her mom got sick, but people would still talk to her. They wouldn't talk to Murphy and Abel, though, not unless she assured them it was safe. "I'm coming with you."

"No." Murphy was adamant.

"No way," Nate said at the same time.

"That's not a good idea—" Abel started.

Gemma held up a hand to silence them. "I know those streets—and the people who live and work on them. I was one of them for a lot of years. Some of my friends are still down there. They don't like strangers, and they don't respond well to authority. You two won't get far without me. With me? People will tell you what they know about Russell because they trust *me*."

The frown creasing Murphy's face made him look intimidating again. Gemma was not backing down on this one. It was her life on the line, and she wanted to kick over every rock possible.

"I don't like it," he finally ground out. "But you're the client, and you do have the most at stake. Fine, you'll accompany us to introduce us to some of the people Russell knew. I don't want you taking unreasonable risks. Proving you innocent doesn't do any good if you're injured, or worse."

. . .

GEMMA ZIPPED up her leather jacket to ward off the cold and damp of the late-winter evening. March in Vancouver this year was colder and wetter than normal, and Gemma wished she'd worn a sweater under her jacket before setting off on this foray into her past.

She was flanked on either side by Murphy and Abel as she led them through the dark corners and back alleys of Vancouver's Downtown Eastside, known to locals as the DTES. Their protective hovering was almost humorous, considering these streets had been her home for so many years.

Since she'd left, Russell had made a lot of enemies as he grew into a major player on the Vancouver drug scene. Clients he'd sold bad drugs to, people who owed him money and couldn't pay, people who'd been blackmailed into sex work to cover their drug debts and feed their habit. A familiar surge of gratitude washed over her as they passed a young woman huddled under a tarp, her hands shaking as she tried to find a vein in her arm. Without her mom, that might still be her. Or she might already be dead.

Their first stop was a shelter and drop-in centre called New Hope Mission. Kimmy Walters, the night manager, was an ex–sex worker who had worked the streets at the same time Gemma had, and who had gotten into a treatment program about six months before Gemma did. Her success in treatment had been inspirational for Gemma, helping her stay focussed when kicking her habit. Gemma still connected with her regularly. Kimmy knew everything about everyone who lived and worked on the Vancouver streets. If she couldn't point them in the right direction, no one could.

Gemma pushed open the doors to the mission, the scent of too many unwashed people crowded into the main dining hall bringing back unpleasant memories. More than once this had been the only place she'd been able to get food or shelter when she was living and working on the streets. New Hope provided food, a safe space to sleep, and even facilities to shower and do laundry for people who had no other options. Run mostly by volunteers, and on donations and minimal government grants, it was nowhere near large enough to meet the demand. Kimmy and her team did their best.

A glance around told her that hot meal service had ended, although there was still coffee, sandwiches, fruit, and cookies out for anyone who wandered in hungry, or who wanted to grab something to go. Which meant Kimmy would be either in the back helping clean up the kitchen, or in the dorm area figuring out how many beds were left.

Gemma waved at one of the volunteers she knew, who smiled at her. He gave her companions a suspicious look. Not surprising. Murphy and Abel both looked too much like police, and police at the shelter usually meant trouble. "They're with me. Where's Kimmy?"

The man jerked his thumb towards the back rooms and continued working. Gemma led Murphy and Abel past the kitchen to the dorms, searching for Kimmy. It didn't take long to find her rearranging cots to make room for more people. Kimmy's eyes widened in surprise when she saw Gemma and her entourage. "If you keep pulling off the impossible and fitting more people in here, the city will never give you more funding to expand, you know." Gemma grabbed the other end of the cot Kimmy was fighting with, helping her slide it into place.

Kimmy flashed her a grin. "Nah, they'll give me the money just to get me to shut up and stay out of the news."

Gemma let Kimmy pull her into a hug, allowing herself to relax for a heartbeat before she pulled back to get a better look at her friend. Kimmy's hair was clipped short, her blond spikes tinted with blue and green. When she'd worked the streets, her hair had been long, but now she kept it short to prevent it from becoming a weapon when she had to break up fights at the shelter. Her heavy makeup couldn't quite conceal the long scar that ran down one side of her face from her hairline to her chin, where a customer had tried to extract a refund with a knife. Gemma had helped her clean it up and got her to a hospital the night it had happened. Sadly, the man had never been arrested.

Around forty, Kimmy's years on the street battling addiction had left her looking older than she should. She was only a few inches over five feet and very slender. There was a faded bruise around her right wrist, probably from being grabbed by someone, and otherwise she looked healthy. Tonight, Kimmy wore green eye shadow that matched her sweater and brought out more of the green in her hazel eyes. The purple shadows under her eyes were barely there, a sign that things at the shelter had been stable recently. Some of the guilt Gemma had been carrying lessened knowing that. When her mother's illness became terminal and required additional care, Gemma had to reduce the amount she volunteered, and it had been months since she'd seen Kimmy. Now she was back, except instead of being there to help, she was the one looking for a favour.

Gemma stepped back from Kimmy, not objecting when Kimmy kept hold of one of her hands. "I'm guessing you know about Russell?"

Kimmy squeezed her hand. "I heard he was dead, and that you were arrested for killing him. What the fuck, Gemma? How did you get mixed up with Russell again?" She stared at Gemma, and Gemma knew immediately what Kimmy was wondering.

"I'm not using again. Still five years sober." Kimmy pulled her into another hug. When Gemma pulled away, she gestured at the two men behind her. "This is Murphy and Abel, friends of a friend. Can we talk in your office? We need some information."

"My office is too small for all of us. The back storeroom is private. Follow me." Kimmy had started to turn to lead them down the hallway when a shadow fell over them, and her lips pressed tight together.

A frisson of awareness skated over Gemma's skin, and her muscles tensed.

"How can I help you, Constable Foster? Are you looking for someone?" Kimmy's attitude had shifted a full 180 degrees from the friendly greeting she'd given Gemma, now cold and aloof as she spoke to Matt Foster.

CHAPTER 9

Gemma stood between the two men, her dark hair hanging down her back. Her stance had widened and her shoulders stiffened when Kimmy greeted him, and he wanted to reassure her that she didn't need to be afraid of him, that she didn't need to be ready to run. Not that she needed to run with the muscle protecting her. Both men were unmistakably ex-military. They were tall, although not quite as tall as his six feet, four inches. The older man exuded power and control, commanding respect with his silent self-assurance. It was the other man that set Matt's teeth on edge. He was standing close to Gemma, using his body to protect her from any threat coming from behind. His dark hair was almost as long as hers, and he had the kind of face that turned women's heads, with dark eyes and high cheekbones. Even in outerwear designed to protect against the chill and damp of a West Coast winter night, the younger man had broad shoulders that hinted at powerful muscles, and muscular thighs. These were not men to get confrontational with, even if he didn't know what they were doing with Gemma.

"I'm looking into Russell's murder. Unofficially," he added. "I wasn't expecting to find you here, Gemma. Who are your friends?"

The older man gave him an appraising look before answering

Matt's question. "I'm Murphy. I own True North Security, and we're helping Ms. Milani. This is my colleague Abel. Care to explain what you meant by 'unofficially'?"

Matt nodded at both men, filing away the information to verify later. A private security firm? Where had Gemma come up with the money to hire these guys? It was one more thing to look into. First a high-priced lawyer got her released; now she had private security protecting her and looking into the murder for her.

"I'm currently not actively working the Molloy homicide, but it never hurts to ask some questions." Matt delivered the half-truth confidently, hoping it would end the questions. He didn't want to admit his temper had cost him access to this case. He wasn't about to let his fight with Morin stop him from digging for the truth. He trusted Rebecca completely, and his gut was telling him that something about this case wasn't what it seemed. Gemma stirred up all kinds of emotions. Her past reminded him too much of his mother, bringing out his protective streak. His admiration at how she'd turned her life around made him more determined to follow his hunch that she was being framed. That was what this felt like, a setup.

Murphy crossed his arms across his chest and stared at him. "You and Rebecca Sutton were the lead investigators. Why are you off the case?"

Matt hid his surprise at Murphy's statement as he ran one hand through his hair. "I'm currently suspended from VPD," he admitted. "I'm not going to explain why, although it is related to the case. I'm not one hundred percent convinced that Gemma is guilty."

Embarrassment burned through Matt at this admission. His suspension was humiliating, although if admitting to it meant that he could build some trust, some good would come of it.

"You were suspended because of me?" Gemma sounded incredulous.

"Not because of you. I did something stupid, and now I'm paying for it." Matt didn't want Gemma to find out what really happened and learn that half the Sex Crimes Unit had seen the video and had been mocking her victimization. It would pile more pain and humiliation on top of everything else she was going through. "I want to find out what really happened, which means talking to the same people, walking the same streets as you are right now. It seems to me, it makes more sense for us to work together."

He held his breath as she looked at him with suspicion. If she refused to work with him, his investigation would be a lot harder. He wanted her to know she could trust him, that he was looking for the truth. His instincts were screaming that she was innocent. He wanted her to see not all cops were corrupt.

Finally, Gemma shrugged. "You're here. You might as well hear what Kimmy has to say." With that, she followed Kimmy down the hallway, with Murphy and Abel close behind.

Matt hurried after them, relieved that Gemma had given in. Maybe this meant she didn't hate him. He tried not to notice how Gemma's jeans hugged the curves of her ass. He was doing this because it was the right thing to do, not because Gemma was incredibly hot. Plus, if she caught him staring, he would lose any progress he'd made.

Once they were all crowded into the storage room, Murphy and Abel began questioning Kimmy. With a nod of permission from Kimmy, Abel turned on his phone to record the interview.

"Can you tell us what you know about Russell's business dealings?" Murphy asked.

Kimmy's hands shook as she pulled a piece of gum out of her pocket. "Nicotine gum," she explained. "Another habit I'm trying to kick. I swear it's almost as hard as the heroin was." She rolled her eyes, then popped the gum in her mouth. "I don't know how much you know. What I've heard and seen is that Russell had become the biggest dealer in this section of the city, and he was working on taking over distribution in other neighbourhoods. He wasn't affiliated with any specific gang, though he was partnering with some type of organized crime. I've heard gangs, I've heard Russian mafia, I don't know. I do know he was running a huge stable of sex workers. Mostly women, not all. Every one of them was addicted to something, though. He was squeezing out anyone who wasn't working for him, or finding ways to blackmail them into working for him. It was getting pretty ugly. Several of his 'employees' have overdosed in the past year, and a couple have committed suicide. Working for Russell was no picnic. I've heard there was at least one family out for revenge. I've also heard he had a few cops on his payroll. That might be worth exploring, although good luck getting past the blue wall." Kimmy glared at Matt.

Matt shrugged. He'd already known much of what Kimmy had told them, although the mysterious overdoses and angry families were worth checking out. He and Rebecca dealt in sex crimes, and while there were some crossovers, he didn't deal with a lot of drug arrests or overdoses anymore. As for dirty cops, that was no surprise either. It was a poorly kept secret that there were still dirty cops on the force, and proof was scarce. If he could find evidence, maybe more good might come out of his suspension after all. Irrefutable proof against dirty cops would be his ticket back into the good graces of the new police chief, who was on a mission to clean up the force. She was fighting an uphill battle. "Any suggestions about where I should start? I've heard rumours, but people on the street would know more than I would. I can't do anything if I don't know what I'm looking for."

Kimmy snorted. "No one will tell it to your face, Constable Foster. You're one of them."

Matt knew her use of his official title was intentional. As much as he loved his job, the people down here had every reason to hate cops, and most didn't hesitate to let officers know how they felt. Matt kept his frustration in check. He couldn't prove who killed Russell if he alienated the people who might help him.

"We don't know any of the players here, and we have no loyalty to anyone except our client: Gemma. So anything you share with us will be used to help prove her innocence, and we will never reveal where it came from." As he spoke, Murphy used his voice and body language to project calm competence, while still creating an air of protection around Gemma.

Matt was impressed. Murphy had swiftly defused the automatic hostility Kimmy had towards the police, and reminded her that clearing Gemma was what they were working toward.

Kimmy cast another dubious glance at Matt, finally turning to Murphy and talking again. "The cops on his payroll took bribes to turn a blind eye to the prostitution. There were rumours that a couple actively worked for him. As for Russell's drug pipeline? He may have been getting it from one of the big gangs, but his contact was a cop who was working for that gang. That guy seems to be untouchable, because he's been doing it for years, and no one has ever caught him."

Matt's heart rate notched up, and he balled his hands into fists. He'd known about dirty cops on the force, and this made it sound like they were in deeper than he'd suspected. How had the force never taken action on this? He was usually proud to wear the badge. This made him feel physically sick.

"We're going to need names," Murphy encouraged.

"I don't know 'em all, I can only give you a few names I've heard. The one who's mobbed up? That one I know. Claude Morin was an asshole when I was working the streets, and now he's built a power base no one can touch."

Kimmy's words hit Matt like a punch in the gut. He *knew* Morin was dirty. Nothing would make him happier than proving it.

"I may be able to help with investigating Morin," Matt said slowly, not wanting to seem too excited. The chance to get some payback for his suspension was personal, and to protect Gemma's feelings, he didn't want them to know why he hated Morin.

Gemma faced him, staring with a mixture of curiosity and skepticism. Matt tried not to let her hostility bother him. He would have to prove himself before she would trust him the way he wanted. Right now she still had no reason to.

"What are you suggesting?" Murphy gave no clue what he was thinking.

"For the sake of the force, I would love to find some real evidence that Morin is a dirty cop. I remember some of the cases he's worked on, including a couple where evidence mysteriously disappeared. No one could prove anything at the time. Maybe those cases will provide clues. If we run into something I don't know, I can call in a few favours to find out. I could do this alone, but I think we'd be more effective together. I propose we team up to investigate both Russell's murder and Morin's potential involvement."

Matt hid how much he wanted this. He was used to being part of a team, and while he was confident he could investigate on his own, having additional resources would help. An additional benefit was that evidence discovered by private security firms wasn't always admissible in court. If Murphy and Abel found anything that could help, he could loop Rebecca in to prevent evidence contamination. Matt wanted to clear Gemma, and he also wanted the real killer to face justice.

Even as Matt spoke, Gemma was shaking her head. "No one will talk to us if you're involved. And I don't trust him," she directed at Murphy, clearly referring to Matt.

Matt resisted the urge to defend himself. Nothing he said would help his cause, and it might hurt.

"If you really don't want us to work with him, we won't," Murphy told Gemma. "I think any information he can provide, both about this Morin and anyone else Russell had contact with, would be valuable to our investigation. I'd like to hear what he has to say."

Gemma was still frowning, and Matt allowed himself a sigh of relief when she shrugged. "If you think he can help, fine. I'm done for tonight. I've got an early shift tomorrow." She leaned over and gave Kimmy a hug, then pushed her way out of the storage room.

Matt followed the group out of the shelter, turning Gemma's statement over in his mind. She was going back to work tomorrow? She'd been released from jail only that morning. It seemed a little soon to him, considering the emotional wringer she'd been through for the past forty-eight hours. He wasn't about to say anything and jeopardize his new relationship with her team. This partnership was about the only thing that had gone right for him today, and it might be his best chance to get Claude Morin gone for good.

CHAPTER 10

Gemma jumped when someone touched her shoulder, her earbuds and the noise from the vacuum blocking any sound of their approach. Nate stood behind her, waiting as she turned everything off.

"Abel thinks he's found something in the room Russell was killed in. He wants to show you, and ask you a few questions."

Excitement buzzed through Gemma, making her walk faster as they wound their way through the maze of hallways and corridors that made up Harbourview. The men from True North had been investigating for only one day, and Abel had found something already? Nate was right, these guys were *good*. Her excitement dimmed slightly when they arrived at the suite she and Russell had used on Saturday night. The memory of that video had fury roiling in her belly. She wasn't ashamed of what she'd done with Russell; her motivation had been to save her mother's house, and survival was all she had cared about. Knowing that the video could have been seen by a lot of other people without her consent was the violation. The door swung open and Gemma stepped inside, stopping dead. Standing with Murphy, Abel, and Matt was Rebecca.

"What is she doing here?" Gemma was pleased to hear her voice come out calm and even, with no sign of her instinctive distrust of the police. She still didn't love Matt working with Abel and Murphy. She was trying to believe he might actually be on her side. Rebecca was still an unknown quantity. As far as Gemma knew, Rebecca was still trying to prove her guilty.

"I called them," Abel said. "If I'm right, I've found evidence that might prove not only how someone got into the room without being seen, but that someone actually did do so. I don't want to jeopardize any possible future prosecution of the true guilty party."

Abel's explanation made sense, and Gemma relaxed slightly. He wouldn't have called Rebecca if he didn't think he'd found something important. "What did you find?"

Abel turned to Rebecca. "Since he's on suspension right now," he jerked his thumb towards Matt, "can you record everything so it's official?" He waited while Rebecca took out her phone.

Curiosity warred with hope as Abel opened the closet door. "There's an access hatch in the ceiling of the closet." He shined a flashlight up, and Rebecca trained her phone up after it.

Gemma scuffed the carpet with her running shoe, frustrated that because the space was so small she couldn't see anything clearly.

"We found it," Rebecca said. "Our techs found no evidence that it had been used recently. There were extra pillows and blankets directly under it, blocking access. Besides, only employees would be able to open it."

The spark of hope that Abel had inspired was almost squashed by Rebecca's certainty. She seemed so positive that this was a dead end. As she processed Abel's words, Gemma realized there was a problem. Something in the room wasn't right.

"Did your techs look in any of the other rooms?" Abel asked.

Matt cocked his head to one side, craning to see into the closet. "I don't think so. This room didn't connect to any others, so there was no reason to."

Abel nodded. "I think our suspect was counting on that. This is a suite, with a pullout couch and a wardrobe. I looked at four other suites today, and do you know what I found?"

"We keep all the spare pillows and blankets in the wardrobe," Gemma said. She'd worked in housekeeping at Harbourview for long enough that she could put it all away blindfolded. No pillows or blankets should be in that closet.

Abel stepped back out of the closet and looked over at Gemma. "Can you tell us where everything belongs? Rebecca, for the sake of preserving evidence, can you move things to where Gemma tells us?"

Gemma stepped closer to Abel and studied the contents of the closet while Rebecca snapped on latex gloves. "Like I said, the pillows and blanket should be in the wardrobe. The ironing board should be leaning against that wall." Gemma pointed to the right side. "The robes should be hanging in front of the board."

Rebecca made the adjustments. When she was finished, she reached for her camera and recorded the new positions.

"Now look at the ceiling." Abel pointed up. "The hatch is easily accessible. And it wouldn't be hard to pull the blankets and pillows under the hatch on the way out. There's something else I want you to see, though." Abel pulled himself up on the closet shelf and pushed open the access point. "No one looked in here." Abel backed out so Rebecca could climb up and film inside the ductwork. "What do you see?"

Rebecca's voice rang hollow as she moved deeper into the ducts. "The dust has been disturbed. The ducts are surprisingly clean, but it looks like someone crawled through here. And I see one dark smudge, looks like it could be dried blood." Rebecca dropped back to the floor and turned to Nate, her lips turned down and deep grooves framing her mouth. "I'm taking custody of the room again. We need to take samples. If that dark stain proves to be blood, and DNA can connect it to Russell Molloy . . ." she said. "Fuck. This could be a problem."

Gemma's pulse was racing, her heart beating so hard she was sure everyone could hear it. Someone had crawled through the ceiling access? How was that even possible? Was Russell's murder random? It would be painfully ironic if her new life was ruined over a bit of bad luck. After all her poor decisions, the chances she'd taken living on the streets, and now this? "So this could prove that someone else did it? That I'm innocent?"

Abel put a hand up. "Slow down. I don't want you to get too excited yet. If DNA testing proves the blood is Russell's, it should be enough for Brent to cast doubt on other evidence collected by VPD. That might get you a not guilty verdict, but I don't want to rely on this blood alone. What it *does* do for us is provide another avenue to investigate. Who left the blood there? Was Russell the target? How did they gain access to the ductwork? This discovery creates more questions than it answers. In our opinion, yes, it's good for your case."

Gemma paused. If he was right, this wasn't the smoking gun she needed. Besides, she didn't trust VPD. "How are we going to prove the evidence wasn't planted? VPD released the room, which means anyone could have come in and moved the pillows, smeared the blood in the ducts, right?" The little bit of hope she'd been feeling washed away, disappearing with every word out of her mouth. There was no way the Crown would accept this. If *she* could poke holes in it, the Crown would have a field day.

A large hand settled on her shoulder and gave it a reassuring squeeze. She looked over at Nate, who wore a smug smile. "We thought of that. Surveillance footage will show no one entered the room from the time the crime scene techs left to when we opened the door this morning to search for additional evidence. Plus, to be safe, Abel and Murphy recorded everything they did, from when they broke the police seal until they called Rebecca to come see what they found. Brent will get the evidence admitted, even if the Crown objects."

His faith in her innocence and his confidence in his friends that they would be able to prove it suddenly overwhelmed her. Nate had no reason to believe in her word, and to pull in so many favours for her? Gemma clenched her teeth and fought the urge to cry. Tears wouldn't help her right now. She nodded an acknowledgement and managed to get her emotions under control.

"If the Crown is reasonable, they may look at this evidence and drop the charges entirely," Murphy said. "I don't want to rely on that.

While Constable Sutton may be ready to believe that someone else may have been in the room, I don't like leaving my client's fate in the hands of someone else. Once she has everything she needs from us, Abel and I will be going out tonight to investigate further."

Gemma bit her lip. "I can't come with you tonight. I have an exam in one of my classes. I can't miss it, or I could fail the course." She had spent most of last night studying after getting home from the shelter, and as much as she wanted to help them, she was not going to miss this exam. Even though her grade in the class was decent, skipping tonight was not an option. Graduation was too close.

Murphy shrugged. "Don't worry too much about that. Between you and Kimmy spreading the word last night, there should be a few people willing to talk to us."

"I'll come with you tonight."

Murphy looked satisfied as he acknowledged Matt's offer.

"Your shift is almost over. Why don't you clock out and head home?" Nate said.

"Thanks," Gemma said gratefully. There was nothing she could do here, and she still had to go home and grab her books. The police had released her house earlier that day, after she had been at work already. An extra couple of hours to tidy up any mess they had left behind was welcome. "You'll let me know if you find anything?"

"You'll be my first call," Murphy promised.

CHAPTER 11

Gemma parked her car and reached for her backpack. Her nursing exam tonight had been long and difficult, and all she wanted was to shower and crash. She slammed the car door, checking the handle to make sure it was locked, then turned and trudged across the gravel driveway towards the house. A few steps away from the car, she paused. Something wasn't right. The yard was pitch black. The motion detection lights should have kicked on by now. She knew exactly where they were located, exactly when they should turn on. She should, as she was the one who had installed them when she had started taking night classes, to make her mother feel better about Gemma coming home so late.

With growing unease, she reached for her phone and turned on the flashlight app. This could be a simple power outage, if not for the lights on at her neighbours' houses. She scanned the yard, looking for anything out of place. Finding nothing, she kept moving forward. Another few steps toward the house allowed her to see that the floodlights had been removed, the bare sockets mocking her as she shined the light up at them. What the fuck? Who would steal her floodlights? Crime was out of control in Vancouver, but the tiny house she shared with her mother was in a quiet neighbourhood that always felt safe.

She wanted to believe it was just kids out looking for trouble. It was the kind of thing she might have done when she was thirteen or so. Except she and her friends would have thrown rocks, broken the lights, then tagged the house. They wouldn't have gone to the trouble of unscrewing the bulbs.

Anxiety ratcheting higher, Gemma continued moving slowly toward the house. She searched for other signs that this was the work of teens, quickly losing hope that this was a random act of vandalism. There were no signs of spray paint or broken windows.

Even with the light from her phone, the dark was eerie. Gemma tried to ignore her fear, reminding herself this was nothing compared to how she used to live. Had all the years since her time on the street made her soft? She rounded the corner of the house cautiously, feeling ridiculous when there was nothing there. She was being paranoid. She edged closer to the door, reaching for the keypad lock she had installed to punch in her code. When she touched the first number, the door pushed open, unlatched. She turned and raced for the safety of her car, punching the auto-lock button on her key fob as she ran.

She slid into the car and smashed the lock button, shaking in her seat once she was safely inside. Someone had broken into her house. Gemma habitually checked her locks when she left her house, and she knew that the house had been secure when she left for school earlier. As much as she wanted to believe it was a coincidence, she wasn't stupid. The odds of the first break-in on the street in years to be at her house, right after she was accused of a murder she didn't commit? She had been targeted. As she backed out of her driveway, she called Murphy.

IT TOOK SURPRISINGLY little time for Murphy to arrive and park the sleek, dark SUV behind her battered Toyota in front of her house under the bright streetlights. Gemma hadn't wanted to leave, and staying in her dark driveway had been too risky. Three men stepped out of the vehicle. Matt's appearance with Murphy and Abel did little to help Gemma's equilibrium. His very presence made her feel safer, even when her past experiences and her survival instinct told her she couldn't trust law enforcement. Matt had done nothing personally to earn her suspicion, even if the badge he carried made her doubt his motives for helping them.

Gemma exited her car and greeted them. The air was chilly and damp, but it was fear that made her shiver as she explained to Murphy everything she'd observed. This might look like a simple break-in, except too many things pointed to this being one more attempt to make her look guilty of killing Russell—especially after their find at Harbourview that afternoon.

"You were right to call us." Murphy turned to Abel, who was distributing high-powered flashlights and latex gloves that he had unpacked from the SUV. "I want you to do a full sweep of the yard before we go inside. Photograph anything that looks unusual. Don't touch anything with your bare hands."

"We should call VPD," Matt said.

Gemma fought the urge to roll her eyes. Of course he wanted to call his buddies. There was a reason her call had been to Murphy, and not to the police. If this turned out to be nothing, there was no reason to involve them. She would feel a little silly about overreacting, but no one would know except the four of them. If it turned out to be related to Russell's murder, then they could decide if they would involve VPD. She didn't want cops in her home again. They'd already invaded her privacy when they'd searched her house after Russell's murder. Inviting them in again was something she wanted to avoid at all costs.

"Not yet. Let's see what we find first. I want to know what they were looking for," Murphy said. They all put on the gloves, then Murphy motioned for Gemma to stay near him as he followed Abel up the drive.

As Matt fell in behind them, Gemma heard him grumbling about contaminating evidence. He went silent as the beam from his flashlight swept the backyard. The trees formed hulking shadows. The gusting wind made the leaves rustle eerily. The whole scene gave Gemma the creeps.

After Abel finished prowling the yard and gave the all clear,

Murphy led Gemma to the unsecured door. "Stay behind us. Abel, Matt, and I will go in and make sure whoever did this is gone. I want you to stay close. Understand?"

Gemma nodded, tucking herself behind Murphy's broad body as Abel and Matt took point and entered the house. Her stomach rolled, and her eyes burned as she fought to blink back tears at the destruction inside her home. The house was a 1950s bungalow, with a front door that opened directly into the tiny living room. The room was in chaos. Cushions had been pulled off all the furniture and cut open, the stuffing spilling over the floor. Books from the bookcase were everywhere, and the drawers to her desk hung open, the contents scattered haphazardly around the room.

The deeper they moved into the house, the sicker Gemma felt. Whoever had done this had been searching for something, but she wondered whether they'd wanted to hurt her too. Some of the destruction felt random and wanton. Picture frames had been smashed, and glass littered the floor. Relief warred with confusion at the fact her mother's room was barely disturbed. The contents of this room were the last things that her mother had touched, and the thought of losing them was devastating.

Her own room had been destroyed. Every drawer was empty, her clothes scattered and cut to ribbons. Her jewellery box was looted, not that there had been anything of value in it, and all her makeup was smashed and smeared on the walls. Scrawled on the mirror of the bathroom in bright red lipstick was "TALK AND YOU DIE, BITCH." Fear had Gemma freezing in front of the mirror, and a trickle of cold sweat ran down her spine.

Murphy turned and met her gaze. "Any idea what that means? Is there anything you haven't told us?"

There was no accusation in his voice, so Gemma tamped down her automatically defensive response. Gemma reread the message. Who could have done this? She didn't know anything. Russell had never shared secrets with her; she hadn't wanted him to. They didn't have the kind of relationship that led to pillow talk.

"I have no idea what that means." Gemma nervously twisted a lock of hair around her finger. "My best guess is that someone thinks Russell told me something. He didn't. I don't even know for sure it's about Russell, but nothing else makes sense. My life has been nothing except school and work for years, until my mom got sick."

"We need to call VPD," Matt repeated. "This is clearly not random. You're in danger." He sounded worried, almost like he was scared for her safety. Gemma couldn't believe that. Her past experiences told her that the blue brotherhood came first. Always.

When Murphy added his agreement, she nodded. "Fine, call them. Even with the threats, it's a property crime, so I don't think they'll care much," she grumbled as she walked back down the hall.

The living room bothered her. Whoever had done this had destroyed most of the house, leaving only the kitchen and her mother's room without too much damage. In her room the destruction felt random, but not out here. They had been looking for something, something small enough it could be hidden in a book or inside a cushion. But what? It could be anything—a USB drive, a piece of paper, even a photograph. Something worth killing over, clearly. The problem was, whatever it was, she didn't know anything. Russell had never shared secrets with her.

"You can't stay here tonight. It's a crime scene, but it's a property crime. Even though it's connected to a murder, VPD won't come until tomorrow to investigate."

Gemma jumped at the sound of Matt's voice behind her. How had such a big man snuck up on her without her noticing? For all that he resembled a bear, he moved like a jungle cat, all quiet and stealthy. Sexy. *Whoa, where had that thought come from?* Finding Matt Foster attractive was a recipe for heartbreak. She took a step sideways before turning to face him, needing the extra space. "I know. I'll find a place."

She hadn't actually thought that far ahead. For tonight she'd see if Harbourview had a room. She'd worry about tomorrow night later. Wanting to get the night over with, Gemma looked up the police nonemergency line and dialled.

CHAPTER 12

"You take Gemma back to Harbourview when she's finished with VPD. Matt and I will secure the house before I take him home," Murphy said to Abel as Gemma reported the break-in.

Matt needed to let Rebecca know what had happened too. This was probably connected to her investigation, and if they left it up to Property Crimes, clues might be overlooked.

"Fuck!" Gemma kicked a shredded couch cushion across the floor after she ended the call.

"What's the problem?" Murphy looked at her curiously.

Gemma ran a hand through her hair, and Matt noted the dark circles under her eyes. She had to be exhausted.

"VPD wants to meet in the morning, and I have to be there. I was hoping they would agree to talk to you instead, but no, it has to be me, and that means missing another shift at work." She let out a long sigh. "It's fine. I hate asking Harbourview for any more favours after everything they're doing for me, that's all."

"You need some sleep. I want you at Harbourview tonight, for your own safety. Abel will go with you, and we can all come back tomorrow to meet VPD." Murphy spoke like the ex–military commander he was; he expected Gemma to follow his instructions.

"That was my plan anyway," Gemma agreed. "I'm ready when you are."

"Let's go," Abel said.

As the front door closed behind them, Murphy was already headed for the kitchen. "I'll secure back here if you want to start on the bedrooms."

Matt went into Gemma's mother's room first, checking the locks on all the windows before turning to leave. It struck him again how odd it felt that this room had been left alone, considering the destruction throughout the rest of the house. Maybe whoever broke in hadn't had time to search this room, had been spooked when Gemma arrived home from class. He flipped the light off and moved to secure the rest of the house before meeting Murphy at the front door. Using the keys Gemma had provided, Murphy locked the dead bolt and they walked to the SUV.

"Gemma's mother's room is bugging me," Matt said as Murphy pulled away from the curb.

"Agreed. Abel will take another look through the entire house tomorrow before VPD gets there. We need to check the attic and the crawl space, see if those were searched too. Plus I want to ask Gemma some more questions when she's a little less rattled."

Murphy's plan made sense. Gemma might remember something that would explain the break-in. From observing him tonight, Abel had a knack for finding connections between two seemingly random pieces of information. "How long have you and Abel been working together?"

"Abel joined True North three years ago when he left the military. He served under me when he was first starting out, before I took early retirement. When I heard he was looking for work, I gave him a call. He fit right into my team."

"Who else do you have working for you? Rebecca told me you offered Nate a job. Is everyone ex-military?" Matt wanted to know more about who Nate trusted more than VPD to look out for Gemma.

"Not everyone, no. Most of us are, though. I've got a couple of ex–law enforcement too. My primary criteria is that either I've worked with them before, or one of my people vouches for them. It hasn't let me down yet." Murphy spoke with pride when he talked about his people. "When I started TNS, it was just me and my office manager, Andrea. She's ex-military, too, and the smartest, most organized woman I've ever met. I was badly wounded and given two choices, ride a desk or take early retirement. I didn't know exactly what I wanted to do. I'd planned on being in the military my entire career. Andrea got called home to deal with a problem on her family's ranch. Her brother had been shot and a bunch of their cattle stolen. We flew home from Afghanistan together, and by the time the plane landed, she'd talked me into going into private security and letting her join me. That was ten years ago. Now we have a dozen agents, and we do personal protection, insurance fraud investigations, cybersecurity attacks, you name it."

Matt listened intently. Murphy was acting casual, like this was simple small talk, as he talked about TNS. If this was a subtle attempt to recruit him, there was no harm in listening and considering his options. "You have enough work to keep everyone busy?"

"We do. We're based in Alberta, so we don't get a lot of calls from Bay Street, but the oil execs keep us busy. Add in the cyber division, and our insurance work? It has built our reputation to the point that sometimes we have to turn work away. It's a decent living."

Their arrival at his apartment building ended the conversation, and Matt exited the SUV with a promise to meet them back at Gemma's house in the morning.

THE NEXT DAY, Matt shoved his wallet into his pocket and grabbed his truck keys, heading for the parking garage. He had to get moving if he was going to get to Gemma's house before the police arrived.

Matt had spent a restless night, sorting through everything they had uncovered talking to people on the DTES last night. He'd also spent some time viewing the pictures he'd taken of the damage at

Gemma's. Something didn't add up. Russell had made a lot of enemies—more people wanted him dead than alive. That helped Gemma's case, because any of them could be plausible suspects. Unfortunately, most of them didn't have any access to Harbourview, and especially not the hotel's HVAC system. Now it looked like Gemma was more than a convenient fall guy. The message on her mirror had been personal. It made Matt rethink everything they'd seen in the hotel room, and every bit of evidence they'd collected since. Had the killer wanted to kill both of them, and Gemma had left before they could access the room? Or had the killer planned to have Gemma play the patsy, giving them time to find whatever evidence they thought she had? Most importantly, was Gemma telling them everything?

Matt stopped long enough to swing into a drive-through and order coffee for everyone before resuming his mental gymnastics. Everything about this case felt wrong, including the way he responded to Gemma. She was a beautiful woman who'd gone through some hard times and had found her way out of them. In the course of his career, he'd met a lot of women with similar stories. She was different. He'd never been attracted to a suspect or a victim before, and at this point, Gemma was both. He was drawn to her, instinctively wanting to provide a safe haven for her, to shelter her. On the surface, Gemma was independent and self-sufficient. Her years on the streets had left her with a tough, jaded exterior, yet under pressure Matt had glimpsed hints of vulnerability. It was that vulnerability that drew him to her, made him determined to help her.

Her lack of trust in the police, and by extension, in him, made it harder. Objectively, he could understand her feelings. The police had a bad habit of ignoring and dismissing sex workers and addicts in Vancouver. If they weren't being ignored, they were being hassled, arrested, even blackmailed by dirty cops. Deeply entrenched attitudes were hard to change, and there remained a large segment of the force that held opinions like Morin's, that marginalized people were the dregs of society. All Matt could do was work to change those attitudes and prove through his actions that he was not one of those cops.

Maybe then Gemma would start to trust him, view him as more than his badge. He wanted her to see him as a man.

Matt parked on the front street in front of the house, walking the perimeter before knocking on the front door. VPD hadn't arrived yet, but Murphy's black SUV was parked behind Gemma's sedan in the back driveway, so someone was here. The door swung open and Murphy waved him in, taking the tray of coffees from him.

"They're late," Matt observed as he toed his shoes off. He really didn't need to, considering the condition of the house, Still, his mother had drilled good manners into him his entire life, and some habits were impossible to break.

Gemma frowned at him. "Did you really think they were going to take this seriously?" She took the cup that Murphy handed her. "Thanks for the coffee, though. At least the morning isn't a total waste of time."

Gemma was seated at the small wooden table in the dining room, her laptop open in front of her. The chairs that matched the table were just about the only furniture still usable, so Matt helped himself to another one and sat down. "They didn't get your laptop?"

Gemma continued typing. "Nope. I had it with me in class last night, thank god. I've got another class tonight, and two papers due next week. Even though I keep everything stored in the cloud, it still would have sucked to lose this."

Matt tilted his head towards the laptop. "Think that was what they were after?"

Murphy nodded as he swallowed a mouthful of coffee. "I'd already considered that might have been their target. We took a closer look this morning, as Gemma started putting together a list of what was missing for the police and the insurance company. They took anything that connects to the internet, or that could store data. The missing items include her tablet, every USB drive in the house; they even took a couple of old cell phones."

"And my e-reader," Gemma griped. "That one really sucks. It was brand new and fully loaded with books. At least I can download the books again." She turned her attention back to her laptop.

Matt scanned the room again, visualizing the search now that they knew what the vandals had been looking for. The search in the living room had been methodical, checking the books, drawers, etc. Even the shredded sofa cushions could be explained. The chaos in Gemma's room had been a message. That had been less about finding whatever it was they were looking for, and more about making Gemma feel violated and scared. He hated that Gemma couldn't feel safe in her home, that after what Russell had put her through with the video, she was being re-victimized. He wanted to be the one who caught the perpetrators, who ensured that Gemma got justice. This was personal for him now. "Where's Abel? Chasing down another lead?"

"You could say that. I sent him up to the attic to see if anything had been disturbed. Considering our murderer doesn't mind crawling through tight spaces, it seemed prudent."

A knock on the door prevented Matt from responding. VPD was finally here. Rebecca entered, followed by two other officers he knew. "Thanks for taking this seriously." Matt shook hands with the two officers from Property Crimes. "This is Gemma Milani, the homeowner. These are Constables Shin and Kaur. We've worked on other cases together."

As Murphy introduced himself and began explaining his role, Matt pulled Gemma aside. "They're good officers. I trust them." Gemma frowned, not arguing.

"Ms. Milani, can you show us the threatening message first, please?" Officer Shin asked.

Once Murphy and Gemma were occupied walking the constables through the house, Rebecca pulled Matt aside. "You shouldn't be here. If Michelle finds out you're still working on the investigation while you're suspended, even the union might not be able to save you." Worry lines creased her forehead and pulled the corners of her mouth down.

Matt shrugged and barely refrained from hugging her. Rebecca was his best friend. She was doing what she thought was best, trying to look out for him. "Thanks for caring. I'll be fine. What's the status of your complaint against Morin?" Matt had been suspended for days, and the thought that Morin had received no punishment for his behaviour infuriated him. Sure, he'd used physical force. He deserved a heavier punishment. If Morin had skated, it would encourage him to keep treating victims like trash.

Rebecca snorted. "If I hadn't filed a formal complaint, Michelle wouldn't have done anything. I don't know what kind of leverage Morin has over her; she acts like he's a department superstar when we all know he's the worst cop we have. So either he's got dirt, or she slept with him and is afraid it will come out and she'll face a disciplinary hearing." Rebecca shuddered. "Which is more nauseating than him blackmailing her, to be honest. Human Resources got involved, though. Morin has to redo the sexual harassment seminar, and he got assigned desk duty for a week. It's something. Plus my complaint is on his official file. Another incident and he'll be suspended."

A week of desk duty. The injustice of the entire thing galled him, but at least Morin had to redo the harassment seminar. Matt had been in the same session as Morin last time they'd done it, and Morin had been miserable. The thought gave Matt some satisfaction. "I almost wish I could be there to watch him suffer."

"Has anyone talked to you about when your suspension will be lifted? I want my partner back."

Matt grimaced. "The union called me yesterday. My disciplinary hearing is scheduled for the Monday after next. With any luck, they'll decide two weeks is enough, and I'll be back to work as soon as the hearing ends."

"If they don't? They could kick you off the force. What will you do then?"

"They won't fire me. There's too much precedent. Other cops have done a lot worse and kept their job," Matt said, hoping he sounded confident. It was the truth. In the bad old days VPD had turned a blind eye to all kinds of terrible behaviour. They had been working to clean up that reputation recently. Matt's infraction was minor compared to many others. He'd survive this.

Rebecca looked sideways at him. "Sure, if all we're talking about is the incident with Morin. What if they find out you're still working the case?"

The return of Gemma, Murphy, and the investigators saved Matt from having to answer Rebecca.

Abel tossed a tangle of black plastic and wires on the small table they'd clustered around. The lens of a camera winked as the light bounced off it. "I found these in the attic. There were several cameras installed throughout the house, along with a wireless transmitter that was piggybacking on your Wi-Fi connection," he said to Gemma. "Someone has been watching you."

CHAPTER 13

Gemma swallowed the wave of nausea Abel's words brought on, clinging to her anger to get her through without breaking down. The thought of some random stranger watching her in the one space she'd always felt safe made her blood boil. "Someone has been spying on me? Could this have been Russell?" Please, please let it have been Russell. It still sucked, but he'd already violated her once, and those videos had been far more humiliating.

"I have no way of knowing. I can tell you they weren't installed last night. The insulation upstairs showed no signs of being recently disturbed, and the cameras had a thin layer of dust on them. My best guess? You're looking at a time frame of a few weeks to a few months. When did your mother pass away?"

Oh god. Had the cameras been present to witness those horrible last few weeks of her mother's life? Her mother either in excruciating pain, or so numbed with pain medication that she was barely conscious? The idea brought the nausea back, bile rising in her throat. Her mother hadn't asked for any of this. Gemma had made sure she never found out about her arrangement with Russell. She'd told her mother that she'd taken out a loan to help with their financial situation, and that she'd taken a casual job to help make the payments.

Gemma had considered it a half-lie. Having sex with Russell had definitely been work. "Two months ago. She was at home right to the end. She refused to move into palliative care."

Abel nodded. "I'm going to guess the cameras were installed after that. It would have been too hard to get in and out undetected with someone home almost constantly. That narrows down the time frame."

Gemma's anxiety eased slightly. At least whoever had done this hadn't victimized her mother too.

Rebecca pulled on a pair of gloves and began poking through the mess on the table. "I wish you had left everything in place, let us look at it for ourselves. I'll send it to our cybercrimes division and see if they can track down where the video was being streamed to."

"I took photos of everything before I pulled it out," Abel told her. "I'll send them to you. I've already sent everything to Jett, boss. She'll let us know what she finds."

"Who is Jett, and what did you send her?" Rebecca asked suspiciously.

Murphy's smile was almost predatory. "Jett is my cybersecurity expert. I'll wager she figures out who is behind these cameras before your department does."

Gemma sank into a chair and tuned out Abel and Rebecca as they started talking about the technical specifications of the equipment found in her home. She didn't care what brand of camera had been used. All that mattered was who was doing this, and why.

Matt crouched down by her chair, heat radiating off him, his big frame invading her space. Tension coiled through her muscles, her instinctive response always fight or flight. Flight had kept her alive for most of her life. She worked hard to control her breathing so Matt wouldn't know he was affecting her. "Yes?"

"When was the last time you had something to eat?"

His question was so normal it caught her off guard, and she needed a moment to remember. "Last night before my exam. I grabbed some cheese and crackers as I was running out the door. I haven't felt like eating."

His loud sigh sounded exasperated, though his next words were gentle. "Grab your laptop. We're going for a late lunch."

Gemma let out a gurgle of laughter. "Lunch? Who are you kidding? I can't leave now. Who knows how long this will take?" She waved her hand vaguely at all the people currently taking over her house.

Matt stood and offered her his hand. "You're shaking, probably a combination of low blood sugar and too much caffeine. If I'd been thinking, I would have brought you a muffin with your coffee this morning. There's nothing else for you to do here. VPD will need the house for a while, so you can't start cleaning up. You've given them your statement. You might as well have a sandwich and work on your paper for a few hours, somewhere with fewer distractions."

The fact Matt had realized she needed a calmer environment to focus on her paper gave Gemma a buzzy feeling, like the bubbles in soda on her tongue when she took the first sip from a fresh can. It was such a small thing. No one except her mother had ever truly worried about taking care of her. With a small nod, Gemma gave in to the urge to let someone else carry the burden for a few minutes. She took Matt's hand and let him pull her to standing.

"We're going for lunch," Matt announced. "I'll drop Gemma off at school when we're done. Call me when you're ready to do some more digging," Matt said to Murphy.

"I'm not sure she should go to school. One of us should be with her at all times," Murphy said.

"I'll be fine. I'll be surrounded by people, and my campus has security," Gemma pointed out.

"I'll pick her up when her class ends. Then except for the class itself, she won't be alone," Matt offered.

Gemma opened her mouth to object, stopping because there was no point. Murphy was already agreeing with Matt. She grabbed her jacket and laptop, and followed Matt out the door. She climbed into the passenger seat of Matt's truck, taking in her surroundings. The truck was an older model, the interior was spotless, and it started as soon as Matt turned the key. It was definitely in better shape than her old Toyota.

The truck suited him. A bigger vehicle, a little rugged, dependable. Everything Matt did proved he was dependable. He was a big man, but she didn't feel crowded by him. As they drove, she snuck glances at him, taking in how his big hands cradled the gearshift, how his sleeves rode up and exposed the dark hairs scattered over his wrists. He was a good-looking man. The silence in the truck was comfortable, which she appreciated. She'd needed to get away from the chaos that her home had turned into.

When they arrived, Gemma slid into a booth opposite Matt. The diner he'd brought her to was halfway between her house and the nursing school she attended, and yet she didn't think she'd ever noticed it before. Named Caroline's, it was very 1950s retro, with red vinyl booths and Formica tabletops. A counter ran the length of the building with stools lining it, all with matching red vinyl seats. More importantly to Gemma, the food smelled divine. She hadn't thought she was hungry, hadn't felt hungry until she walked in the door and was hit with the scent of frying hamburgers and hot coffee.

She muffled a groan, her mouth already watering. "You were right. I'm starving," she admitted. "This place is amazing. I had no idea it was here. How did you find it?"

"My aunt and uncle own it. In fact—"

"Matt Foster, don't you think you can sneak in here without saying hello to me." A woman Gemma guessed to be in her late fifties had approached the table, carrying a pot of coffee and a menu that she set in front of Gemma. Her blond hair was cut into a short bob, and her blue eyes sparkled with happiness when she looked at Matt. She was all of about five feet tall, and looked nothing like Matt. Maybe he was related to the husband?

"Coffee, dear?" She waved the pot at Gemma, giving her a wide smile. Gemma nodded.

"I wouldn't dream of it, Aunt Caroline." Matt grinned and stood to accept the hug she offered him, his large frame swallowing her as he wrapped his arms around her.

Gemma couldn't stop staring. This was a side of Matt she hadn't expected. His police persona was a combination of stern and gentle;

now he was relaxed and happy. It was a nice change. Gemma needed some relaxation right now.

Matt sat back down, his cheeks flushing a dull pink under his tanned skin. "Gemma, this is my aunt, Caroline Foster. Aunt Caroline, this is my friend Gemma."

"Pleased to meet you, Gemma." Her smile was friendly and kind, if tinged with curiosity.

"It's nice to meet you, Caroline." Gemma closed the menu she had barely glanced at. "Everything smells wonderful. Matt tells me this is your place. What's the house specialty?"

"That depends. If you're vegetarian, we make a mean homemade veggie burger. If you're not, our pulled pork sandwich is the way to go. I make the brioche buns myself, and it comes with hand-cut fries and slaw."

"The pulled pork sounds perfect." At that moment, her stomach rumbled again, loudly.

Caroline laughed. "I'll get that right out for you. Don't you dare leave without saying hello to your uncle," she warned Matt before she hustled away.

Gemma was confused. "She didn't ask you what you wanted. Aren't you eating?"

"I'm their guinea pig. When I come in, I either get the pulled pork, or if they're testing new recipes, I get to try them. We'll see what comes out today." He shrugged. "I don't mind. I'll eat anything, and even the dishes that don't make it on the menu are pretty good."

His easy acceptance of his family surprising him with trial recipes was one more piece of the puzzle that was Matt. He was more laid back and trusting than she'd expected. "You're close to them. Did you see them a lot when you were growing up?"

Matt nodded. "My parents adopted me as a baby, and I'm their only child. Caroline and Ron had two boys my age, and we grew up together. They're more like my brothers than cousins, and my aunt and uncle are like second parents. What about you? Are you close to your family?"

Gemma shook her head. "My dad died when I was little. Car accident. Mom never remarried. She had one sister, who moved to Australia after college and hasn't been home in years. My father's family never liked my mother, and they cut all ties after he died. So it's just me."

She glanced out the window, hoping Matt hadn't picked up on how alone she felt, and that he wouldn't ask deeper questions. Ever since her mother had died, her life had been untethered. After making it through rehab and finally sticking with the program, she had allowed herself to dream and plan for the first time in years. Going back to school had been a major step in making those dreams reality, and then her mother's cancer had come back. This time there had been no hope of a happy ending. Now she was alone, adrift. She still wanted her nursing degree, still wanted to specialize in addictions, to help people who were struggling like she had. After that? She had never allowed herself to want a relationship. The kinds of guys who could overlook her past were usually not the kind who made good partners in the long run. She'd found that out the hard way shortly into her recovery, when she'd thought dating might be something she could handle. As soon as a guy found out about her past, they either bailed or expected her to get kinky with them. Or worse, got paranoid and possessive, assuming she would cheat on them at the first opportunity. Eventually she had decided being alone was easier.

The rattle of a plate being set on the table in front of her shook her out of her melancholy. Her life was what it was. She had a few good friends, like Kimmy and Nate—and, surprisingly, more support at Harbourview than she ever thought she did. It was enough.

Gemma focussed on the plate, taking in the fluffy brioche bun filled with steaming, juicy pork, the huge pile of golden fries, the green coleslaw flecked with bits of orange carrot. "This looks amazing."

The plate in front of Matt was filled with a grilled sandwich that was oozing pulled pork and cheese out the edges, with a side of fried eggs and hash browns, and a ramekin of maple syrup.

"Your uncle is playing with a pulled pork version of a croque monsieur. This one has provolone, and the maple syrup is for dipping.

Let me know what you think," Caroline told Matt after she topped off their coffee.

The smile Matt flashed his aunt was full of love and appreciation, and for a split second Gemma wished he would look at her the same way.

"It looks delicious, and I promise to be honest when I tell Uncle Ron what I think." Matt picked up the sandwich as Caroline was called away to another table. He dipped the corner of the bread into the maple syrup, then sank his teeth into the bite. Pulled pork squeezed out of the sides of the bread, and a glistening drop of maple syrup clung to his bottom lip as he chewed. For a split second, Gemma was tempted to lean over the table and lick it off. She shoved the thought away. He was a cop. She had to remember that. Even if he was a good cop, a decent man, her history meant there could be nothing between them.

Instead, she picked up her own sandwich and took a huge bite, hoping to satisfy her cravings with food, if nothing else.

The first bite of her sandwich made her eyes water. The bun was pillowy soft and buttery, a sharp contrast to the spicy bite of the sauce on the pork, which was melt-in-her-mouth tender. It might have been the best sandwich she'd ever eaten. She had barely swallowed when Caroline was back, this time delivering two old-fashioned milkshakes heaped with whipped cream and topped with a cherry. "This will help with the spice." She smiled as she placed the glasses on the table. "I wasn't sure if you were a chocolate or a strawberry person, so I brought one of each. Matt likes both." She winked.

Gemma reached for the strawberry and took a sip, the bright fruit flavour and rich creamy texture cutting the spice from the barbecue sauce, cooling her taste buds. "I haven't had a strawberry milkshake since I was a kid," she admitted. "This reminds me of Saturday afternoons with my mom. Thank you. And the pork is amazing. I'll definitely be back." Sharing the cherished memory was impulsive, but for the first time since she'd lost her mom, it didn't hurt when she thought about her.

"What did you think of the sandwich?" Caroline asked Matt.

"The pork and the cheese are perfect, but I think you need a bread with more structure. The French bread you used got a bit too soggy." Matt pointed to where the middle of the sandwich was tearing apart. "Too hard to pick up and eat. Maybe a rye bread would work better?"

His aunt took a closer look at the sandwich and nodded. "I'll send your uncle out to look at it. Do you want me to have him make something else?"

Matt pulled the plate closer to him. "No way. I'll eat it with a knife and fork. It tastes too good to waste." He forked another bite into his mouth, making Caroline laugh as she walked away.

"You know your food," Gemma said, popping a fry into her mouth. "I wouldn't have known another type of bread would make a difference."

Matt cut another bite of the sandwich and dipped it into the syrup. "Remember, they've been testing food on me for years. I even cooked in their kitchen with Uncle Ron for a couple of years when I was in high school. Here, try this. Tell me what you taste, and think about how it feels in your mouth." Matt held the fork out for her to take a bite.

His actions were so casual, but to Gemma they were incredibly intimate. No one had ever fed her, not that she could remember. It was such a personal gesture. She leaned forward and closed her lips over the bite he was offering.

The pork was dressed with the same spicy sauce that hers was, while the sweet maple syrup cut the spice. She let the flavours and textures play over her tongue before she tried to describe it to Matt. "The syrup blends with the barbecue sauce. It's not as spicy as mine. The cheese is kind of stringy, a bit chewy. Not in the same way as the pork, though. I can't quite name the texture, but I like it. I see what you mean about the bread. Even though the eggs gave it a rich flavour, the bread got soggy, and didn't crisp the way French toast usually does. A different kind would fix that?"

Matt grinned at her. "A different bread will hold up to the egg better. Uncle Ron can experiment until he finds the right combination. Once he does, we can try it again, and you can tell me what you think."

Gemma broke eye contact with Matt and took another long sip of her milkshake. His offhand remark about bringing her back to the diner stirred up impossible feelings. They didn't have that kind of relationship. Hell, they didn't have a relationship, and they had no future together. "I need to work on my paper. Will it be okay with your aunt if I monopolize this booth?"

Matt studied her long enough that she wanted to squirm in her seat, then eventually nodded. "That's why I brought you here. Work as long as you want; then I'll drop you off at your class."

Gemma pulled out her laptop and tried to ignore the man sitting across from her. It was a harder task than it should have been.

CHAPTER 14

Matt parked his truck on a side street off Hastings, the DTES main drag, and headed for the spot where he was supposed to meet Murphy and Abel. He'd dropped Gemma off for her class after spending the entire afternoon at the diner with her. She'd worked on her homework and carefully avoided talking to him; he'd done a little research of his own, into True North Security. It was always good to know who he was working with. Even though Nate's trust spoke volumes, Matt liked to make up his own mind about people. Everything he'd found so far had reinforced his initial impression. Murphy and his team were professionals with ethics. Matt loved being a VPD officer, but it never hurt to have a backup plan. If things went south over his incident with Morin, working for Murphy might not be so bad.

Murphy and Abel were sitting in a coffee shop, chatting with someone Matt recognized immediately as a sex worker and addict who worked for Russell. They'd been trying to talk to her all week and hadn't been able to find her.

Matt seated himself in the last chair at the table for four, noting the half-eaten doughnut in front of the woman, along with at least eight empty sugar packets. At a guess, she was in desperate need of her next high and was trying to curb the cravings with sugar. She was thin, the knobs of her wrists sticking out from her coat sleeves, and her dark hair was lank and greasy. Her heavy makeup did little to hide the deep circles under her eyes, and her hands shook as she stirred more sugar into her coffee. She was close to thirty, about the same age as Gemma, but they couldn't look more different. The contrast between the two women made Matt grateful Gemma has been able to get away from this life.

"Hey, April. Thanks for talking to us." Matt had arrested her before and knew it wasn't her legal name. Using her preferred name was a simple courtesy too many cops refused to give.

"Gemma's in trouble," she said, as if that explained everything.

"April was telling us stories about when she used to work with Gemma," Murphy said. "It sounds like they were pretty close, once."

April ducked her head. "Gemma did good. She got into treatment, got herself clean. She still checks on me sometimes, makes sure I'm okay. Not everyone does that." She fidgeted with a braided bracelet, twisting it back and forth on her wrist.

Matt wasn't surprised. He'd seen the title of the paper Gemma was writing, and it didn't take a rocket scientist to figure out she was studying addictions. Trying to help her friends sounded like something she would do. He'd seen the loneliness when she talked about her lack of family, which would make her friends even more important to her.

"Do you know anything that could help Gemma? Anything about people who might want Russell dead, or to hurt Gemma?"

"Lots of people wanted Russell dead. He was a bastard. Most pimps are, most dealers are, and he was both. If it was only that, someone would have killed him years ago." April looked around the restaurant, shrinking lower in her chair before speaking again. Her voice was barely above a whisper. "I don't know who he was working with. I overheard a conversation once, when I was picking up my fix. Whoever he was talking to, they were arguing about money. The guy told Russell that he was taking too big a cut, and if he didn't start paying everything he owed, they would have someone else take over running the business. Russell noticed me right after that, sent me outside. I've been hiding out since I heard Russell was killed, in case they came after me."

Matt's excitement at the prospect of a lead was tempered by concern. April was right to be afraid. If the person responsible for killing Russell thought April knew who they were, she would be a target. Matt leaned closer to April, keeping his voice quiet. "Do you know who 'they' are? Who was threatening Russell?"

April shook her head vigorously. "No way. I don't even know who I should be afraid of. I'm out of money, and I need a fix. I gotta work." She glanced around once more, then met Matt's eyes. "I do know one thing. Russell had cops on his payroll. More than one. Some of the girls had to entertain them sometimes." April smirked. "I never had to do that. I'm not their type."

Matt felt sick to his stomach. He'd heard about cops coercing sex workers for sex in exchange for lenient treatment, and he'd really hoped most of that had been cleaned up. If April was being truthful, they had a bigger problem. Could a cop have killed Russell? Had Russell done something stupid like try to blackmail one of them? "Can you give us any names, April? I'll make sure it never comes back to you," Matt promised. Everything he was doing was off the record. No one ever needed to know he got his lead from April.

April gave him a seductive smile. "Why, Officer Matt . . . I thought you knew. Rumour has it that you were suspended for attacking one of those wonderful officers. If I were you, I'd start there." She pushed back from the table, swaying slightly as she stood to her full six-foot height. He didn't like how exhausted April looked.

Morin was involved? He shouldn't be surprised, and yet. Anger warred with outrage. How far would Morin go to protect his career and still keep dirty money and free sex flowing? Matt was determined to find out. "Will you be okay? Do you need anything?"

"I'll be fine. I just need my fix. I'll see you around. Tell Gemma I said hi." Without another word, April swayed to the exit, her legs looking impossibly long and thin in her skinny jeans and high-heeled boots.

"This keeps getting more complicated," Murphy said. "Dirty cops are tough to track down, and tougher to root out. Are you up to this? And are you willing to sacrifice your career?"

Matt leaned back in his chair, crossing his arms over his chest. Was he willing to give up his career to expose corruption? Damn straight. If the force wouldn't get rid of bad cops, he didn't want to be part of it. "Am I right that you've been hinting there might be room for me at True North?"

Abel looked surprised when Murphy smiled. "I'm always looking for good people. Nate vouched for you, you're good people. I've been trying to branch out to Vancouver for years, and Nate keeps turning me down. No pressure, but there's an exit strategy available if you want one."

The brief flare of excitement Matt experienced was tempered with regret. He loved VPD, had wanted to be a cop his entire life, and he didn't want to be forced to give that up. If it meant cleaning up the department, it might be worth it. It was good to know he had options. "I'll think about it. I looked into you, and your organization has an excellent reputation. Nate speaks very highly of you too." Matt's phone buzzed, demanding his attention.

> GEMMA: I've got to stay after class to work on a project. I'll catch a rideshare home to pick up my car.

Matt smothered a growl as he read the message. A rideshare? No way. When he'd dropped Gemma off for her class earlier, he'd told her to wait for him by the building entrance. Matt knew she wanted to take care of herself, but this was not the time for her to prove her independence. His sixth sense had been on high alert ever since Abel had pulled the cameras out of Gemma's house. Someone was watching her, and worried about what she knew. That made her a target.

> MATT: I'm picking you up. Let me know when you need a ride.

"Something we need to know?" Murphy looked pointedly at the phone.

"Gemma has to stay after class and wants to take a rideshare home."

Murphy was shaking his head before Matt finished speaking. "Not happening. One of us needs to pick her up. After the break-in at her place, she's a target. Whoever is after her probably knows her schedule. That means she's in danger."

"I told her that. I'm picking her up."

Abel let out a low whistle. "We have a problem, boss. Jett located the website the cameras were being broadcast to. She was able to hack in, start reviewing the saved recordings. There's nothing suspicious so far, but she was also able to hack into the account that owns the videos. It was registered to Russell Molloy."

The website could belong to Molloy, except that none of the video clips had been taken from Gemma's house. Russell spying on Gemma didn't make sense, when he could get more explicit recordings whenever they were together. If the website had really been Russell's, it wouldn't be an issue. What was Abel concerned about?

Murphy looked worried. "You said we have a problem. If the videos actually belonged to Molloy, we wouldn't have a problem, so I'm guessing she found something else?" Murphy asked.

"The account is in Molloy's name, but the email isn't his, the contact information is fake, and the account has a prepaid credit card listed as the method of payment. Jett also called VPD, talked to Rebecca. Rebecca confirmed that Molloy's computer and phone had nothing on it to link him to this website. Molloy wasn't the type to hide this kind of activity. Jett's almost positive Molloy had nothing to do with this."

"Which means the person who put the cameras in Gemma's place is probably the same person who killed Russell Molloy," Matt said. "If they've killed once, they won't hesitate to kill again if they think she's a threat." Matt drained his coffee and stood. "I'll go find her. We'll meet you back at Harbourview. We have some planning to do."

"Keep her safe, and don't let her out of your sight." Murphy followed Matt out the coffee shop door, Abel close behind. "Whoever is orchestrating this clearly doesn't want to be found, and has some serious resources to play with. Now that the cameras are deactivated, they'll know we're looking for them. Gemma is in danger."

Matt had already figured that out. "I'm on it." He climbed into his truck and headed for Gemma's school. He checked the time and calculated how long it would take to get there, and what time Gemma's class was supposed to end. How long did she plan to work on the project? He wanted to get there before she tried to ignore his text and leave on her own. Traffic was heavier than normal for this time of night, and his frustration grew as the minutes ticked by. Finally, he made it past the accident that was slowing traffic, and he pressed his foot down on the accelerator, racing towards Gemma.

Matt slowed his truck to a crawl and scanned Gemma's school campus, assessing any possible threat. Even this late, parking was at a premium, so he circled the building where he'd dropped her off, watching for her. He was at the end of the block, preparing to turn around, when he saw her coming down the steps, talking to another student. A dark van roared past him, speeding down the narrow street towards the steps. Matt yanked the steering wheel and did a 180 turn to follow. The van screeched to a halt in front of where Gemma and the classmate were standing. As if in slow motion, Matt watched the side door slide open and an arm reach for Gemma.

CHAPTER 15

Gemma shrieked and pulled back, digging in her heels. Gasping for breath, she twisted to break free.

"Get in the van, bitch!" The man pointed a pistol directly at her. Gemma closed her eyes to block out the sight of the sleek, black gun; then she went limp and fell to the pavement.

The dead weight threw her kidnapper off balance, and he lost his grip on her wrist. Gemma rolled away before he could grab her again. She could hear her lab partner screaming, but all she could focus on now was escaping.

"Just shoot her!" someone yelled as the van started rolling again.

Gemma braced for the impact of a bullet. Instead, she heard a howl of pain and the slam of the van door. Tires squealed, and Gemma watched the van careen down the street and out onto the main road, then disappear into the night.

"Gemma! Gemma, are you all right?" Matt leaned over her, running his hands over her gently, checking for injuries.

Panic and fear made her jerk back, until his voice penetrated. Confusion mingled with relief. She hadn't texted Matt to pick her up, and she was grateful to see him. "Matt? What are you doing here?"

"I was waiting to pick you up. I was at the end of the road when the van stopped. I got here as fast as I could."

As her heart rate decelerated, Gemma noticed aches and pains where Matt was probing. Her wrist and shoulder hurt where the gunman had grabbed her, and her hip hurt from where she'd crashed to the ground. Her jeans had protected her skin, and she hadn't hit her head. She pushed herself up to a sitting position, taking in Matt's truck illegally stopped on the sidewalk with the door hanging wide open, and her lab partner Grazia leaning over her. "I'm fine, really," Gemma told her reassuringly.

"You're fine? You need to call 9-1-1! They were pointing a *gun* at you!" Grazia trailed off, a horrified look on her face.

Gemma was glad no one had witnessed this except Grazia. She didn't need an audience. At least Grazia hadn't been hurt. "I know. I don't need to call 9-1-1. This is Matt. He's a police officer. He'll take care of everything."

Matt looked away from Gemma long enough to acknowledge her lab partner. "You should head home. I'll make sure Gemma is okay. Do you have a car? Are you good to drive?"

Grazia looked from Gemma to Matt and back. "My brother is picking me up. I'm meeting him at the restaurant across the street." She pointed at a brightly lit fast-food place. "That's his car pulling in now. I'll text you about the assignment," she told Gemma as she hurried away.

Gemma let Matt help her up from the ground. She was going to have some nasty bruises, but physically she would be fine. The bigger question was how she was still alive. The driver had ordered her to be shot. What had stopped it?

"What happened? How did you stop them from shooting me?"

"I rear-ended them, and that caused the van door to slide shut. I guess it caught the shooter's wrist before he could take a shot. Truthfully, you did all the work. Dropping like that was smart. It saved your life."

Matt's words slammed into her, bringing her back to reality as he helped her into his truck. Someone had tried to kill her, and they had almost succeeded.

She was starting to shake. Shock was setting in, she thought abstractly. Matt pulled a blanket from behind the seat and draped it over her, and she burrowed deep into the warmth. It smelled like him, clean and woodsy. Why a big city cop always smelled woodsy mystified her. She liked it, though.

"Let's get you back to Harbourview. We need to let Murphy and Abel know what happened. This changes things," Matt said, speaking firmly. Gemma paid little attention. She was too tired and too wired to deal with whatever "things" Matt was talking about right now. Later was soon enough.

Gemma woke, disoriented, when a heavily muscled arm slid under her legs. Fear came crashing back as she remembered the attempted kidnapping, and she struggled to get free.

"It's me," Matt said quietly as he lifted her out of the truck like she weighed nothing. Gemma stopped struggling and let herself relax against him, enjoying the temporary contact. She must have fallen asleep on the drive to the hotel, and she was exhausted and sore. She didn't have the energy to argue that he didn't need to carry her. She hoped no one she worked with saw her like this. She ducked her face closer into Matt's chest to hide her identity. Matt cradled her in his arms and carried her to the elevators. His arms were like steel bands under her legs and around her shoulders, while his chest was firm and warm under her cheek.

When they arrived at the suite Nate had assigned True North, Abel swung the door open and said nothing as Matt carried her into the room and settled her on the sofa.

"How are you feeling?" Murphy handed her a cup of tea as she sat up. "Matt called us and told us what happened. Did you recognize either of the kidnappers?"

Gemma sipped the tea and tried to remember everything about the incident. It had happened so fast. "Even though they were both wearing masks, I could see the guy who grabbed me was white. He had brown eyes. He was strong, but I don't think he was really tall.

Not like Matt. I'd guess maybe my height? Five eight? I think they were both wearing black. They were definitely wearing gloves. The thing I did notice was his boots. They looked a lot like yours." She pointed at the black boots Matt wore. Gemma stared at the thick rubber soles and flashed back to seeing those same boots as she fell to the ground, trying to get away. She gripped the cup harder to keep her hands from shaking. She'd come so close tonight to dying.

"Police issue," Matt said, frowning.

"April did say Molloy had cops on the payroll," Murphy pointed out.

"You saw April? How is she?" Gemma sat up straighter. April had been a good friend to her over the years, and street life was hard on her.

"She told us to tell you she says hi," Matt said. "She's not looking great. She's too thin, and Russell getting killed has her scared."

Gemma bit her lip and looked away, blinking back tears.

"If we assume it was an officer who attempted to kidnap her, what was the plan?" Abel wanted to know.

"To kill me." Gemma fought to keep her fear from showing. Inside she wanted to cry, and she had never missed her mother as much as she did right now. She would get through this. She was strong.

"Why not shoot you, then?"

"A shooting on a college campus attracts all kinds of attention," Matt pointed out. "The disappearance of an addict who dies of an overdose? It was dark, and she was alone except for one other person. If they had succeeded, who would have known? We would have found her body somewhere, and it would be chalked up to another relapse, or be associated with the current gang wars. My guess is that was the plan. They were likely following her until they had a chance to grab her with few witnesses. They only tried to shoot Gemma when they couldn't get her in the van."

"Very plausible," Murphy agreed. "They won't stop. Whoever is behind this seems positive you either know something you shouldn't, or Russell gave you something incriminating. You might not be as lucky next time. We need to get you somewhere safe."

"What? No." Gemma shook her head adamantly. "I can be safe in Vancouver. I can stay here at Harbourview. Now that you know how Russell was killed, you can make sure the room is secure. I won't go anywhere except work and school."

"It's too risky. You can stay here tonight in our suite, where we can protect you. They tried to grab you from campus, so they clearly know your routine. You're not safe at home, at work, or at school. Whoever is behind this is getting bold, or desperate. If you stay here, you're putting other people at risk too. The best answer is to get you out of town." Murphy turned to Abel. "Call Andrea, get her to book something for a few weeks, maybe somewhere in the Okanagan? Driving distance from Vancouver, far enough away that Gemma will be harder to find. See if Kylie or Roman is available to help. She'll need security, and we need to stay here to find out who's behind the threat."

"Hold on," Gemma objected. "This is my life you're talking about. You want to send me to some rental somewhere, with strangers? No way. I can't go. I have commitments. I have classes, projects. If I miss too many classes, or don't hand in my work, I'll fail. I've been offered an internship, and if I fail a course, I lose it. I'm not letting that happen." She folded her arms across her chest stubbornly. They were trying to keep her safe, but they needed to understand that her future was at stake. There had to be another way.

"I may have a solution," Matt offered. "My grandfather has a cabin in the mountains. It's remote—and secure. No one knows about it. I could take Gemma, stay with her. That way she's not with a stranger. Since I'm suspended anyway, no one will notice I'm gone."

"A cabin in the middle of nowhere? Also, no." Graduation was so close. Her internship was for her dream job, one that hardly ever came up. If she failed a course, she could repeat it. If she lost her internship, she might lose her chance to work for her dream addictions program forever.

Murphy gave Matt a long, assessing look. "Won't people be able to trace it back to you? Through property records, if nothing else? We're dealing with trained investigators with all kinds of resources available."

"The cabin belongs to my biological grandfather. My adoption was sealed, and even on my original birth certificate, there is no record of my father's name—it's listed as unknown. I tracked my grandfather down a few years ago through a genealogy website. The only people who know I found him are my adoptive parents, and I never told them about the cabin. I never even told them his name. No one can trace it back to me. It's perfect."

If it weren't for school, disappearing to Matt's cabin for a few days didn't sound too bad. Spending those days alone with him made her nervous, although not because she didn't trust him. She did. In three days, Matt had proved that he was a good guy, and she could rely on him. No, her problem was she didn't trust herself. It would be too easy to delude herself into thinking that Matt's concern for her was more than professional. Allowing Matt to fill up some of her loneliness was a mistake. It was one more reason why going to his cabin was a bad idea. Too bad none of them were listening to her.

Murphy nodded. "You should leave at first light. Grab the supplies you need, plan for being gone for at least a few weeks. Hopefully we can get this taken care of quickly. Just in case, you need to be prepared to stay off the grid for a while. How remote is this place? I don't want you using your cell phones, too easy to trace."

"There's no service out where we'll be. Electricity is all from a generator. Heating is wood. It's in good shape and it's winterized, if a little rustic." Matt met Gemma's eyes and grimaced apologetically. "You'll need boots and a warm coat. We'll have to get you some basics, and we can't run all over the city stocking up. You may have to live with department store stuff."

Gemma set her tea down carefully, needing to get through to them about why this couldn't happen. She reminded herself they were doing this to protect her, but it had been the second-worst day of her life and she was tired. "I don't care about the clothes. I spent too many years being grateful for clean socks and a warm sweater to care about what I wear. You need to listen. My internship means everything to me. I can't go anywhere until I'm done school."

Murphy was scowling, but she was no longer nervous around him, and she wasn't backing down.

"What if we had Rebecca contact the school and tell them that you were being put into protective custody? That you can't attend classes until the situation is resolved. You could still complete your assignments, and you wouldn't be penalized for missing classes." Matt's suggestion made Gemma pause.

"That could work," she said slowly. "I'd still need an internet connection to upload my assignments."

"There's a public library in Williams Lake, about half an hour away from the cabin. I could drive you there when you need to upload them."

"I can live with that," Murphy said.

Gemma knew when it was time to give in. "If Rebecca can get the school to agree, then I guess you can drag me into the wilderness in the morning. Now I'm exhausted and I'm going to bed." Without another word, Gemma walked into one of the two bedrooms in the suite and closed the door behind her.

CHAPTER 16

Gemma's restless pacing was setting Matt's teeth on edge. She'd barely said a word in the car on the long drive up to the cabin, sitting silently in the passenger seat, working on homework with headphones on to discourage talking. When they'd arrived, she'd walked the small space that made up the one-room building, raised an eyebrow at the solitary double bed in the corner of the room, thrown her backpack on the sofa, and began pacing. Silently.

The threat to her safety had them all wound tight, and her obvious discomfort at being stuck in the cabin with him bothered him. There was no other option. None of them trusted VPD to keep her safe, not after the second attempt to silence her. All signs pointed to the danger coming from inside VPD itself—either the force had a leak, or the killer was a cop. In either case, it had meant whisking Gemma away to a location no one else knew about. The cabin was perfect.

Half of him wanted to be in Vancouver, trying to figure out who on the force was the threat. Every investigative instinct he had told him it was Morin, though he wondered if he was too focussed on Morin because of his personal feelings. Morin was a bad cop, and he was connected to Russell, but so were a number of others, according to the people they'd interviewed. They didn't know who they could trust. With the hearing regarding his suspension scheduled for the end of next week, Rebecca was working on figuring out who the mole was. She would relay any information to Murphy. No one had the number to the satellite phone Murphy had given Matt, except Murphy himself. They were truly cut off from civilization.

The closest town to the cabin was a twenty-minute drive, and it was small enough they might attract unwanted attention. Williams Lake was a little farther away and a little bigger, though they still needed to restrict any trips there. The cabin was not in a popular tourist area, which made it perfect for hiding out. It also meant they could be identified as strangers. His grandfather had used the cabin frequently until his Parkinson's had worsened significantly a year earlier. Now Matt drove up a few times a year to make sure everything was kept in good condition, even though he knew his grandfather would never be able to use it again.

Matt tried to see the cabin through Gemma's eyes. To him, this cabin represented the bond that had developed between him and his grandfather after Matt had tracked him down with the help of a genealogy site. Finding out his father had died decades earlier had been disheartening, but his grandfather had been thrilled to find out about Matt's existence, and together they had built a relationship that had only grown stronger over the years.

To an outsider, the cabin could be considered quaint. It was built from rough-hewn wood, with plank floors. The big windows made it hard to keep out the bitter winter cold, though they made the cabin brighter with natural light. The single room was dominated by a big fireplace that was surrounded by built-in bookshelves. A double bed covered in a handmade quilt occupied one corner, and a small kitchen ran along the back wall. There was a table with two chairs, hand carved by his grandfather decades earlier, and finally an old sofa in front of the fireplace. He found it rustic and homey, although he could see where Gemma might view it as rough, little more than a hut in the woods. At least his grandfather had built an addition that included indoor plumbing. Most important, no one would find them here.

With a sigh, Matt began unpacking the groceries he'd purchased before they left Vancouver, while Gemma had been clothes shopping with Murphy's protection. He surveyed the food in front of him, trying to decide what to make for dinner. The first thing he'd done when they arrived was fire up the gas-powered generator that provided electricity, followed immediately by starting a fire in the fireplace for warmth. The generator allowed them to run the pump for running water from a well on the property, and for a small refrigerator for the perishables he'd bought. The cabin was built into the side of a mountain, and there was expanded cold storage just off the kitchen. Considering the season, the cold storage would keep milk, eggs, and meat fresh for several days. That meant that he could reduce their reliance on the generator and ration the gas he'd brought for it.

The cabin's kitchen area had a propane stove for basic meals, and Matt had made sure to purchase mostly nonperishable foods. He found the shopping bag filled with marshmallows, chocolate, and graham crackers, and stashed it in one of the cupboards to surprise Gemma later. They might be stuck in the wilderness, but the least he could do was make things a little brighter for her. A bonfire and s'mores in the evening might take her mind off the threat hanging over her. If it got too cold for an outdoor fire, they could still do s'mores in the fireplace.

When Matt finished unpacking, he turned to face Gemma. "Let me show you the rest of the cabin."

The cabin was the definition of one-room efficiency, but Matt still had one surprise to show her, one that he hoped would help her unwind and relax a little. She'd been through more than any person should have to in the last five days. She needed to de-stress.

Gemma stopped pacing and followed him to a door off one side of the kitchen. When Matt swung it open, she gasped quietly. Inside was a bathroom with a basic sink and toilet, and a big iron tub.

"It's not much, but it has indoor plumbing. No hot water, though. In the summer, the water gets warm enough to use without heating it. This time of year we'll have to heat water for a bath."

"Who built all this?" Gemma slipped past Matt to explore the small room.

The subtle scent of orange blossoms trailed behind Gemma and made Matt want to see if all of her smelled that good. "My grandfather built it all," Matt said proudly, noting the solid construction of the walls and the careful use of space. His grandfather had put a lot of time and effort into making this place comfortable and welcoming. The furniture in the main room was handcrafted, and the small open cabinet that stored soap and towels exhibited the same craftsmanship. "He did most of the work before I met him. The way he tells it, after he retired, he wanted to spend as much time as possible out here. My grandmother put her foot down, said she would only come with him if he installed a septic field and piped in running water. You can see who won."

Gemma trailed a finger along the edge of the iron tub. The deep tub had a ceramic coating, glossy smooth and inviting. "This looks like heaven."

"Say the word, and I'll start boiling water." Matt headed back into the main room, and Gemma followed. When she moved to pull the door closed, he stopped her. "You should leave it open. Let the heat from the fireplace warm it up."

Matt was pleased to see that Gemma looked a little less anxious when they returned to the main living area. "Feeling a little more relaxed?"

Gemma walked around the room once again. "If I weren't weeks away from graduation, this wouldn't be a bad place to spend a weekend with my boyfriend. A cup of tea and a book in front of the fireplace? Sounds like my kind of getaway. But we're not here for a weekend, and you're not my boyfriend."

Matt pushed her gently towards the sofa and sat beside her once she took a seat. "I know you're worried about school. Your professors were all understanding when Rebecca talked to them this morning, weren't they?"

Gemma dropped her head back against the couch. "Yes. Before we left Vancouver, I received emails from all of them, including alternate assignments and instructions on revised due dates. I appreciate everything you're all doing. I still worry."

Matt's heart broke at her genuine surprise that anyone would care enough to take care of things for her, especially something she cared this much about. Gemma was too used to doing things on her own. He wanted to show her she could lean on other people and they wouldn't let her down.

"And here I thought you were cranky about the idea of sharing a bed with me," Matt teased, bumping his knee against hers.

Gemma's head snapped back up, and her eyes went dark and far away as they roamed slowly from his face down his body and back up again. "Payment for services?" she asked suggestively. "What's your pleasure?"

Matt grasped the hand she placed on his biceps, holding it gently. He thought she was teasing him, and this was not something he could joke about. Not with her. "No. That's not what I meant, and I think you know it. If not, then hear me say it. I will never, ever ask you for sex as payment for anything. You're incredibly attractive, and under normal circumstances I'd love to get to know you better, take you on a date. The fact is, you're being hunted, and you're accused of a murder you didn't commit. That's a lot of trauma to process. I'm a cop. The breach of ethics and power imbalance would be unfair to both of us." Matt paused, waiting for Gemma to absorb his message, searching her face for some kind of reaction. Her bitter laugh was not what he was hoping for.

"My life will never be normal. I'll always be a former sex worker and addict. Dating me would ruin your career. I can be your dirty little secret, but your girlfriend? Never going to happen. I'm not girlfriend material. Guess I'll be sleeping on the couch."

Gemma turned away from him, not fast enough to hide the flash of pain on her face. She really believed that her past made her unlovable? That she wasn't girlfriend material. The vehemence in her words told him more than she knew. She'd been hurt before, and she wasn't willing to risk being hurt again. As much as he wanted to prove how wrong she was, he could not make a move until she was safely back in

Vancouver and all threats against her had been eliminated. As for her past ruining his career? She was right to worry. If he stayed with VPD, their lives could be difficult. People could be cruel. If he joined True North, Murphy wasn't the type to hold someone's past against them. His family wouldn't care. They only wanted him to be happy.

"You're not sleeping on the couch. The bed is plenty big, and we're both adults. Besides, it can get cold here at night. Makes more sense to put all the blankets on one bed and share." Matt hoped he didn't sound as eager as he felt. The thought of sleeping next to Gemma, even platonically, had him half hard and aching in the best way.

Gemma rolled her eyes at him. "You expect me to believe that?"

"Believe what you want. I'm telling you the truth." Matt shrugged, acting casual. Gemma was still anxious and stressed, but she was beginning to loosen up. "We need to eat. I'm making chicken for dinner. How about you come help me prep it, and then we can take the rest of the night off?"

CHAPTER 17

Heat crawled up Gemma's cheeks. She was being unfair to Matt. He was a truly decent man who didn't deserve to have her take her fear out on him. Her emotions were stretched as tight as they'd ever been. Even her mother's death hadn't been quite like this, mostly because she'd been sick for so long that by the end, it was almost a relief her pain was over. Finding herself in a one-room cabin, with only one bed, with Matt Foster? A guy she'd like to strip down and make a meal of? It was the last straw in a series of events that had been impossible to control. So she had reverted to the hard shell that had protected her emotions when she was working the streets. If she pretended nothing mattered, then nothing did.

In her attempt to deflect, to make a joke out of this, she'd upset him. "I'm sorry. I shouldn't have said that. I know you weren't expecting anything from me. You've been nothing but kind to me through all of this. How can I help with dinner?"

Matt accepted the offered olive branch with a simple nod, and once again Gemma recognized that he was different from most cops she'd dealt with. Her lack of faith in him had hurt him. Somehow it was like he knew her better than anyone. It had only been a few days since Russell's death, yet the week had stretched on forever. At every turn, Matt had been there for her, defending her reputation and protecting her. That alone told her more about who he was than anything else could have.

Wordlessly, Gemma followed Matt to the tiny kitchen area.

"I'm making chicken cacciatore. Can you chop the vegetables?"

Gemma accepted the bag and knife Matt handed her, her skin tingling when his fingers brushed hers. She couldn't control her body's response to Matt. The aching need he aroused in her was one of the reasons she'd baited him. If she could push him away, there was less temptation.

When she looked in the bag, she discovered mushrooms, peppers, and onions, and the earthy smells made her mouth water. It had been a long time since the sandwiches they'd eaten on the drive up, and surprisingly, she was hungry. Matt was right—dinner was a good idea. She edged past him to get to the small sink to wash the vegetables, then took them over to the two-person table to chop. The kitchen was too cramped for both of them to work comfortably. His huge frame filled the tiny space, and if she stayed close, there would be no way to avoid bumping into him at every turn.

Gemma kept an eye on Matt as she chopped, appreciating his economical movements. His time in his family's diner had paid off: He was a pro in the kitchen. In less time than she'd needed to chop the vegetables, he'd cleaned and cut the chicken, heated the oil in a large cast-iron skillet, and started cooking. In short order, the chicken was browned, the veggies were sautéed, and everything was combined back in the skillet with tomato sauce and seasoning. The rich scents took her from hungry to ravenous, and her stomach growled loudly.

Matt twisted a dial on the stove and turned to face Gemma. "The chicken needs to simmer for a bit; then I'll cook some pasta to go with it, but you sound hungry. Want a snack?"

Gemma accepted the apple Matt offered her and surveyed the small cabin again. It was quaint and comfortable, and looked well loved. "You said your grandfather built all of this, to spend time with your grandmother. Do they still come out here?"

Gemma turned in time to see the sadness that flashed across

Matt's face. "My grandmother died shortly before I tracked my father's family down. My grandfather was the only one left. We used to come up here a few times a year. Now he has Parkinson's, and it's progressed to the stage he needs constant care. He's in a facility now. He refused to come to Vancouver, so I get up to visit him as often as I can." Matt sat back down on the sofa in front of the fire.

Sitting next to him, Gemma wanted to know more about who Matt Foster really was. "You said you were adopted. Tell me about your family?" She'd met his adoptive aunt and uncle, who were obviously affectionate towards Matt. Everything he'd said about his parents told her he adored them. And yet he'd clearly wanted to know where he came from if he'd sought out his birth family through genealogy sites.

Matt kicked his feet up on the polished surface of the wood coffee table, angling his body so he was looking at her as he answered. "My adoptive parents are amazing. I had a great childhood. My parents were always honest about me being adopted, never made a big deal about it. They didn't want me to find out later and be angry at them for lying to me."

Gemma let out a small hum, encouraging him to continue. She wanted to know more about this man who had dropped everything to protect her, when it wasn't even his job. No one had ever done things like that for her before.

"Which doesn't mean I was the perfect kid." Matt laughed ruefully. "I went through an angry phase, bitter that my birth mother hadn't wanted me enough to keep me, furious that my adoptive parents thought they could replace that blood connection. It was stupid, and juvenile, and I know it hurt them, my mom especially."

"That doesn't sound too different from the abandonment I felt growing up without my dad," Gemma said. "I was so angry with him for dying on me. How did you work it out? Was that why you tracked your biological family down?"

Matt grimaced. "Nothing like that. I flunked my grade eleven social studies assignment—you know, that one where you have to look after an egg like it's a baby? Epic fail. I splatted the egg inside my backpack on day two, fighting with another guy from my school. I almost got expelled for the fight, but for some reason it was the egg that really infuriated my mom. She decided since I wasn't going to take it seriously, she'd make it more real. She rented one of those actual computerised baby simulators and made me take care of it for an entire week. Told me if I couldn't keep it alive and healthy for seven days, I would be grounded for months and would have to quit the hockey team I was playing on." Matt paused.

Teenaged Matt sounded so different from the man in front of her now, though she shouldn't be surprised. She was a very different person from who she had been at seventeen too. Matt's adoptive parents had obviously done their best for him. He'd turned into a good man because of it. "How did it turn out?"

"It was the hardest week of my life to that point. Although my mom and dad helped a little, they made me do almost everything, including finding a babysitter every time I wanted to go do anything. By the end of the week, I couldn't give that doll back fast enough. I also figured out real fast why my birth mother gave me up. My parents told me she was fifteen when she had me. She was not prepared in any way to be a mother. In the end, it was the best decision she could have made for me. Completely changed my mindset about her, and my adoptive parents." Matt grinned at Gemma. "I found out later that the idea to give me the doll came from the therapist my mother was seeing to help her cope with my behaviour. It worked perfectly. I won't say I changed immediately, but I wasn't so angry anymore, and that meant I didn't lose my temper as much, which led to fewer fights . . . you get the idea."

Matt's smile made her feel warm all over. "It sounds like your mother's therapist was pretty smart."

"No kidding. I decided I wasn't ready to have kids for a long time."

Gemma studied him from under downcast lashes. Matt was clearly still single, and he seemed like an inherently good man. She was about to ask what he knew about his birth mother when Matt continued.

"I wanted to know more about my mother, so when I turned nineteen, I registered with the adoption reunion registry. If my mother ever registered, we would be reunited. I wanted to find out where I came from."

Matt's matter-of-fact delivery told Gemma all she needed to know. "She never registered, did she?"

Matt's smile faded. "No. That was seventeen years ago. I've done a bit of investigating on my own, and never got anywhere. When these genealogy sites started to get popular, I decided to see if I could find out more that way. I didn't want to disrupt her life, but I wanted to know if there are any hereditary illnesses I should watch out for. And I wanted to let her know I understood, and that her decision worked out." Matt shrugged. "I uploaded my DNA and waited. A few years ago, I found a paternal relative, a cousin of some kind. That led me to my grandfather. He helped me fill in the rest."

"You never found your mom?" Gemma kept her voice steady, hiding the sadness that hit her at the thought some woman didn't want to get to know the man her son had turned into.

Matt rubbed his hand over his beard, and Gemma noted that the circles under his eyes were deepening as the day progressed. As much as she was wound up and stressed, Matt clearly hadn't had a restful night, either, and then he'd driven all day to get them to the cabin while it was still light out. "You don't have to answer that."

Matt grimaced. "No, it's fine. It just doesn't have a very happy ending. I mentioned my mother was fifteen when she had me—the hospital and adoption organization told my parents that much. They also said she refused to identify the father. Claimed she didn't know who he was. Turns out she was in foster care, and was probably being abused by her foster family. She had a boyfriend, and DNA proved he was my father, but she had no way to find out back then. If she was being abused, reporting her foster family likely wouldn't have done any good. Their abuse was finally uncovered a decade later after two other foster kids reported them. Turns out they'd been abusing any teenage girl who was placed with them for years. I doubt my mother was any different, although we'll never know for sure."

Gemma's heart broke for Matt's mom. She'd met too many women on the streets with similar stories. While her own addiction had been horrible, at least she'd always had her mother to lean on. Home had always been a safe place for her.

"After she gave me up, her life spiralled. She was arrested a few times for drug offences, she dropped out of school, she ran away a lot. She disappeared one night when she was only seventeen. She was last seen hitchhiking along the highway out of town. She wasn't even reported missing for weeks, and they've never found her." He swallowed hard. "As for my dad? He was killed in a bar fight a few years after my mom disappeared. When I found my grandfather, he was thrilled to find out about me, and I have the best adoptive family anyone could ask for. I was lucky."

Gemma nodded, at a loss for words. Matt's past held more tragedy than she would have guessed. Losing both his parents to violent deaths before he could ever meet either of them? His story could have belonged to many of the people she'd known when she worked the Vancouver streets. Maybe that was one of the reasons he'd been kinder to her and others like her when he was working in the DTES.

They stared into the fireplace, and silence surrounded them, broken only by the crackling of the fire and the simmer of the pot on the stove. It was slightly unnerving for Gemma, who had never lived anywhere except the city, where she was surrounded by light and sound. It was peaceful, until her stomach gurgled again, loud enough for both to hear. Matt laughed and swung his feet down onto the floor.

"Sounds like that apple didn't help much. You're hungry. I'll start the pasta."

While Matt put the finishing touches on dinner, Gemma unpacked her limited supply of clothing and placed it into the tiny dresser beside the bed, which was covered by a thick, handmade quilt. It definitely looked more comfortable than sleeping on the couch, even if every time Gemma thought about curling up next to Matt, her skin felt hot and tight. He was a big man, and even in a bed this size there was no way she could avoid touching him. The visual of that big body next to hers, of being able to touch him—Gemma whirled away from the bed, eager to escape her thoughts. When her gaze landed on the bookshelves, she almost ran to them and began examining the titles. She quickly realized they were organized by genre, with large collections of mysteries, history books centred mostly on the Second World War, and nonfiction. The biggest collection stopped her in her tracks. There was an entire bookcase filled with romance novels. Most of them dated back to the 1980s, though some of them had been published in the last decade. They must have belonged to Matt's grandmother. Gemma smiled to herself, thinking about Matt's grandparents sitting in this room, reading together. It was a sweet picture. She scanned the rows of books, pulling out a couple that caught her attention and setting them on the top of the dresser. She couldn't do homework all the time, and reading something for fun would be a treat.

"*Sweet Temptation*," Matt rumbled from behind her, making her jump. "That's a good one. The next book in the series, *Sweet Indulgence*, is good too. Let me grab it for you." He wandered over to the bookcase and picked up the book in question, depositing it on the stack Gemma was building.

"You've read these?" Gemma masked her surprise that a tough cop would read romance novels.

Matt shrugged. "I've been coming up here for a while. I've read almost all of these books. With no electricity, reading is the best way to pass the time. The opportunity to unplug, to leave the city and my job behind? Priceless. Now come eat some dinner."

CHAPTER 18

Gemma set the novel she had been reading on the small table beside her and tried not to stare at the man sitting on the opposite end of the couch. Matt appeared totally relaxed, absorbed in a book. His dark Henley showed off his broad shoulders, and his muscular thighs stretched his jeans tight. She turned her head towards the fireplace, looking at anything except Matt.

The cabin was cozy and warm, with the light from a kerosene lantern mingling with the glow of the fireplace making the room bright enough to read. She was safe here, and the fear and anxiety that had consumed her since Saturday had eased up, but then the storyline in the book had hit a little too close to her next dilemma. The couple had found themselves stranded at an inn with only one bed, and she wasn't ready to think about her own sleeping situation yet.

The lone bed against the wall on the opposite side of the cabin had been lurking in the back of her mind ever since they'd finished dinner. Everything Matt had said made sense: The cabin would get cold at night, they were both adults, and the bed was big enough for both of them. Still, sleeping beside him felt intimate. Sex she could depersonalize—she'd learned to do that for survival. She hadn't actually slept in the same bed as a man since her first boyfriend over a decade ago.

Even with the men she'd dated since getting sober, she hadn't trusted them enough to be that vulnerable.

"Not enjoying the book?"

Gemma shifted her attention from the flames flickering in the fireplace. "I can't concentrate right now. I'll try again tomorrow."

A wrinkle creased Matt's forehead, but he didn't push her for more. "It's still early. Do you like board games?"

"What were you thinking?" A game might be a better distraction than the book she'd been reading.

Matt stood and went over to a small cabinet beside the bookcase. "I don't have a lot, and most of them are from when my grandparents came up here. We've got chess, backgammon, cribbage, or Scrabble."

"Scrabble," Gemma said instantly. She loved Scrabble and had played it frequently with her mom both when she was in rehab and when her mom was sick. This could be fun. "I'm going to grab a snack. Want anything?"

"Whatever you're having is good with me." Matt began setting the board up on the coffee table.

Gemma poked through the food Matt had unloaded, finally settling on a bag of popcorn and some cookies. Matt had brought a variety of snack foods, more than enough to last them for the week or so they hoped they would be up here. She grabbed two bottles of water and brought everything back to the couch. She handed one bottle to Matt. "I didn't think we needed coffee this late."

"Water's fine. If you want something hot, there's tea too."

Gemma bit into a cookie. "Quit stalling and play, Constable. Unless you're chicken?"

Matt arched his brow at that taunt, but all he did was hand her the bag of tiles. "Pick a letter."

Gemma reached into the fabric bag and pulled out the small wooden game piece, hiding it until Matt had also pulled one. He showed an *O*. When Gemma set her tile down, it was an *E*.

"You go first," Matt said.

Gemma pulled six more letters and arranged them on the tray in front of her: *EEEMTDO*. Not great letters, although she could have worse. She quickly spelled *emoted*, making sure the *M* landed on the double-letter tile, netting twenty-four points. She pulled a notebook and pen out of her backpack and wrote her score down as Matt studied his tiles, rearranging them on his tray.

"Schooled," Matt said as he laid his tiles on the board. "Which is what I'm going to do to you. That's fourteen points, plus two double-word scores, is fifty-six, and fifty bonus points for using all my tiles." His smile was annoyingly smug. "Who's chicken now?"

So that was how this was going to be, was it? "Game on, buddy, game on." Gemma recorded Matt's score before focusing on her next move. Matt's play had left her at a disadvantage, but she wasn't going to give up. There were a lot of tiles left to play.

Gemma managed to catch up to Matt's score before the game was half over, and they battled for the lead as each of them got more creative with their words. Matt played *subpoena* on a cramped triple-word score by using two letters from the board. It blocked her from using the space, so she got him back with *catheter*, which used all her letters for a fifty-point bonus.

With only two tiles left on her tray, and down by ten points, Gemma searched the board for somewhere she could use her letters. She'd pulled the *J* in her last group of tiles and was searching for any spot she could use it and score enough to win. Matt had played his final tile on his last turn, so if she could find at least eleven points, she would win. Her problem was her only other letter was a *U*. There was a *T* open that she could make *jut* with, except that would only tie the game. She wanted to *win*. She kept looking, and then she spotted the open *G*. "Jug," she said triumphantly. "That's eleven points. I win!"

Matt laughed. "You win," he agreed. "Want another game?"

Gemma nodded and started clearing the board. Matt placed another log on the fire, and they pulled new tiles to start again.

By the time the second game ended, Gemma was yawning. She was exhausted and still a little freaked out about tonight. The friendly rivalry that had grown as they played had worn down her defences, and that made the idea of sharing a bed with Matt even harder. No man could be this perfect. Not only was he stupidly gorgeous, but he was smart, and funny, and kind.

"You're tired. You should have said something," Matt said as he put away the game.

"I was having fun. I am tired, though," Gemma admitted. "I think I'll get ready for bed." She stood and went to grab her pyjamas before Matt could see the blush she felt heating her cheeks.

Knowing the cabin was remote and the weather in the mountains would be colder than Vancouver, Gemma had bought thick, fleecy sleepwear when she and Abel had been shopping, and now she was grateful. She hurriedly brushed her teeth and pulled on the pyjamas. The reflection in the mirror almost made her laugh out loud. Her choices at the store had been pink with red hearts, or a cow print. Gemma had grabbed the cow print, and now she looked ridiculous. There was nothing sexy about these. Good. She was warm, and the temperature in the bathroom was already several degrees lower than it had been earlier in the day. If the cabin temperature dropped like this, this fuzzy outfit would be a godsend.

She was stalling. She stood straight and reminded herself that this was only a bed, and he was just a man. No big deal. She picked up her clothes and went back to the main room.

Matt had taken the time she was in the bathroom to change his own clothes, and she was amused to see he was wearing *Star Trek* bottoms. His plain grey T-shirt was a different story. It was old and well worn, and the fabric looked soft where it clung to every curve and muscle. And Matt had muscles. It was weird, because his physical strength could have felt threatening, but it never did. He was definitely easy on the eyes. The heat pooling between her legs had her reconsidering the couch for her own sanity. If it was this hard on the first night, she didn't want to think about trying to resist him after they'd been here for days.

"I didn't take you for a *Star Trek* kind of guy." Gemma folded her jeans over the back of the couch and tossed the rest of her clothes into the suitcase she had bought that morning. "*Star Wars*, maybe."

"My cousin's idea of a joke. We exchange gag gifts every year at

Christmas; this was mine from him last year. The joke's on him. I love *Star Trek*." He squatted in front of the fireplace and began spreading ash over the coals.

"What are you doing?"

"Banking the fire so it will be easier to get a good fire going in the morning." Matt finished and stood. "I'm going to wash up. Take whichever side of the bed you want."

He closed the bathroom door behind him, and Gemma looked over at the bed again. Letting out a small sigh, she climbed in and punched the pillow until it felt right. The quilt was heavy and warm, and she was almost comfortable when Matt blew out the lamp and the cabin plunged into near pitch darkness. The mattress shifted as he lay down beside her, and she couldn't stop herself from rolling towards him before the bed settled again. He was so big he took up more than his share of the bed, and Gemma scooted over to ensure there was space between their bodies. Matt radiated heat, and as tempting as that was, she didn't want to blur the lines.

"Good night, Gemma."

"Good night, Matt." Gemma burrowed deeper under the covers and hoped sleep would come quickly.

CHAPTER 19

Matt lay awake, staring at the ceiling, intensely conscious of Gemma sleeping scant inches away from him. It had taken her almost no time to fall asleep, and she'd slept soundly all night. Not so much for him. So much had happened in the past few days that he was struggling to make sense of it all. If it was confusing him, it was no wonder Gemma was defensive and overwhelmed. Her resilience impressed him, and he would keep her safe.

Part of what was keeping him awake was the nagging feeling that they were missing something obvious. It didn't help that he was hours away from the scene of the crime. Protecting Gemma was his first priority, but he wanted the puzzle of who actually killed Russell to be solved. Gemma wouldn't be safe until the killer was caught and they understood the motive behind his death. Being up at the cabin made it difficult for him to contribute.

In Matt's mind, the key was access. VPD got called out to incidents at Harbourview all the time, and they knew most of the security and surveillance personnel. But knowing them was very different from having full access to the back areas, especially without an escort. Even if Morin was behind the murder, it was unlikely he could have done it himself. Morin could have bribed someone, especially since, knowing

Morin, he wouldn't have wanted the risk of being caught doing his own dirty work.

Plus, how could he have known that Russell was at the resort that night with Gemma? Unless he was also hacking Russell's electronic communications, he couldn't know for sure when Russell would be there. It all seemed very improbable.

That meant there had to be an inside connection. Someone who had access to guest registration data, so they would know Russell was there. Matt had investigated enough hotel incidents to know that didn't narrow down their suspect list much. Front desk was the obvious choice, and housekeeping always had to know which rooms were occupied and for how long. Would they have had customer names with that list?

Would housekeeping or front desk have access to the ducts? That was the piece that nagged at him. Whoever had done this needed to be able to move around without suspicion, and they also needed to have some connection to whoever had ordered the hit. Matt wondered idly if Harbourview employed twenty-four-hour maintenance people. That would be the kind of position that could move around the hotel and casino with impunity, and no one would think twice. Would they have access to registration data? He would have to ask Gemma when she woke up. If nothing else, it was another line of investigation he could provide to Murphy when he checked in with him this morning.

Light began penetrating the gloom of the room as the sun rose, chasing away the shadows. He'd banked the fire last night, and while the cabin had been warm when they went to bed, there was a chill in the air as Matt tried to slide out without disturbing Gemma. She moved under the blankets, but her breathing stayed even. Good. She needed the sleep. He pulled on a sweatshirt and began gathering what he needed to get the fire going again.

He was crouched in front of the fireplace, coaxing the coals back to life when Gemma spoke. "What's on the agenda for today? *After* you get this place warm again."

Her accompanying laughter took the sting out of her words, and Matt couldn't blame her. You could almost see your breath in the air, it was so cold in the cabin. Matt turned towards the bed and swallowed his own laugh. Gemma had wrapped the blankets around her like a cocoon, and only her eyes and nose were visible. "It's not that cold in here. I'll have the fire going in a minute, and it won't take long to warm up. I don't have any plans beyond breakfast. I have to call Murphy. After that there's nothing else to do but wait."

Matt hated that all they could do was wait, and he was sure Gemma felt the same. At least she had homework to keep her busy. He was going to have to find things to do, because sitting around doing nothing wasn't in his DNA. He continued working on the fire, and soon it was crackling loudly and heating the cabin air.

Gemma let out an audible grumble. Matt heard her feet hit the floor, and she padded into the bathroom without another word. When she finished, Matt took his own turn and came back out to the scent of bacon frying.

Gemma was in the kitchen, still in her fleece pyjamas. Matt let his gaze linger on the way the fleece hugged her curves, showing off her incredible ass as she leaned across the counter. One large black spot from the cow design covered her right butt cheek and was practically begging him to give it a squeeze. His fantasy ended when Gemma spoke.

"Scrambled eggs good for you?" She had a skillet on the propane stove and was cracking eggs into a bowl.

"Sure. You didn't have to start breakfast. I'd have taken care of it."

Gemma shrugged. "You made dinner last night. I'm not as good in the kitchen as you, but I can do breakfast. Near the end of her life, the only thing my mother could eat was eggs. I learned to cook them every way imaginable." She began whisking the eggs with a fork as Matt grabbed the coffee percolator and began scooping in grounds.

"I wanted to ask you a couple of questions about Harbourview."

Gemma raised an eyebrow. "What do you want to know?"

"Who had access to the computer system that would show which guest was staying in each room? Did anyone besides the front desk have that information? Did you have it in housekeeping?"

Gemma shook her head slowly as she answered him. "I didn't. My supervisor might have. All I got as an attendant was a printout with which rooms were occupied, which were checking out, that kind of thing. Sometimes there would be special information or requests, but we still didn't have guest names, or anything that would identify them. Why?"

"I'm trying to figure out who else besides the front desk might have known Russell was in that room, and waited for you to leave before killing him."

Gemma dished up their breakfast and handed Matt a plate, frowning thoughtfully. "You need someone who had access to the registration software and could also get into the back areas to crawl around the ducts."

"Exactly."

"Well, obviously the managers have access to pretty much anywhere. I can't see it being any of them; they all have to go through ridiculous levels of background checks to get their jobs. It would have to be someone who is at least somewhat familiar with where the cameras are. There aren't a lot in the hotel, though there are some. Same with the areas restricted to employees. So it would need to be someone who didn't look out of place on the cameras."

As Gemma took a bite of food, Matt outlined his list of potential suspects. "As much as I'd love to rule out the management team, they need to be investigated first. I'm sure Rebecca and Murphy are already working on it. While it would be suspicious for someone from the front desk to get caught in the maintenance areas, it's not impossible, so they'll need to be checked out. I was wondering if Harbourview had maintenance staff on duty twenty-four hours a day?"

Gemma's response was immediate. "Definitely. Most of the team work during the day, but there were always a few people scheduled around the clock. Clogged toilets, leaky faucets, heating or air-conditioning that stopped working. Somebody had to be on shift to take care of emergencies."

Matt filed that information away to share with Murphy. In truth, he was sure Murphy and Rebecca had already started looking into Harbourview staff, but he needed to feel like he was doing something.

"I need to work on homework today," Gemma said, pulling Matt out of his head. "My laptop is charged, and the battery will only last so long."

"You work until you need to charge it, and then I'll turn the generator back on. I've got to do some maintenance on the cabin anyway. I noticed a few missing shingles as we arrived yesterday. I need to replace them. I'm surprised there isn't water damage already."

Gemma picked up his empty plate and put it in the sink with hers. "You go fix the roof. I'll wash these after I'm done."

Matt grabbed the satellite phone and went outside, where the reception was better to call Murphy. He didn't want to distract Gemma from her homework unless it was necessary, and if Murphy had news, it could wait until she was done. Murphy picked up immediately.

"Murphy."

"Just checking in. We arrived last night, no difficulty. No one followed us. I took several back roads where we were the only car for miles, so I'm sure we were alone," Matt said.

"Excellent. Unfortunately, there's no change here. Abel and I are still questioning Gemma's contacts, and Jett is trying to trace the recording equipment. It's proving more difficult than we anticipated." Murphy didn't show much emotion, yet Matt could hear his frustration.

"Have you started looking into Harbourview employees?"

"We have. Rebecca officially pulled the employee lists and the schedule from the night of the murder, and Nate made sure we got copies. We have a few names we're running down leads on. I'll let you know if anything pans out. I did want to pass on one rumour. Gemma's kidnapping was not because she got bail. The killer messed up. It looks like Gemma was a target too. She was supposed to be in the room, and it would have been staged to look like a murder suicide. It seems that while Gemma didn't want anyone knowing about her arrangement with Russell, he bragged about their deal. He'd even told a couple of people about the videos he'd made. To our knowledge, no one had ever seen them, but people knew they existed, and that

Russell intended to force Gemma back into working for him. There was also a wild rumour that she meant more to him than simply a potential source of income. A few people speculated he actually cared about her, in his own twisted way. Apparently he talked a lot about how Gemma had kicked her drug habit, how she was clean now. Either way, Gemma was seen as a threat."

"That bastard." Matt paced in front of the cabin, anger warring with concern. Russell had put Gemma in danger by bragging about their connection. The reason didn't matter; the end result was the same.

"Getting her out of Vancouver was the best thing we could do," Murphy said. "You keep her safe, and we'll find out who's responsible so you can bring her back. We'll talk tomorrow."

CHAPTER 20

Gemma saved her files and closed her laptop. She had worked all morning and made good progress. Without access to the internet, she'd been forced to rely on her downloaded textbooks for the last few answers she normally would have googled, but her paper was coming along. Thankfully she'd finished most of the research before they fled Vancouver. She set her laptop aside and went looking for Matt.

She found him outside, chopping more firewood. It had warmed up since the frosty early morning, and Matt had stripped down to his T-shirt while he worked. The light-grey knit clung to every muscle, and Gemma's mouth went dry as she watched those muscles ripple with each swing of the axe. It should be illegal for any man to look that good.

She clamped down her surging desire. This was not happening. He was a cop, for fuck's sake. No matter what Matt had said yesterday, nothing could happen between them. Maybe if she kept telling herself that, she'd start to believe it.

"Hey," Gemma called out as Matt reached for another hunk of wood to split.

"You're done already? Or are you out of battery?"

"Out of battery. It's an older laptop, so the battery is only good for three hours, max. I got a lot done and can do more later." Gemma skirted around Matt to begin picking up the split wood that had collected in front of the chopping block. "Do you need to do more logs? I can take this into the cabin while you keep working."

Matt set the axe down and bent to help Gemma with the wood. "No, we have enough. I didn't realize how late it was. By the time I talked to Murphy and fixed the roof, most of the morning was gone. Once we get this put away, let's grab some lunch. I've got something to show you this afternoon."

They worked quickly, stacking the split logs in front of the cabin, and over lunch Matt filled her in on his call with Murphy that morning.

"They think I was a target?" Gemma shivered, her nails digging into her palms as she tried to keep her hands from shaking. For the last few years, her entire world had been school, work, and recovery. Even after her mother had been diagnosed, she had stayed on track. Then she had asked Russell for a favour. It was like she'd invited the devil in and would be paying for it with her life.

"It's a possibility," Matt said gently. "Unfortunately, your bargain with Russell was no secret to some of his contacts. That, coupled with the rumour that he might actually care about you, had more than a few people on the street wondering how much you truly knew about his business."

Gemma couldn't believe anyone really thought Russell cared about her. She was no different from any of the other women and men trapped into working for him, except she'd gone into her deal with him with both eyes open. Even then, his recording their encounters and blackmailing her had been a shock. Sweat trickled down her back and pooled at the base of her spine, making her feel cold and clammy even though the room was hot from the fire. "That's bullshit. I don't know why anyone thought I was more to him than any of his working girls, and he never told me anything."

Matt grimaced. "I believe you, and so does Murphy. That doesn't take the target off your back. Someone still wants you silenced. Until

Murphy and his team figure out who that is and find a way to stop them, you won't be safe. Staying here is the best option."

Matt pushed away from the table and picked up their empty plates. "I have something planned for this afternoon that might help distract you. Go put on your hiking boots."

"You tell me that someone put out a hit on me, and you want me to go *hiking* with you?"

"Yes. I want you to go hiking with me. Come on, get ready. It'll be fun." Matt smiled, his eyes crinkling at the corners. The smile did nothing to hide the intense way he was looking at her, promising without words to keep her safe, making her insides go all soft and gooey. She could get used to having someone totally committed to looking out for her.

Gemma opened her mouth to protest again, then snapped it closed and shrugged. They were stuck in a cabin in the middle of nowhere, off the grid. It's not like she could do anything, and the odds of the killer, or killers, tracking her down up here were slim. Hiking wasn't her favourite thing, but it sounded better than sitting around worrying. She stood and moved to the dresser to find warmer socks.

"Where are you taking me?"

"There's a lake not far from here. It's beautiful in the summer, and an easy hike. I want to see if the ice is off the lake yet."

Gemma shivered at the mention of ice. This hike was starting to sound cold. They were still in the mountains, and it was freezing at night. If Matt thought it was worth it . . . she finished dressing and followed Matt out the door.

The air was crisp and cool, yet not uncomfortable. The sun was high in the sky, bright yellow against blue in shades that were rarely seen in Vancouver this time of year. Matt led her around the rock face and down a wide trail. Small piles of snow against the base of trees were the only reminders that it was still early spring. Most of the trees were evergreens, adding to the illusion that winter was long over.

The path was muddy from the melt, and Gemma's boots squelched with each step. Matt was walking swiftly, and it didn't take long before Gemma was panting slightly as she struggled to keep up with him. She hadn't thought she was out of shape, but she was no match for Matt. "Can we take a break?"

Matt looked back at her and frowned. "I'm going too fast. I'm sorry I didn't notice." He waited for her to catch up, then handed her a water bottle before taking a drink for himself. It gave her the time she needed to catch her breath without feeling bad about slowing him down. "We're almost there. Can you keep going? I'll go slower."

Gemma took one more deep breath, then nodded. This was ridiculous. She could do this. "I'm ready."

They started again, and true to his word, Matt set a slower pace by shortening his steps to match hers. The occasional birdcall broke the silence, a perfect soundtrack to the afternoon.

The trees began to thin, and they entered a clearing at the edge of the lake. Water licked at the shore, yet about ten feet from shore there was thick, white ice covering the centre of the lake. "I would have thought it would be melted by now," Gemma said.

"Not yet. It's early this year, and the ice often doesn't melt for another month or more. I used to come ice fishing up here, but I didn't make it this winter. No fishing now until the ice is gone." Matt pulled a thick blanket out of the pack he'd been carrying and spread it over a large rock. He climbed up and patted the spot next to him. "Come sit. We'll rest a bit before heading back." He held his hand out to her.

Gemma stared at the hand in front of her, hesitating. With everything else Matt had done for her, this shouldn't feel like a big thing. When she placed her hand in his, his fingers wrapped carefully around it, and heat shot through her. His hands were big and strong, matching the rest of him, with palms that held calluses from hard work, while his touch was gentle. Placing one foot on the side of the stone for leverage, she let Matt pull her up beside him. Everything was so quiet compared to her life in the city. She closed her eyes and let the sun warm her face. "My mother would have loved this place."

"Tell me about her?"

The customary wave of pain that came whenever she thought about her mother was surprisingly absent. Instead, happy memories crept in to remind her of the good times. "She was beautiful. I don't mean physically, although she was that too. She was a beautiful person. As a child, I remember her as always being happy. Even when money was tight, she always found ways for us to have fun. She loved the outdoors, so we would go to the park or a playground all the time. Her laugh was contagious. She was always laughing about something. You would have thought she might have been bitter or angry because of my dad's death, and his family turning their backs on us, but she wasn't. All she ever said was it was their loss." The sadness was edging its way back in, and Gemma opened her eyes to the sun to try to chase the grief away.

"It sounds like she was special."

"She was. And similar to you and your adoptive mom, I was not an easy child." Gemma paused and took a sip of water from the bottle Matt pulled out of his pack again.

"Mom got some life insurance when my dad was killed, and she used it to put the down payment on the house I live in now. She got hired at a restaurant and worked her way up to manager over the years. Restaurant work means weird hours, so I was alone a lot. When I was twelve, I switched schools and met some kids who got into a lot of trouble. It started off relatively harmless: breaking curfew, skipping school, tagging stuff. When that got boring, we branched out. Petty shoplifting, some vandalism. I started trying drugs when I was thirteen. At first it was edibles, mostly. Lightweight stuff. Then someone swiped a bottle of prescription opioids from one of their parents."

Like it was yesterday, the feelings came flooding back. Her boyfriend had crushed the pills, then shown Gemma how to snort them. The immediate feeling of euphoria, of flying, was nothing she'd ever felt before. Once had been all it took. Her thirteen-year-old self had wanted to fly forever.

"There's no way to describe how it makes you feel. I've tried, so many times. Part of my recovery was coming to terms with never feeling that way again. I didn't know that then. All I knew was I needed more. So at thirteen I started doing anything and everything to get my next fix. I hid it well. My mom didn't even know I was addicted for the first year. I was able to hide a lot of the physical symptoms from her because of her work schedule, but she figured it out. Money was disappearing from her wallet, and my grades tanked. She put me in rehab the first time when I was fourteen." Her eyes burned as guilty memories rushed back, of her screaming horrible things at her mother, of her mother crying.

Matt's hand covered hers, making her jump. His touch offered comfort and encouragement, and Gemma savoured every bit. It was something she'd had little of since her mother died. "I'm assuming rehab didn't work?"

"Not for long. I came out clean; then pretty soon I was hanging out with all the same people, and the next thing I knew, I was using again. Another stint in rehab, another relapse, rinse, repeat. I went to rehab four times total before I was seventeen. And three of those times were private rehab. Expensive private rehab. Mom borrowed money, then remortgaged the house to pay for it." Gemma took another long swallow of water, her throat tight as she struggled to fight back her tears.

"I was seventeen, and after relapsing again, Mom told me she was trying to find me another spot in rehab. I kept running away and using. I came home after a night of partying, totally wasted. I found my mother asleep at our dining room table, surrounded by bills. Some were already past due. She was drowning in debt all because she was trying to save me, and I didn't want to be saved. I grabbed a few things and ran. Left her a note telling her not to worry about me, I'd take care of myself. I couldn't let her lose everything because I couldn't get my shit together."

"Is that when you wound up on the streets?" Matt rubbed his thumb over the back of her hand, making no other move to offer physical comfort, as if he could sense she might shatter if he was too kind to her.

"Pretty much. I stayed at my boyfriend's place for a few nights; then his parents kicked me out. I bounced around, finally found a place to crash. At seventeen, with an addiction and no job, I had no options. I'd already traded sex for drugs, so it wasn't a big leap to start trading it for money. You know the rest."

Gemma struggled to keep her voice even, not wanting to fall apart completely as she remembered her shame. Somehow, sleeping with someone who was willing to share his drugs with her hadn't seemed that bad, but the first time she'd had sex for money had left her feeling hollow and ashamed. It had created a never-ending cycle of needing drugs to mask her pain and needing money for more drugs to chase the pain away.

Matt wrapped an arm around her and pulled her against him, and Gemma crumbled. There was nothing sexual in the move, and that alone allowed Gemma to let the tears come. She'd mourned her mother during the long months she had been sick, and after her death too. Somehow, she'd never allowed herself to mourn the loss of her childhood, and the damage that had caused.

She cried until she had no more tears, with Matt doing nothing except stroking his hand up and down her back in comfort. His large frame blocked the chill in the air, and she let herself daydream about what it might be like to actually build a relationship with this gentle man. To have Matt by her side, encouraging her to chase her dreams, to share in her successes. To do the same for him, celebrating each time he was able to help someone. It was an impossible, wonderful fantasy. When she felt ready to face Matt again, she pushed away from him and wiped her face on her sleeve.

"Feel better?" Matt slid off the rock and offered her his hand to help her down.

"I do. Thank you for listening." Gemma ducked her head, not wanting Matt to see how raw her feelings still were. She did not want to set off another round of tears. He had been so easy to talk to, and she didn't want to come to depend on him. Eventually they would go their separate ways, and the closer they became, the more painful that would be for her.

Matt's hand cupped her chin and tipped up her face so she couldn't look away. His blue eyes were the same colour as the sky, and they reflected sincerity. "I'm glad I could be here for you. Ready to head back?" Matt let her go when she nodded, then pulled his pack over his shoulders.

Gemma inhaled deeply through her nose, the fresh outdoor scent clearing out the last of her tears. Matt's compassion had allowed her to release some of her grief, and she was grateful. She was ready to start putting her past behind her. "Let's go."

CHAPTER 21

Matt set a log on the tree stump he used as a chopping block and swung the axe over his head, bringing it down with enough force to split the log in half. The physical exertion helped him clear his head and kept him from staring at Gemma like a teenager with a crush while she worked on her homework. This morning, he'd woken to her slender form curled around him, one leg flung over his, her hand resting on his abdomen. It had been for warmth, and not intentional, but he was a man, not a saint. His body had responded like any straight man would to a beautiful woman wrapping herself around him. He had wanted to roll her over and press her into the mattress underneath him, strip off those adorable cow pyjamas, and explore every inch of her. Instead, he'd forced himself to carefully peel her limbs off him without waking her, and had then gotten up to start the fire.

He wasn't sure how Gemma would have responded if she'd woken up and realized she was clinging to him in the night. Every day since their arrival, she had dropped her guard around him a little more, giving him glimpses into who she really was. After the first night, she hadn't said another word about sharing the bed with him either. She was beginning to trust him, and sometimes he caught her looking at him in ways that made him think she might be attracted to him too. He'd been doing everything he could to encourage that possibility.

He set up another piece of wood and brought the axe down again with a satisfying thunk. Four days after their arrival there had been no major breaks in the investigation, which meant he and Gemma wouldn't be leaving yet. He still had a week until his suspension hearing, and if no progress had been made by that point, he would have to return to Vancouver to argue for reinstatement.

The sat phone started vibrating in his pocket, and he dropped the axe. "Foster."

"There's been another murder," Murphy stated. "A maintenance man at Harbourview named Jacob Yap. Rebecca told me last night that they were planning to interrogate him for Russell's murder today. Now all of a sudden he turns up dead of an overdose. It's too convenient. You predicted they would do this with Gemma, and you were right."

"Shit." Matt whistled. "A maintenance man? If anyone would have access to Harbourview's heating ducts, it would be maintenance. What was his connection to Russell?"

"He was another recovering addict that Nate's program sponsored, and he was new. It looks like Molloy was his dealer at one time. My guess is, someone else either hired him to commit the murder, or blackmailed him into it. Now that suspicion was landing on him rather than Gemma, whoever was behind it needed to tie up loose ends. We still can't prove that it was anyone within VPD."

Matt paced the clearing. Proving Gemma's innocence was good, but they needed to find out who was calling the shots, or Gemma would never be safe. The news about another murder was going to drive her anxiety even higher. "What did Rebecca say? Did anyone outside VPD know this guy was a suspect?"

"Rebecca is positive the leak came from inside the department, if there was a leak at all. The only people outside the department who knew this guy was a suspect were myself, Abel, and Jett. I'm wondering if the original hit was ordered by someone inside the department, who knew about Russell and Gemma's arrangement and decided she made a good scapegoat. I'm not about to accuse VPD without more evidence, so I wanted you to know what I'm thinking. The only upside to all of this is that we're closer to isolating who wants Gemma silenced. We'll find them." Frustration echoed in every word.

Matt kicked a stray piece of kindling. None of this helped either him or Gemma. Gemma was still in danger, and his suspension was still in effect. "When we talked to April, she hinted that Morin might be involved. Have you been able to find anything that would prove he's dirty?" His gut told him April hadn't told them everything, not that he could blame her. If word got out that she was helping the cops, she could be in danger. More danger than her addiction already put her in.

Murphy snorted. "Rumours and innuendo, mostly. Morin's dirty, I guarantee it. Proving it is going to be tough. He's been smart enough to not get caught up to now, and it sounds like he's been dirty for a long time. Everything from coercing sexual favours from sex workers in exchange for dropping drug charges, to trafficking, bribery, and extortion. No one has proof, and no one wants to talk to the police. They don't believe VPD will do anything to stop him, even if they do report him and can provide proof. He's too powerful and has been getting away with it for too long. We only know what we do because Gemma vouched for us, and we have no affiliation with VPD. People on the street are scared."

"Does Rebecca know all of this?"

"Not yet. She's got enough to deal with, and considering her harassment complaint against Morin was minimized, it might seem like sour grapes if she went after him for this too. When we have proof, we'll loop her in. No point having both of you under a cloud right now."

Matt grunted. He couldn't fault Murphy's logic. And Rebecca might be more even-tempered than he was, but she wasn't someone who would back down when she thought she was right. "What does this mean for Gemma? Even with the real killer dead, she might still be in danger."

Selfishly, Matt didn't want their little escape to end. Going back to Vancouver, both of them resuming their lives again—he wasn't ready. He was only beginning to crack the hard shell Gemma used to block everyone out of her life, and if they went back now, she'd slam that door closed.

"It's too soon to bring her back," Murphy agreed. "It's only been four days, and Morin might not have been working alone. We'll reassess in a few more days. Unless there's a reason you need to come back?"

"Not if it means Gemma might get hurt. We've got enough supplies for a while." If they started to run low, Matt would risk a trip to Williams Lake and restock before he put Gemma in danger by taking her back home.

After getting a few more details, Matt ended the call and went inside to bring Gemma up to speed.

Gemma looked up expectantly from her homework when Matt opened the door. Murphy called around the same time daily, and she always wanted to know everything. She waited until he'd stacked the load of firewood before asking, "What did Murphy have to say?"

"Do you know a person at Harbourview named Jacob Yap?" Matt threw the question out casually, searching for any clue that Gemma had some type of history with the dead maintenance worker.

Gemma pursed her lips and nodded. "Sure, I know who he is. He works in maintenance. He's another person hired through Nate's rehab connections. Why?"

Dammit. Matt had hoped Gemma didn't know him. She had already lost her mother, and if she was close to Jacob, it would be another big loss. "I have some bad news. VPD found Jacob's body this morning. It looks like he overdosed."

The grooves around Gemma's mouth got deeper, the only outward sign the news had affected her. "That's sad, but I didn't know him that well. Sometimes people relapse. What does it have to do with me?"

Her matter-of-fact delivery seemed genuine, and the tension coiling in his muscles dissipated slowly. Delivering bad news was part of his job, but it was a lot different when you had to tell someone you cared about that they had lost someone close to them. He didn't want to hurt Gemma again. "Rebecca and VPD had connected Jacob to Russell and were planning on bringing him in for questioning today. It looks like he might have been the one to kill Russell, and once he realized you weren't in the room, he set you up to take the fall. Coincidentally, he just happened to relapse and overdose the night before they questioned him."

"Are you kidding me? They actually had another suspect, and now he's dead?" Colour darkened Gemma's cheeks, and Matt could almost hear her teeth grinding as she clenched her jaw.

Matt nodded. "Even VPD thinks this was too convenient and are treating it as a suspicious death. Murphy and Abel are chasing a couple of leads, trying to find out who might be behind all of it. Because if Jacob killed Russell for someone else, then that person is probably also behind the attempted kidnapping."

Gemma threw her head back against the couch and let out a noisy huff. "Which means even if they prove Jacob killed Russell, I still can't go home yet. You said Murphy and Abel are working on leads? What kind of leads?"

Matt paused, choosing his words with care. He didn't want to get Gemma's hopes up. At the same time, maybe she could add something to the investigation. Even though she'd been off the streets for years, her connections there were solid. "The leak about Jacob had to come from within VPD—no one else knew he was a suspect except Murphy and his team. While they were interviewing people on the street, a couple of names kept turning up. Without evidence to prove their suspicions, they can't take it to Rebecca. Not only would no one believe them, if the suspect finds out, he could destroy evidence. It might also lead to more deaths. He's killed more than once to cover his crimes."

Gemma sat up and glared at Matt. "Within VPD? So a dirty cop."

Even though he'd expected this reaction, Gemma's automatic acceptance that there was a dirty cop at the centre of this mess hurt him. He refused to latch onto the "not all cops" excuse. The fact was, as long as decent cops ignored bad behaviour, there would be dirty cops. Even his record wasn't spotless: as a rookie, he'd seen things he should have reported, things he wanted to report, and had known if he did break ranks, his career would be over before it started. So he'd pretended he didn't see and worked to make sure his own record was clean. He was proud of his record, yet he could have done more. Not wanting to upset Gemma further, Matt drew on all his conflict training to keep his feelings hidden as he responded.

"Yes, a dirty cop."

Gemma ran her hand through her hair, pushing the thick dark strands away from her face and tucking them behind her ears. Matt followed the path of her hand, aching to touch her, to comfort her.

"They have a name, but you're not telling me. Why not?"

CHAPTER 22

"I wanted to see who you thought it might be, and I didn't want to prejudice you. Maybe you can come up with a name no one else has yet."

"There were a number of cops to be avoided at all costs when I worked the streets. Some would shake us down for sex, others for money. Some simply enjoyed treating us like the dirt they thought we were." Gemma muttered under her breath, not wanting Matt to hear her call his colleagues assholes, even if that was what they were. She didn't want to hurt him again, to make him think she didn't see him as different from them. He'd proved himself to be a good man, which was why she was willing to share these memories with him. What she was describing wasn't even the worst thing that had happened. A couple of officers had been caught running their own prostitution ring, forcing women to work for them in exchange for making arrests disappear. At least those pricks had been caught, and the union hadn't been able to save them. Crown prosecutors had seen that they did a little jail time for their multitude of crimes.

"Can you remember any names? Do you know if any of them are still working for the department?"

Gemma nodded. "Most of them are. I know there were a few high-profile firings, and those hardly made a difference. Then you all had your own internal issues to deal with, so the problems on the street took a back seat. At least I was out by then. If you want names, the ones I remember, that I know are still a problem from talking to friends? A guy named Peters, another named Dhillon. They're mostly involved in shaking down girls for sex. And, of course, your nemesis and mine, Morin. If anyone is behind this, it would be him. Not only was he always looking for sex, I heard he was extorting some of the dealers and the local businesses for money. Was he working with Russell? I don't know. Russell never named names. Not that Morin would know that, or believe me even if I told him. Am I getting close?"

When Matt looked away first, Gemma knew she'd hit a bull's-eye. "So it *was* Morin. Have Murphy and Abel found anything to tie him to this?" The thought of Morin getting away with murder made her skin crawl. She'd hated Morin since the time he had arrested her, then offered her a trade to release her: sex for her freedom. She'd told him to go fuck himself and gone to jail instead. When he'd tried to manhandle her, she'd bit him for good measure. If he thought she could put him away for murder, she would be a target for the rest of her potentially short life.

The silence stretched before Matt finally answered. When he did, he looked as frustrated as she felt. "Nothing concrete. I was hoping you might have some ideas about where they could look, maybe find a link between Morin and Russell?"

Gemma closed her eyes and tried to think of what kind of insurance Russell would have wanted against Morin, and where he would have hidden it. There was no way Russell would have worked with Morin unless he had some type of guarantee that if he went down, he'd take Morin with him. Not all their hookups had taken place at Harbourview, as much as Russell would have liked them to. Some of them had occurred at one of his places. "I'm guessing we're looking for something digital, like a flash drive or memory chip. The way they tore up my house? They were looking for something small. Russell kept a safe in his office; I've seen inside it. There was nothing in there except money. He never kept drugs on the premises, in case he got raided. Or at least that's what he said," she said wryly. She opened her eyes to find Matt watching her, a worried frown on his face.

"What about his house? Have you ever seen inside?"

"His new place? A couple of times. Never for more than a few hours. Knowing Russell, that's where he'd have kept any evidence. He'd want it close. Honestly, he was smart enough that he probably had a couple of copies, so that if one was discovered, he would have a backup. He was a bastard, but he wasn't stupid." Gemma chewed at a fingernail, a nervous habit she'd developed in rehab. She'd kicked it for a long time; then, as her mother's illness had progressed, she'd slipped back into it. The situation she was in now was not helping. At least she hadn't started smoking again.

"Russell had a few properties," Gemma continued. "I can't see him stashing something like this at any of those places; too many people passed through them. So I assume it would be at his home." Gemma closed her eyes again, visualizing the modern high-rise penthouse Russell had bought himself as he became more powerful in the Vancouver underworld. It had been all sleek lines and glass windows with a great view, and even that hadn't been enough to give Russell the veneer of respectability he was trying to build. Whenever she'd been there, there would be dirty dishes in the sink, dirty laundry on his bedroom floor, and a stale odour permeating the place. The unit had two bedrooms, one of which Russell used as an office. But that would be too simple. "You searched his place, of course." Gemma peeked back at Matt to see him nod in confirmation.

"We did. We found no records pertaining to his business anywhere except his office in back of the cheque-cashing business he ran. Even then, everything was coded. It's going to take our forensic accountants some time to figure out what was legit, and what was illegal. Last I heard, Rebecca was still sorting through holding companies, trying to figure out if they had found every location Russell owned."

The cheque-cashing place had been his front for dealing drugs and laundering money. Russell had also run a seedy boarding house, rented mostly to the sex workers and addicts he did business with. He would never have kept any type of insurance there. If one of the residents had found it, there would be too much risk they would blackmail him with it—he would believe that even if it wasn't true, simply because that was what he would have done. No, he would have wanted to keep the evidence far away from anyone he didn't trust, which, for Russell, was everybody. Even though he'd bought himself the fancy penthouse, Gemma knew he'd rarely ever had people over. The only reason they'd hooked up there a few times was that Russell would have her come over and clean up for him, before they wound up in bed. Plus, he had a few BDSM pieces there that weren't portable, and he'd enjoyed using them on her.

The BDSM pieces had included a spanking bench and a restraint chair, and hidden within their construction were secret detachable pieces that could be used for sexual torments. They would also be excellent hiding places for things Russell didn't want anyone to find. Unless you knew where to look for them, they were not easy to locate. "I might have an idea."

Gemma sat forward and reached for the notebook sitting on the table. Her classmates thought she was old-fashioned, choosing to take her notes on paper during their lectures, but the act of writing the words helped her remember the information better. Now she flipped to a blank page and began sketching. Matt leaned closer to see what she was drawing, and she tried to ignore the way his breath ghosted over her skin and raised goose bumps on her flesh. This was important, and she needed to focus. A few more quick strokes from her pencil, and she'd drawn a reasonably accurate rendition of the spanking bench and circled two spots on one end of the bench. "Tell Murphy to look here." As she looked at the drawing one last time to see if she needed to add any details, a sense of freedom stole over her. She would never be strapped down to it again. The act of drawing it had given her control over the memories. Maybe she should try that with a few of her other memories. She handed the sketch to Matt, her fingers tingling when they brushed against his.

Matt studied the drawing. "What should I tell him to look for? This looks pretty straightforward."

"It is, except in those two spots. Those spots are supposed to be quick-release levers for the wrist restraints, something you can reach with your fingers if you need out of the cuffs and no one is around to let you out. It's a safety feature. Russell showed me how to use them, then warned me if I released myself, he'd make me pay worse than if I simply took the beating." Gemma rolled her eyes. "He liked to play the big man. Now that I know he was recording our sessions, I think he wanted to show off for the camera."

Matt's brows furrowed as she described the abuse Russell had inflicted on her, and when he started to protest, Gemma reached over and placed a finger against his lips. The warmth of his lips sent a jolt through her, but it was the anger and concern reflected in his eyes that had her melting. How was it that this man could turn her insides into a puddle with nothing more than kindness and caring?

"He never did anything to me that I didn't consent to. I knew what I was getting into when I made my deal with him. None of that matters anymore. The important part is, one night as he was releasing me, he accidentally bumped something beside the quick-release button, and a tiny panel slid open. All I saw inside was a baggie. I assumed it was drugs and never thought anything of it. If Russell was bringing other women up to his place for sex, some of them would have wanted a fix. What if that baggie didn't have drugs in it?" The sliver of hope this idea generated was tiny, but it was *something*. And she'd had so little hope lately that anything was welcome.

Matt looked like he wanted to protest again, then thought better of it. "I'll call Murphy back, tell him what you told me. He and Abel may not be able to access Russell's place. Rebecca can. If they don't find anything, at least we tried."

A glimmer of hope forced Gemma to stand and move restlessly in the small space of the cabin, needing to do something. Hope was good, but she worried this wouldn't help enough. She needed this to end. It was close enough to lunchtime, and she'd done enough homework for the day. Matt had been taking her out adventuring every afternoon, and today that was just what she needed to take her mind off the chaos her life had turned into. Up here, she could almost forget she was accused of murder and the target of a hit man.

"I'll make lunch while you call Murphy. After you do that, how about we hike to the lake again?"

Matt's eyebrows shot up. "You're actually asking to go, instead of me making you? Who are you, and what have you done with city-slicker Gemma?" His laugh rumbled deep in his chest, wrapping around her like a warm hug.

"Don't make me regret asking."

Matt laughed harder. "Never. We can go to the lake if you want, but I've got another place I'd like to show you."

Gemma cocked her head, intrigued by the hint of wistfulness in Matt's voice. "It's your mountain. I'm game to go wherever you want to take me."

CHAPTER 23

Gemma stepped carefully over a fallen tree, following Matt's footsteps through the dense underbrush. Their hike to the lake had followed a well-used path, but wherever Matt was taking her today was not as heavily travelled. This was the third fallen tree blocking the path, and more than once Matt had held back heavy branches for her to pass through an overgrown spot. Even at this time of year, there was still a lot of snow scattered through the forest. There were a lot of upsides. It was quiet and serene, something Gemma appreciated more than she thought she would. The scenery was beautiful, and sometimes they'd catch a glimpse of local wildlife. So far she'd seen deer, rabbits, foxes, and even a lynx in the distance. Not that she'd known what all of them were, so Matt had identified the different animals when they spotted them. Plus following behind Matt was no hardship. The way his jeans hugged his butt and thighs was pretty easy on the eyes.

The trees were starting to thin out when Matt halted ahead of her and put a finger to his lips. "Listen. Do you hear that?"

Gemma concentrated on her surroundings, trying to hear what Matt heard, to hear what was different. Yesterday it had been a bird call that had caught his attention. Today, all Gemma heard was a low rumbling sound. It didn't sound like any animal she'd ever heard; it sounded more like . . . traffic? "Is there a road around here?"

Matt's smile was playful. "Guess again."

Gemma closed her eyes to block out other distractions and listened again. The rumble was steady and constant. So not traffic. It didn't sound artificial, so what was it? The nonstop rumble became part of the forest, blending with the birds, drowning out any sound made by the light breeze. "Water? Not the lake, though. The lake was much quieter." Gemma opened her eyes to find Matt beaming at her proudly.

"I'll turn you into a country girl yet. We're near a river. Come on, we're almost there." Matt turned and continued down the path.

With every step, the sound grew louder, until there was a break in the trees and they stepped out onto the riverbank. There, the water rushed past them, white foam gathering around the rocks that broke the surface. As Matt led her along the bank, a slight spray of cool water misted her face. The raging river was a stark contrast to the serenity of their forest hike, and watching the water move was hypnotic. When they reached a bend in the river, Gemma gasped. Rising up in front of her was a majestic waterfall nestled in the side of the mountain. From where they stood, the cliff rose at least fifty feet in the air, and water crashed over the edge. Here, the spray was no longer a mist, was instead heavy droplets, and the noise from the waterfall was overpowering.

"Amazing, isn't it?" Matt yelled over the roar.

Gemma nodded, speechless. Sure, she'd seen stuff like this on television, but she'd never spent any real time outside Vancouver in her life. She'd never been camping, or taken a weekend to go to a resort in Tofino or the Okanagan. *This* was what she'd been missing? The foaming water cascading over the rocks, the wildly swirling pools at the base of the cliff. The scent permeating the air, a fresh scent, and yet earthy and timeless. The rocks lining the pathway along the side of the cliff were frosted with moss and lichen, and sunlight refracting off the water cast rainbows everywhere. It was magical.

Matt crooked his finger, beckoning her to follow him. Excitement over what other wonders he might share with her had Gemma scrambling after him as he led her along the cliff wall until they reached the spot where the water poured over the ledge. The narrow path continued behind the falls themselves, and Matt stopped and reached for Gemma's hand. She slid her hand into his, savouring the warmth, the way his large hand engulfed hers.

"Follow me."

Matt tugged on her hand and pulled her along as he slipped behind the water. Gripping his hand and fighting off a sudden chill, Gemma picked her way over the slippery rocks until the water was roaring in front of her, and then stepped behind the falls.

It was dark behind the water, with only a little sunlight making its way in, and much quieter. Gemma's nerves relaxed once she stood beside Matt. There was a black shadow behind him, and he pulled out the heavy-duty flashlight he always carried and flicked it on. The bright light illuminated the small space, outlining the cave-like depression Matt stood in. The walls were glistening with moisture, and the air felt warmer here, sheltered by the water.

"Now tell me this isn't better than hiking to the lake again," Matt teased.

Gemma laughed, and the sound bounced off the walls of the confined space. "I bow to your superior experience in the wilderness." She ran her fingers along the walls of the cave, tracing the crevices and noting how silky smooth the rock was under her touch. "How did you find this place?"

Matt set the flashlight down on the cave floor and began moving rocks near the back of the opening. "My grandfather showed it to me. He and my grandmother spent a lot of time out here together." With a tug, Matt pulled the last loose rock away from the rear of the cave, leaving a small opening. He reached inside and pulled out a bundle of canvas.

"What's that?"

Matt unwrapped the canvas to expose a wooden box with delicate carving decorating the top. "My grandfather made this for my grandmother. Every year, they would add another treasure to the box to commemorate their anniversary." Matt slid the lid open, revealing an assortment of items: rocks, dried flowers, small pieces of paper with writing on them. "After she died, he still came out here every year and added something to the box in her memory. The last time I visited him I promised I'd retrieve the box and bring it to him in his care home. He wanted to have it with him since he can't make it out here again."

The love and devotion evident in the story behind the box sucked the air out of Gemma's lungs. What would it be like to have someone love her that much? So much that he would continue to mourn her and celebrate their love even after she was gone? "It's a good thing you're doing, bringing that back to him."

Matt grimaced. "I wish I could have brought him out here to get it himself, but his disease progressed too fast. We thought we'd have more time. This was the least I could do." He reached into the box and fished out a small, polished rock. "This is a piece of my father's headstone. My grandmother took his death hard, and that's when Grandpa carved this box and started bringing her out here. He wanted her to find some peace, some happiness again. This piece of marble was the first thing they put in the box together." Matt's voice was husky, with grief visible in the lines around his eyes and mouth, even in the dim light of the cave.

Gemma swallowed hard, fighting back tears. She gave his shoulder a squeeze in wordless comfort.

Matt dropped the stone back in the box and slid the lid shut. He wrapped the canvas around the box again before placing the package in his backpack.

He stood and brushed off his jeans before shrugging the backpack over his shoulders. The grief had left his expression, and the smile he gave her made her tingle all over. "Ready? We need to get back before nightfall. It gets cold and dark fast up here."

Gemma wasn't ready to leave, but they needed to get back. She hated to think she might never be back here. She moved closer to the wall of water that created this little piece of magic, reaching out to allow the water to splash over her fingers. The shock of the cold had her yanking her hand back with a laugh. "It's colder than I thought." She wiped her fingers on her jacket and reached for her gloves, stopping when Matt grasped her hand between both of his, rubbing it to warm it up.

The icy tingling was replaced by burning heat, and it wasn't only her hand that was on fire. Every time Matt touched her, it was like her entire body heated from the inside out.

"Better?" Matt stopped rubbing but didn't let her hand go, and he laced his fingers through hers.

Matt had turned the flashlight off as he'd prepared to leave the cave, and the dark shadows made it hard to read his expression. Gemma felt like she was balancing on the edge of a cliff. What would happen if she leaned into him, instead of pulling away? The tension building between them was getting harder to ignore. Maybe she didn't want to ignore it anymore. As she was about to lean into him, Matt brushed a brief kiss over her knuckles before he released her hand.

The moment was gone, so Gemma turned and began making her way back out from under the water, with Matt following close behind. She kept one hand pressed against the cliff face for balance as she made her way back across the slippery path, until something sparkled off to one side of the trail. When she looked closer, she found a crystalline rock that glittered in the sunlight. She leaned down to pick it up, wanting her own reminder of their afternoon together.

The rock was stuck in the muddy bank of the fast-moving river, and with the help of a nearby stick and a little digging, Gemma dislodged it and rinsed the mud off. She stood and showed it to Matt. "Do you know what this is? It's beautiful."

Matt picked up the rock and turned it over, letting the sun catch the facets of it. "Quartz, I think. There's a lot of it up here, and this looks right. Not valuable, but nice to look at." He smiled and handed it back to her.

"I'm keeping it." Gemma tucked the rock back in her pocket. She didn't care about the value of the stone. It was worth so much more to her. It would remind her of a truly good man. She hadn't met many of those in her life, and even though she would have to let Matt go when this was over, she wanted a tangible reminder of him. Gemma climbed back onto the trail, letting Matt take the lead again. He knew his way around these woods, and she would get lost in a heartbeat if left to lead the way. Let her loose on the streets of Vancouver, though, and he'd never find her.

They walked in silence, the sound of the river fading as they moved deeper back into the trees. Here the sunlight barely penetrated the canopy of tree branches, thick with their perpetually green needles. Gemma was searching for signs of wildlife in their branches when she tripped and sprawled across the trail, landing with a hard thump. "Shit!"

Matt swung around. She scrambled to an upright position, cheeks heating at her carelessness. The fall was her own fault for not watching her footing, and now she was aching all over. Worry lines creased Matt's face as he reached a hand towards her to help her up. Gemma accepted Matt's hand and let him pull her to standing, grimacing and letting out an involuntary cry when she put weight on her ankle.

"What happened? Are you okay?" Fuck, that *hurt*. Gemma gripped Matt's arm and tested her ankle again, but the pain was just as bad the second time.

"It's my ankle. I need to look at it."

Matt helped her over to a fallen tree, where she sat and began unlacing her hiking boot and then stopped. Her ankle was already swelling in the boot. If she took it off now, she'd never get it back on, and then she'd be screwed. "I don't think it's broken; it's probably sprained. Walking back is going to be brutal." Gemma looked around them, searching for something to help her walk. "Can you find me a long, sturdy stick I can use for support? I think I can make it back if I have some assistance, and we go slow."

Matt frowned, gently unlacing her boot enough that he could roll her sock down and look at her ankle himself. Gemma refrained from rolling her eyes—she was the nursing student, and she knew a sprain when she saw one.

"This looks like a bad sprain. You can't walk on this, not even with a walking stick."

"It's not like I have a choice. You said yourself it's going to get cold and dark. We're miles away from civilization, and we don't want anyone to know where I am anyway. So my options are walk or freeze to death? Yeah, I'll walk." Gemma wasn't looking forward to it, but she was a survivor. A sprained ankle wasn't going to take her out now.

"You're not walking," Matt said. "I'll carry you."

CHAPTER 24

The words were out of his mouth before he thought them through, but he didn't see any other option. No matter what she said, Gemma could not walk on that ankle. They were still at least half an hour from the cabin, hiking at a good clip; if she tried walking, it would take them hours. They didn't have hours. At most they had two hours until sunset, probably less. He needed to get her back to the cabin before that happened.

"You'll *carry* me? I don't think you need to do that. I'll be fine walking." Gemma shoved herself to her feet, then buckled back onto the tree when her ankle wouldn't support her weight.

"It's the only answer. You can't walk on that ankle; you can't even stand on it." Matt slid his backpack off his shoulders. "Here, put this on."

Grumbling, Gemma accepted the pack and pulled it on, fumbling with the buckles to tighten the shoulder straps. "What are you going to do, throw me over your shoulder and carry me fireman style? I mean, don't get me wrong, your ass looks great in those jeans, but I don't want to spend that much time up close and personal to it."

Matt bit the inside of his cheek to stop himself from laughing at Gemma's disgruntlement. Her observation about his ass was flattering, though. It was nice to know she had looked. "No, I'm not going to carry you upside down. I was thinking piggyback would work better, since you're conscious."

"Oh." Gemma's cheeks got even pinker. "That actually might work. It's not the worst idea."

"We still won't be able to move as fast as before, but we should make it back before dark. You ready?"

"As I'll ever be," Gemma said, sounding resigned.

Matt squatted in front of the fallen tree, his back to Gemma so she could climb on. Her arms tentatively slid over his shoulders, and he linked them together around his neck. Her body was warm, even through the layers of outerwear between them, and he could smell the subtle scent of her body lotion. The intoxicating combination made him want to peel off the layers and reveal the secrets underneath. He shook off the thought. Gemma was hurt. Now was not the time.

"Hang on tight." With a fluid motion, he lifted Gemma off the log as he stood. Then he gripped her thighs and helped her wrap her legs around his waist. Every move had her rubbing against him, the heat from her core pressed against his lower back where his vest had ridden up. His body responded in kind, blood migrating south until he was half hard, and walking was going to be even more uncomfortable. At least Gemma didn't weigh much more than the heavy packs he trained with sometimes. "You let me know if you need me to stop."

"Let's get this over with."

Gemma's breath blew warm against his neck as she spoke, and for a moment Matt allowed himself to imagine her lips trailing over his throat, her tongue flicking his neck as she moved down his body. Torture. This walk back to the cabin was going to be sheer torture. Matt began hiking down the trail.

Where the silence between them before had been comfortable as they both enjoyed the peace of the hike, now things were awkward. Gemma was holding herself stiff on his back, and Matt had to continually adjust her position to stay balanced. Finally, he couldn't take it anymore.

"Why did you decide to study nursing?" he asked abruptly. He'd been meaning to ask her all week. Every time he'd thought of it, she'd been busy studying. As he watched her study and work on her assignments, her dedication was evident. She had passion for the topics, and he hoped talking about that would ease some of the tension. Maybe he'd been wrong. He was searching for another conversational distraction when Gemma broke the silence.

"A nurse changed my life."

There was another long pause, and Matt stayed quiet, hoping Gemma would say more.

"You know my past." Gemma shifted against him, her arms looping tighter over his shoulders as her body melded against his.

Matt let his own muscles loosen as Gemma relaxed, making carrying her much more comfortable. It was actions like this that proved she trusted him. He wanted her to trust him. He wanted a lot more than that, but he'd start with her trust. He picked up his pace, wanting to get her back to the cabin quickly to take another look at her ankle.

"I overdosed more than once. The last time I did, I almost died. Like, my heart actually stopped, and they had to resuscitate me. When I woke up, there was this nurse with me. Wendy. She was so calm, so kind. She talked to me, asked me questions about my life. No judgement, just let me talk. When I was done, she asked me if there was anyone she could call for me. I started to cry, because I didn't want to live that life anymore. I told her to call my mom. Kimmy had been trying to get me off heroin for a while, and I figured she might be right. It was Wendy who *listened*, who let me talk until I was ready to make a choice. I want to help people like she helped me. It's my way to pay it forward, you know?"

The desire to help others, to repay some of his good fortune, was something Matt related to. Nursing seemed like a difficult way to do it. "Wouldn't have becoming a counsellor been easier?"

Gemma laughed softly. "Yes. Less school, no anatomy classes. Wendy did so much more for me. After I told her I wanted my mother, she stayed with me until my mom arrived. She helped us with the search for a treatment bed. It wasn't easy to find one; she pulled every string she could and finally found a private facility that had space. After six months in rehab, I finally managed to quit using. When I was released, I went to see Wendy. The day I arrived at the hospital, I walked in to find her in the emergency room, working with the team to try to bring an overdose victim back, like I've been told she did with me. Counsellors are a super-important part of the healing process, but what Wendy did fascinated me. Still does. I've never regretted my choice."

After a long pause, Gemma spoke: "Your turn. Tell me why you became a cop?"

He picked up on the underlying distress in Gemma's question. She didn't like cops, and with her history, how could he blame her? Choosing his words with care, Matt tried to answer truthfully, without damaging their fragile bond. "I didn't know what I wanted to do when I graduated from high school. I got good grades and was offered a couple of sports scholarships, so I went to college. Nothing I took held my interest, until I signed up for a criminology course. The puzzle aspect was interesting. I took a couple more, and I was hooked. I majored in criminology, not thinking about what that would mean when I graduated. Turns out, that when you major in criminology, most of your career choices are in some type of law enforcement: police officer, corrections officer, private investigator. I could have tried to get into law school, I guess. That didn't interest me, though. I didn't want to do a lot more years of school to get a degree in social work or psychology either. And with my size? I was fit from playing hockey, so passing the physical tests was easy for me. I applied to the police academy. At the academy, they tell you that you're doing something important. Helping people, protecting them, putting away the bad guys. I believed it. For myself, I still do. I try to model that philosophy, and I know Rebecca does too. We truly want to help the victims, and we want to see murderers and sex offenders put away where they can't hurt anyone else." Matt stopped, self-conscious that he might come across as evangelizing. The fact was, he did want to believe most cops were good. Unfortunately, he'd seen too many cops like Morin break the rules and get away with it. He was certain Gemma had some horror stories from her time on the street. There was little he could say to change her mind.

"I wish more cops were like you."

Gemma's words were quiet, almost wistful, and Matt savoured the pleasure they gave him. It sounded like he was getting her to view him differently, and that was all he wanted. Matt waited for her to continue, but she didn't say anything else. This time, the quiet surrounding them was easier, without the tension from earlier. Gemma had relaxed, making it more comfortable for him to carry her. The sun was setting, and they were close enough to the cabin now that Matt wasn't worried. When they broke through the trees and into the clearing where the cabin stood, Gemma exhaled audibly, and Matt sensed the pain she was covering. Her ankle must be hurting, especially after being bumped and jostled over a rough hiking trail for more than an hour.

"Ready to put your foot up and relax?" he asked as he climbed the stairs leading to the cabin door.

"You have no idea."

Matt carried her inside and over to the bed, where he squatted so she could slide off his back and onto the bed without landing on her foot. "Now let's get that boot off and look at your ankle."

Gemma was already reaching for the laces when he turned to face her. When she rolled her sock down, he tried not to flinch. Her ankle and foot were badly swollen, and the outside of her foot was turning dark purple. "I'll get some cold water to soak it and find you some painkillers. We don't have any ice, but I could try to find some snow to pack around it."

As she set her foot on the bed, Gemma let out an involuntary gasp. "No painkillers. Lots of water is fine. Don't worry about the snow; the well water is frigid. It'll work. I don't suppose you have any compression bandages?"

Matt didn't say anything about her refusal to take the painkillers. They weren't opiate based, but still he respected her desire not to use them. Addiction and recovery were always tricky. "I'll have you know, I was an Eagle Scout. I'm always prepared. Let's elevate your foot while I get the water and bandages." Matt piled pillows at the end of the bed and helped Gemma raise her foot onto them before heading to the small bathroom for a basin of water.

When he returned, Matt helped Gemma into a sitting position on the edge of the bed, then knelt at her feet. He immersed her foot in the icy water, holding her ankle immobile to prevent any sudden movement caused by the shock of the water temperature.

"Fuck that's cold," she said, shivering. She shrugged out of her outerwear and wrapped herself in the quilt from the bed.

With her cheeks flushed pink and her dark eyes shining bright, Matt thought she was the most beautiful woman he'd ever seen.

"I could get used to being waited on hand and foot," she joked.

That sounded good to him. Gemma deserved some pampering, and she was so used to being independent that it was nice to hear she appreciated him taking care of her. Matt set her foot against the bottom of the basin and pulled his hands out of the icy water. He wiped them off on his jeans, then placed one on either side of Gemma's hips, staring deep into her eyes. "As you wish."

Her eyes widened, and a laugh bubbled from deep inside her chest. "Did you just quote *The Princess Bride* at me?"

Matt grinned. "Maybe." Thrilled that his teasing had distracted Gemma from the pain in her ankle, Matt moved to stand. The whisper of her breath on his cheek stopped him. Her lips hovered near his ear, each breath sending shivers down his spine, and these weren't from cold. He was on fire, aching to touch Gemma. He wanted to care for her, soothe her pain, slay her dragons.

"Kiss me."

CHAPTER 25

As soon as the words left her mouth, Gemma wished for them back. As much as she wanted to kiss Matt Foster senseless, this was a terrible idea. Matt must have agreed, because he was shaking his head no.

The sheer longing in his eyes had a fire burning in the pit of her stomach, making her forget about the freezing water her foot was soaking in. Matt began to back away from her, stopping when Gemma grasped him by the shoulders. "You want to kiss me." She prayed he wouldn't deny it.

"Yes." The admission came out as a groan.

Gemma cupped Matt's face and tilted it up, bringing her mouth down to meet his. His lips were firm and warm under hers, and momentarily still. When she stroked her tongue along the seam of his lips, he growled deep in his throat and opened his mouth to her. His hand moved to grip her hips, holding her still on the edge of the bed as she explored his mouth, her tongue tangling with his. Arousal had her heart racing, her blood heating, and an ache she hadn't felt in a long time starting between her thighs. It had been too long since she'd actually wanted a man.

Gemma sank her fingers into Matt's silky brown hair and lost herself in him. His skin smelled like the outside, fresh and clean. Her nipples were hard nubs rubbing against her bra, begging for his touch. Gemma trailed her mouth along Matt's jawline until she reached his ear. "I want you."

Matt froze. Then he carefully backed away from her, adjusting his visible erection as he stood. "That can't happen."

His rejection pierced the bubble of hope that had been growing inside her. What had she been thinking? Of course he didn't want her. Oh, his body responded to her, and he claimed he found her attractive, but in the end? She was damaged goods. Masking her hurt, she gave a casual shrug. "Your loss. We could have had some fun." She leaned down to look at her ankle, the curtain of her hair hiding her face. She would not let him see he'd hurt her. She would not. The ache in her chest was surprisingly painful, and she berated herself for thinking that Matt might actually be able to see beyond her previous life.

Matt's knees came into view as he crouched down in front of her again. "Gemma." He moved closer and tilted her head up, forcing her to look at him. "I want you. Anyone with eyes can see that." He pointed at the outline of his erection still visible through his jeans. "Even if you weren't injured, there is still the fact I'm a cop. And you're—"

"A junkie and a whore. I get it, you don't have to remind me." Gemma jerked her face away, thwarted as Matt's fingers tightened on her chin and wouldn't release her.

Anger flashed in Matt's eyes. "I don't ever want to hear you talk about yourself like that again. You are a recovering addict, which is something to be proud of. It means you lived at a time when too many don't, and you choose every day to stay sober. You are a former sex worker, a job you did to survive. If you had done it by choice rather than out of necessity, that would be fine too. It's a job. It doesn't define you. Most importantly, right now you are a woman being framed for murder. You are being hunted by someone who is trying to kill you, and you are under my protection. Sleeping with you now is crossing a line for me. Once we know you're safe, if you still want me? My answer will be very different. Got it?"

His opinion of her, his innate goodness, chipped away at her defences and soothed the hurt of his initial rejection. They still had no future together, but maybe when this was over, they could at least enjoy each other before they went their separate ways. Gemma nodded. "I understand."

Matt stood and kissed the top of her head, making her stomach somersault. "Good. Now how's that ankle? Do you need more cold water?"

Gemma pulled her foot from the basin of water and gingerly probed her ankle. It was badly swollen. The water had helped, and at least the pain had dropped to a dull throb. "I think another few minutes here, and I'll be ready to wrap it." She slid her foot back into the rapidly warming water, barely flinching this time.

Matt rummaged in one of the cabinets, pulling out a large red plastic box labelled with a white cross. He set it on the bed beside Gemma, and as he ran more cold water for her foot, she went through the first aid kit.

Matt hadn't been kidding about being prepared; this kit had everything. Aside from the basics for cleaning and bandaging minor wounds, it had supplies to treat a fracture and even a small suture kit. Gemma pulled out a compression bandage, and a topical pain cream that could be applied to her skin. After reading the active ingredients, she was satisfied and set it aside to apply once she dried her foot. Not as effective as some of the oral painkillers included in the box, but that was all she was willing to use.

After he changed the water in the basin, making her yelp when icy water hit her skin, Matt put the kettle on to boil. "Tea and cookies, or hot chocolate? You need some sugar."

At the mention of food, Gemma's stomach growled. Matt laughed. "Okay, tea and cookies it is."

Matt's return to their easy camaraderie helped Gemma release the last little bit of tension that had lingered after their charged conversation. She wanted him. He wanted her. This simply wasn't the right time. Besides, her ankle was killing her. Gemma assessed it again and decided it had soaked long enough. She wrapped the towel Matt had brought her around it and swung it back up on the bed, then flopped onto the pillow, frustrated. She needed to get her jeans off before she bandaged her ankle, or she'd be stuck in them all night. And while they were drying out, they were still cold and damp, and would be uncomfortable as hell to sleep in. With a grimace, she unbuttoned them and began wiggling them over her hips. It would be easier if she could stand, but that option wasn't available, and they had to come off. Every move jostled her ankle, and she bit her lip as it started throbbing harder.

"Let me help." Matt set the cup of tea and plate of cookies on the dresser.

"I'd be embarrassed, but honestly? I don't care what you see as long as you help me get these off," Gemma admitted. "Every time I try to lift my hips, I bang my ankle. Can you help me stand?"

Matt helped her up, then held her standing as she shoved the jeans down over her hips. Once they were halfway down her thighs, he set her back on the bed and gently pulled them the rest of the way off. Matt was trying to be totally impersonal, but Gemma noticed the way his eyes lingered on her legs as he peeled the damp fabric from her skin. He studiously avoided looking at the spot where her blue panties peeked out from under her long T-shirt. If only she wasn't under his protection, if only she wasn't hurt. The heat pooling low in her belly was making her forget the pain in her ankle. Too bad she couldn't act on it. Matt had made his position clear.

Once her jeans were off, he helped her pull her fleece pyjama pants over her feet, lifting her long enough for her to pull them up. Once she was dressed, she was exhausted, lying back on the bed, panting. "Pain sucks."

Matt carefully spread some of the topical pain cream over her swollen ankle, his warm hands and gentle touch creating a pleasant diversion that helped distract from the pain. "It does. If you don't let me help you, you could hurt yourself more. So please, next time ask for help?" He wrapped her ankle, then propped her foot up, sliding another pillow under her foot before handing her the tea.

"I'm not used to having someone around to help. For the last few years, it was just my mom and me, and she needed my help, not the other way around." Gemma blew on her tea. "I'll try to do better."

The worried wrinkle that had been creasing Matt's forehead ever since she'd taken her boot off smoothed out. "That's all I ask. Now, what else can I get you? Do you want to read while I get dinner started?"

"No, I still need to finish my homework. Even though Murphy did a great job arranging everything for me, this paper is still due soon. Do you think we could drive to a town with a Wi-Fi connection so I could submit it?" Gemma was surprised at how much she had enjoyed their remote cabin with no modern amenities, but she couldn't submit this paper without an internet connection, and her graduation depended on getting it handed in. Plus, if the town was big enough to have a coffee shop with a drive-through, she wouldn't mind a caramel latte and a fresh muffin. A hot shower would be nice too. She'd settle for thirty minutes of Wi-Fi and a fancy coffee.

Matt passed her the laptop she'd charged earlier, a small frown wrinkling his face. It was kind of adorable. Instead of making him seem grumpy, it deepened the dimples in his cheeks. "I hate the idea of you logging on to anything that someone might be able to trace. How important is it?"

"I won't graduate if I don't submit it," Gemma said earnestly. She needed Matt to understand how important this was. Graduation was the only thing Gemma truly cared about. If she didn't graduate, she lost her internship, and she could not let that happen.

"I'll figure something out. Williams Lake isn't very big, but there are a couple of coffee shops with Wi-Fi, or maybe the public library will have computers with internet access. That would be better. Do you have a USB drive you can transfer the file to?"

Relief flooded Gemma. She'd worried Matt would refuse to even consider letting her get online to submit her assignment, and that would have meant retaking the course, setting her back an entire semester. "I do. I can upload the paper from anywhere with an internet connection, so whatever you think is best. It's due in two days."

Matt still looked worried. "How close are you to being done? Could you submit it tomorrow? The weather forecast is clear for tomorrow, but Murphy mentioned that a storm might be coming soon."

Could she be done tomorrow? "I'll be done if I have to stay up all night."

CHAPTER 26

"We hit the jackpot with the spanking bench," Murphy said as soon as he answered Matt's call the next morning. "There were two secret compartments, exactly like Gemma described. One had drugs, and the other one contained a USB drive."

"Have you found anything on it? Is Gemma in the clear?" Excitement rose as Matt realized Gemma might be out of danger soon.

"Russell was paranoid, and the USB had high-level encryption on it. We're still working on breaking it, which takes time."

Murphy's words penetrated, and Matt's police instincts didn't like where this was going. "Wait. Who is working on the files?" If Murphy's team was doing the work, they risked none of it holding up in court, and he didn't know whom to trust at VPD anymore.

"Rebecca has custody of the original drive, and a copy was provided to our team. Rebecca didn't want our only evidence to disappear. Jett has been working all night on cracking the encryption. She's close, and as soon as she's in, we'll know more. I'm optimistic this is the break we needed. Russell had no reason to go to the trouble of hiding an encrypted USB drive if it didn't have some serious dirt on it."

Matt hoped so. They had less than a week before he had to return to Vancouver for his disciplinary hearing, and he didn't want to bring Gemma back if she wouldn't be safe. He could trust Murphy and Abel to look after her, but she was safer up here, where no one knew where she was. "Gemma needs to go to town to submit her final assignment. The closest town is really small. Williams Lake is only a little farther, and a decent size. It's unlikely anyone would recognize us there, and there's a library we could use. It's the safest option I can think of." Matt had weighed his choices yesterday after realizing how important this was to Gemma, and while driving to Williams Lake would take longer than driving to one of the other smaller communities, it made the most sense.

There was a long pause. "That should work. I don't see any reason anyone would identify her there. She hasn't been reported missing, so no one is officially searching for her. Rebecca is watching out for any mention of her in official communications from VPD, but whoever is behind this is smart enough not to make that mistake."

The cabin door banged, and Gemma limped across the gravel to where Matt stood. "Why don't you tell Gemma the good news yourself?" Matt handed the phone to Gemma and moved away to prepare for their trip to Williams Lake.

MATT PULLED his truck into the parking lot behind the library not quite an hour later. Gemma was almost vibrating with excitement beside him. Unlike their silent trip up from Vancouver, their trip to town had been filled with a discussion about her nursing assignment, and a running argument about which chain made the best coffee. He'd finally surrendered and agreed to take her to her favourite one after their stop at the library to submit her paper.

None of that prevented the trickle of unease about this trip. Something felt off. No one knew where they were. Very few people knew he and Gemma were together. There was no reason to suspect anyone would find them, and yet. He double-checked Gemma's rudimentary disguise before she climbed out of his truck. Her long hair was tucked under a baseball cap that she pulled low, hiding as much of her face as she could. She wore baggy jeans and one of his grandfather's old hunting jackets. Matt had found an old cane of his grandfather's in the cabin, and he'd provided that for Gemma to use because of her sprained ankle. She looked like a cross between a teenage boy, which was the look he'd been going for, and a little old man. Now, even if someone caught them on camera, it was unlikely she would be recognized.

"Let's get this done and go for coffee," Gemma said as she carefully climbed out of the truck. She leaned heavily on the cane. She'd insisted her ankle didn't hurt very much, and it wasn't like Matt could carry her around. Now *that* would get them all kinds of attention they didn't want. Not that he would mind having Gemma's body plastered against him again. He'd slept on the sofa last night for the first time, to make sure he didn't bump her ankle in the night. This morning he'd woken up alone, and he'd missed the intimacy of sharing a bed with her. It had been less than a week, and he knew when this was over, there would be a Gemma-sized hole in his life. He wasn't sure how to deal with that.

Yesterday she'd made it clear that she wanted him, at least physically. Her desire had been genuine. She hadn't offered herself as payment, or belittled the connection between them. If it didn't cross a dozen ethical lines, he'd have jumped at the chance, but until her case was resolved, she was off-limits. Her automatic reaction when he'd refused her had punched a hole in his chest. Her assumption that he would hold her past against her, think less of her, had told him more than she knew. How many people, how many *men*, had treated her as "less than" because of her history?

He'd meant every word yesterday. Fighting her addiction, working to stay sober, took strength. She'd survived some of the worst things life could throw at her, and she still wanted to help people. He wanted her. Once all this was over, he'd fight for her.

Matt held the door as Gemma hobbled into the library, following her inside. It wasn't a large building, though it was well equipped, with rows and rows of bookstacks, a series of computers near the front desk, and a clearly marked children's area in the back, where a group of kids were listening to story time. Most importantly, it was quiet and almost empty this early on a weekday, easing some of the tension he'd been feeling all morning. After escorting Gemma to a free computer, he left her to submit her assignment, confident that he could keep an eye on her while he wandered the stacks. The cabin could use a few new reads, but applying for a library card was out of the question. The town was too small to have its own bookstore, so the grocery store always stocked some bestsellers. They could add a stop there before they headed home, pick up a bit of fresh produce and some reading material. Somehow he didn't think Gemma would refuse a new book or two. She'd been devouring all his grandmother's old romances in the evenings.

He turned back to where he'd left Gemma, and his heart rate kicked up. The kiosk was empty. Where had she gone? He scanned the room, that sense of unease still nagging at him, now mingling with a touch of panic. He'd made sure Gemma knew not to activate her phone unless it was absolutely necessary. He didn't want the device popping up on a local cell tower. There was no reason to think she was in danger, but he couldn't shake the sense this trip to town had been a bad idea. It felt like an eternity before he spotted her near the entrance, looking over a large table of books, even though logically he knew it had been mere seconds. Relief flooded through him, seeing her safe. He was being paranoid. No one knew they were here.

A few strides and he was standing beside her. "You all done?"

"All I had to do was upload the file to my school website." Gemma continued sorting through the books on the table, adding to the growing pile beside her.

"You know we can't borrow those."

"We don't have to. These are for sale, and dirt cheap. Only a dollar each. They're clearing out some of their books and fundraising for new ones." Gemma pointed to a small sign sitting on the table. She resumed reading the backs of the books and putting the ones she wanted on her pile.

Why was it that whenever Gemma was around, he couldn't focus on anything except her? He was supposed to be a detective, to notice things, and he hadn't seen the sign at all. He turned his attention to the table full of books and began sorting through them. Matt selected half a dozen books in an assortment of genres. "Have you read any of these?"

Gemma read the titles and pointed to one of the books. "Only that one, and it was really good. I'm taking these. I've got enough cash on me to pay for them." She pointed to the books she had collected.

Matt hid his smile. There had to be fifteen books stacked in front of Gemma, mostly romance novels. Happiness sparkled in her eyes, and Matt wanted this moment to last forever. The last several days had not given Gemma much to be happy about. She had been strong, determined, committed. She had moments of fear and doubt. Today, she glowed.

"Coffee time?" Gemma was almost bouncing as she asked.

"Let's pay for these, and then I'll get you your sugar bomb." Matt swept up Gemma's stack of books and headed for the counter.

After a quick stop at the coffee shop for Gemma to pick up a caramel macchiato and a chocolate caramel muffin, Matt turned the truck towards the biggest grocery store in town. Even though Gemma had purchased books from the library, this would still be their last chance to grab fresh food.

Gemma bit deep into her muffin and groaned. "This is so good. Here, try a bite." She leaned over to offer the muffin to Matt, but all he could see was the tiny drip of caramel that clung to her upper lip. All it would take would be for him to lean forward the tiniest bit and run his tongue over the sweet droplet. He bet it tasted amazing. He *knew* Gemma tasted incredible.

Matt shook his head and directed his attention back to the road. "You enjoy your muffin. I'll stick to coffee."

Gemma made a face as he sipped. "Plain black coffee. So boring. You don't know what you're missing."

Oh, yes, I do. And waiting until you're safe is killing me.

"You could make a list of stuff you want to buy at the store, make sure we don't forget anything."

Gemma pulled a folded page out of her pocket. "I did that last night. You didn't think I was going to let you bring me to town without picking up a few things, did you? I didn't even use my phone, because I knew you wouldn't let me turn it on." She laughed.

He pulled his truck into the parking lot and circled, looking for a spot closer to the entrance to save Gemma from walking too far on her injured ankle. Taking Gemma into the local supermarket seemed safe enough; it was the largest store in the area, and people from other communities shopped here all the time. They wouldn't stick out here as strangers. Finally settling on a spot at the edge of the lot, he parked next to an old pickup with half a dozen wire dog kennels in the back. They were all empty except one. A furry dog that looked like a husky mix was burrowed into a pile of straw at the bottom of the cage. When the dog spotted Gemma, he bounced up and pressed against the cage, whining to get her attention.

"Hey, puppy," she crooned. "What are you doing back there all by yourself? Where are your people?"

Matt took in the battered condition of the truck, noting that the crates in the back were filled with clean straw, and the dog looked well cared for. Several people in the area still used dogsleds for hunting, and some of them even raced the sleds during the winter. This dog could be one of those dogs, and they were not known for always being friendly. "Careful. He might not be good with people."

"Don't you worry. He hasn't got a mean bone in his body. I wouldn't leave a dangerous dog alone in the truck."

Matt turned to see a frail-looking man who could be anywhere between sixty and ninety approaching from the store, carrying a bag of groceries. As soon as the man had said the dog was friendly, Gemma had held her hand out for the dog to sniff, and now she was scratching his neck and ears through the cage. Matt studied the old man and decided he looked mostly harmless. There was no reason to deprive Gemma of her fun with the dog.

"He sure did take a liking to your girl, though. He's not usually that friendly."

Gemma flashed the man a smile. "Dogs like me. What's his name?"

The old man shrugged. "I call him Winter. I'm Ed."

"I'm Matt, and that's Gemma." It was easier to give their first names, and Matt didn't think they'd ever see the old man again.

"You folks from around here? You look kinda familiar."

Matt winced inwardly. He'd been hoping to avoid questions like this. "No, we're just passing through."

Ed nodded. "Not the best time of year to be up here. Weather can turn on a dime."

"Thanks for the tip. Is Winter a sled dog?" Matt guessed, shifting the subject away from their identity.

Ed's lips creased into a frown. "He should have been. He comes from a long line of racers, and all his littermates were great runners. He's got a bad leg, walks with a limp. Can't race a sled, and no one wanted him, not even for his bloodline. So I kept him for myself. Now I don't know what I'm going to do," he muttered under his breath.

Gemma twisted towards them, clearly listening to their conversation. "About what?" Matt asked casually, dreading the answer.

"I sold my land last month," Ed said, his voice shaking. "I'm getting too old to take care of it, and I'm going to live with my daughter. I can't take Winter with me, and no one around here wants a dog with a bum leg. If I leave him at the shelter and no one adopts him, they'll put him down. He's too good a dog to let that happen to."

Before Matt could respond, Gemma spoke up. "I'll take him."

CHAPTER 27

The words were out before she could think about the consequences, but Gemma didn't regret it. In the few minutes she'd been playing with Winter while Matt and Ed talked, she'd realized that she was tired of being alone, and the thought of returning to her empty house filled her with dread. Until now, her schedule hadn't allowed for time to care for an animal. With the submission of her final assignment, school was done. Her internship would start in a few weeks, and she would have a regular schedule. She hadn't had a dog since she was a child, and she loved animals. This was the perfect solution.

"Do you mean it?" Emotion choked Ed's voice.

Gemma looked over and noticed Matt's frown. She should have asked him before being so impulsive. It was his cabin she would be taking the dog back to. Hoping Matt would forgive her, she pressed ahead. "If you'll let me have him."

Ed cleared his throat, fighting back tears. "It's not up to me. It's up to Winter. He seems to like you fine."

Happiness made Gemma almost giddy, though she moved cautiously because of her ankle. A glance at Matt eased her concern about his reaction; he wasn't scowling. If anything, he looked happy for her. Maybe she'd read his frown wrong. Ed moved to the back of the truck and dropped the tailgate before unlocking the crate Winter was in. As soon as the door swung open, Winter bounded out and jumped down, racing towards Gemma. His bad leg made him look like he was bouncing as he moved. It was silly, and funny, and she loved him already.

"What was the problem with his leg?" Gemma asked as she leaned down and let Winter lick her hand.

Ed shrugged. "It's a bit shorter than the other one. Nothing else wrong with it, but nothing could be done to fix it. It doesn't hurt him, though it means he's not a runner and he's not much good for hunting."

Gemma plopped down on the pavement and let Winter crawl into her lap, careful of her ankle as she sat down. She gave Matt a smile when he held out his hand for Winter to sniff, then scratched the dog behind his ears. "Well, I don't hunt, and I don't need a fast dog either. Someone to keep me company and maybe bark at the squirrels in the yard sometimes is good enough for me. What do you think, Winter? Does that sound like something you can handle?"

Winter licked her chin and let out a woof. Gemma laughed. That was a yes if she'd ever heard one. Ed handed Gemma a leash and a small bag with a couple of toys and some papers inside. "I think you've got yourself a dog, Gemma. I'm thankful we bumped into each other. It broke my heart to think no one wanted him."

Gemma continued stroking Winter's head. She didn't understand how no one would want this sweet baby, bad leg or not. It didn't matter now, Winter was coming home with her, and she would spoil him.

Matt pulled out his wallet, reaching for some cash. "I can't let you just give him to us. Can I at least pay for his crate so we've got one for him to use?"

"You don't have to do that," Gemma said. "I can pay for him. I offered to take him with us." She didn't want Matt to feel obligated to do this for her. It was enough that he wasn't protesting her impulsive action.

Ed waved a hand dismissively. "I'm giving the crates to the local Humane Society. They don't have room for Winter, but they sure do need the extra supplies. If you want one, I can put it in the back of your truck." Ed pulled out a pocketknife and began cutting the zip ties holding the crates together.

"His shots are all up to date, his medical records are in that bag." Ed cut the last zip tie, and Matt lifted the crate out of the truck bed.

"Does he sleep in his crate? Does he have a favourite food? Or toy?" Excitement fizzed in her veins, and Gemma gently lifted Winter off her lap and struggled to stand back up. Matt set the crate in his truck, then reached a hand out. Gemma took his hand, allowing him to pull her to her feet as Winter watched her closely. She squeezed Matt's hand in a silent thank-you.

"He started out sleeping in his crate. Once he was the only dog, I relaxed the rules. Sometimes he sleeps on the bed with me, mostly he sleeps on a blanket on the floor. He'll eat anything, and his favourite game is fetch, even with his bad leg. He likes those tennis balls that squeak."

Gemma knew she was grinning like a fool as Ed spoke. She could picture playing fetch with Winter at the dog park near her house, and it was the closest feeling to pure joy she'd had in years.

Ed leaned down and rubbed Winter behind his ears. "You be good for Gemma, boy. She'll take good care of you."

When he straightened up, Gemma gave him a tight hug. "Thank you. I *will* take good care of him, I promise."

With another sniff and a small wave, Ed shuffled his way over to the door of his truck and drove off. Winter pressed his furry body against Gemma's leg. Gemma rubbed his ears, running her hand soothingly over his head. "I know it's your cabin, and I didn't ask, but I couldn't let him wind up in a kill shelter where he might be put down." She was almost certain Matt wasn't mad, even though she had put him in an awkward spot.

Matt knelt and gave Winter a rub when he nudged Matt's hand. "If it had been a big deal, I would have said something."

Gemma bit her lip. "I suppose we'll need to buy some supplies too.

Will that eat into our cash reserves too badly?" Their need to stay off the grid hadn't even crossed her mind when she'd offered to take Winter. He would need food, and treats, and who knew how much that might cost?

"We have enough for now, and Murphy loaned me a True North credit card to use if we had an emergency that we couldn't cover with the cash. Hopefully they'll find out who's behind the threat well before we reach that point." He frowned as he surveyed Winter, Gemma, and the crate. "I hate the idea of leaving him in the crate while we go inside and shop. I know that's how we found him, but it doesn't feel right."

"I wasn't planning on leaving him. I'm going to stay here and keep him company while you shop. That way I can rest my ankle too." Gemma blinked innocently at Matt. Her ankle was starting to throb again, and the rest would help. Plus this gave her more time to get to know Winter.

"You should have said your ankle was sore. I'm happy to take care of the shopping, as long as you two stay in the truck. I want you in the driver's seat, with the engine running. I don't like the idea of leaving you alone, even if we should be safe here. At least if you're in the truck, you can get yourself away if something does happen." He tossed Gemma the keys. "There's a blanket in the back that Winter can lie on."

Gemma handed Matt her grocery list and pocketed the keys. She moved around to the driver's side and climbed carefully into the truck, trying not to put pressure on her ankle. Matt held open the passenger door for Winter to jump in. Once she was safely inside with the doors locked and the engine running, Matt headed to the store. Gemma scanned the parking lot. They were off to the side and in an open area. No one could sneak up on her here, and with Winter beside her, she felt safe being alone.

As they waited for Matt to return, Gemma investigated the contents of the bag Ed had handed her while Winter explored the confines of the truck cab. He checked out the blanket in the back seat and sniffed under the seats, before jumping back onto the front seat beside her. She handed Winter one of the chew toys, and he settled down contentedly. A scan of the vet paperwork confirmed that Winter was current on his shots, as Ed had promised, and other than his one leg was in perfect health. He was listed as a husky crossbreed, crossed with what Gemma couldn't tell. He looked all husky to her, with his thick grey-and-white fur and beautiful blue eyes. He'd been inquisitive as he explored the truck, and his tail was beating happily even now. When she put the paperwork away and set the bag down, Winter hopped off the passenger seat and rested his head on her thigh. The simple gesture, demonstrating so must trust, made a lump grow in her throat. Other than her mother, no living creature had ever needed her before. She should have thought about getting a dog years ago. She definitely wouldn't be lonely anymore.

A knock on the window snapped her out of her daydreams, and Gemma found Matt outside the truck, weighed down with a giant bag of dog food and other shopping bags. While he secured everything except one bag in the truck bed along with the crate, Gemma eased out of the truck and moved back to the passenger seat. Matt climbed into the cab with the single bag, which looked heavy. He pulled out a bag of dog biscuits and immediately opened it and offered one to Winter, who took it gently, licking Matt's hand.

Gemma laughed. "Please don't tell me that entire bag is full of treats for him."

Matt gave her a mock offended look. "Not *just* treats." He pulled out a harness that he slid over Winter's head and fastened around him. This was followed by a strap that buckled onto the harness and clipped into the truck's seat belt. Winter lay down on the blanket in the back, calmly chewing on his toy. "If he's not going to ride in his kennel, then I wanted to make sure he was safe riding with us." He tucked the bag behind the seat.

An emotion Gemma chose not to name squeezed her heart at Matt's thoughtfulness. "Thank you. I'll reimburse you when this is all over."

"You don't have to thank me, and you don't have to pay me either. I have no idea if Winter will be any kind of guard dog, but having Winter means you won't be alone."

Matt's concern left Gemma speechless, and silence filled the cab of the truck, broken only by Winter's soft panting in the back.

When the silence had reached the point of awkward, and Gemma was searching for some way to respond, Matt finally continued: "Besides, I love dogs. My apartment building doesn't allow pets, and my schedule isn't very stable anyway. Spoiling Winter will help me get my dog fix this month. Otherwise I'd only be buying ridiculous toys for my parents' dogs."

Gemma latched on to the change of subject. "Your parents have dogs?"

"We had dogs the entire time I was growing up, usually mixed breeds they got from the SPCA, and then they got involved with a rescue and began fostering dogs. The rescue would take any kind of dog, but my parents have a house in an area that allows pit bulls. My parents fostered pitties almost exclusively. Sometimes a super-special one would come along and they would foster fail." His affection for the dogs was unmistakable, and Gemma wondered why Matt had never sought out a place to live that would allow him to have a dog, when he clearly loved them.

"Foster fail? You mean they would adopt them?" Gemma had never heard of foster failing as it related to dogs, though some of the people she'd met on the streets had come from the foster system, and had talked about how foster failing could happen to the lucky kids who wound up in stable homes.

"Exactly. My parents tried not to let it happen often. If we adopted them, we couldn't take in as many foster dogs. Sometimes they couldn't help themselves, and when I was going through my problem phase as a teenager, one special girl came in for fostering. She took one look at me and made me her human. Her name was Sugar, and we had her until my final year of university. She was thirteen when we lost her." A sad smile crossed Matt's face. "I moved into my apartment a year later, and considering the rental market, I'm not moving out of a rent-controlled apartment. Which means no dogs for me. My parents have two brothers right now that they adopted a couple of years ago. There was a hoarding situation at a rural breeder, and over a hundred dogs were seized. A lot of rescues got involved in that one, and my parents wound up fostering four dogs. Two were adopted right away, but the two brothers were a bonded pair and couldn't be split up. Eventually they kept the boys. I visit Jed and Leo any time I need a dog fix." Matt glanced at Gemma before turning his attention back to the highway. "They love other dogs. We should introduce Winter to them once we get back, let them play together."

Matt's casual assumption that they would continue seeing each other once they returned to Vancouver was like a body blow. They had undeniable physical chemistry, but she was not the kind of girl he could bring home to meet his parents. There was no point fighting about it now. Once this was over, she'd make him understand.

CHAPTER 28

Gemma walked carefully across the yard with Winter, still limping slightly from her sprained ankle. The two days since they had returned from town had been full of getting Winter acclimated to them and the cabin, and waiting. Even after locating the USB drive, there had been no real progress on her case. Dark-grey clouds filled the sky as the first snowflakes started to fall. The promised storm had held off for an extra day, but it was here now. With the way the wind was blowing, it looked to be wicked. Matt had told her that late-spring storms could be unpredictable.

"Has Murphy made contact yet?" Gemma called out to Matt as he carried more firewood to the cabin porch. She wanted to go home, and they didn't have much time left. Murphy had told them yesterday that Jett had broken the encryption on the drive and was sifting through the thousands of files on it. Russell had kept records of *every-thing* he was involved in. It was a treasure trove of evidence, made nearly useless because Russell was dead. The biggest problem was everything was written in code, and Jett was trying to crack it.

"Not yet. If he doesn't call soon, I'll call him. I'm worried that once the storm picks up, we might not be able to get through, even on the satellite phone." Matt stacked the wood next to the door, stopping when the sat phone buzzed shrilly.

"Foster," Matt answered, and walked over to where Gemma was tossing a ball for Winter to chase. "Murphy wants you to hear this. I'm putting him on speakerphone." Matt held the phone between them.

"You ready to come home?"

At Murphy's cheerful question, excitement exploded inside Gemma, and she threw her arms around Matt, crushing him in a hug. "Yes! I'm so ready. What happened?"

"Jett finally broke the code," Murphy said with pride. "She was able to link Russell to several VPD members, including Morin. The evidence was irrefutable. Plus Rebecca kept digging into the death of Jacob Yap. She backtracked any route Jacob might have taken to get to where he was found, and she located surveillance footage from a private residence. There were two people in the car the night Jacob overdosed, and one of them was Morin. Rebecca convinced the coroner to do a closer examination on the body. They found a puncture wound hidden by one of his tattoos, in a spot Jacob would have needed to be a contortionist to reach. It was enough to prove that someone else injected the drugs. Morin was arrested as he came in to work this morning."

Gemma rocked back, shocked that Morin had been arrested. She had never allowed herself to believe that they would find real proof that Morin was behind all of this.

"Was that all Jett found? You're sure the threat is over?" Matt was clearly as surprised as she was.

Murphy chuckled. "Was that all? Not even close. Russell was doing business with almost every crime family in the city. Considering the evidence she located against VPD officers, the case has been taken over by the RCMP to ensure nothing gets swept under the rug. Jett is working with their cybercrime team to decode everything on the drive. The Crown prosecutor is already holding press conferences about cracking down on the corruption. No matter what, Gemma should be safe."

Another gust of wind whipped past them, and Gemma shivered. She wanted to go home, but not in this storm.

"We won't be going anywhere until this storm is over. The snow is already coming down, and I don't want to get trapped on the highway somewhere. It's safer to stay here and let it blow itself out," Matt said.

After a few more minutes discussing the logistics of getting her back to Vancouver, Matt ended the call.

"I can't believe they actually arrested Morin," Gemma said as they headed for the cabin to get out of the wind. Even though Morin was only one person, it sent a message. She was safe now. It hadn't fully sunk in yet.

The cabin door banged as Matt shoved it closed behind them to block out the wind. "I doubt it would have happened without True North getting involved. Morin had a lot of friends who could have made evidence disappear. That will be harder to do now."

Gemma shook the snow off her coat before hanging it up, amazed at the amount of snow that had accumulated during their phone call. "It's getting bad out there. I can't believe how hard the snow is coming down." She grabbed a rag to wipe up the quickly melting mess.

"Guess we're stuck inside for the day. Good thing we bought all those books," Matt teased.

Gemma stuck her tongue out at him. "I'll get to them, but Winter needed me." She had spent so much time playing with Winter since their return from town, she'd barely touched the huge stack of books she had bought at the library sale. Winter was a young, high-energy dog, but Gemma suspected he'd be perfectly content curled up on the couch with her today as she read a book. Even huskies didn't love blizzards like this. Even now, Winter was dragging his blanket from beside the bed over closer to the fireplace, where it was warmer. After pawing it a couple of times until it met his approval, Winter flopped down on the bed and began to snore.

"Do we have enough wood to outlast the storm?" Gemma had never experienced winter weather like this, had never had to worry about things like heating her home with firewood.

"We should be fine. If we do need more, I'll bring it up onto the porch to split, to stay out of the wind. We have plenty of food and enough gas for the generator. The storm should only last a day or so, and then we can head back home."

Gemma clapped her hands together. "Then let's find some things to do to pass the time. It looks like the storm is only getting started."

By midafternoon, Gemma was almost vibrating with frustration. It had been mid-morning when Murphy had called, and since then they'd made lunch, read books, and even played a couple of board games. She'd given up on reading a romance novel when she'd realized that she was picturing Matt as the hero in every scene. Now she was trying to read one of the thrillers Matt had bought, and it didn't hold her attention either. She'd been waiting for Matt to make a move, to signal that her being safe had changed the nature of their relationship. She didn't need his protection anymore.

Gemma didn't know how to do this. Her dating skills as an adult had never developed; having been a sex worker, she was always hesitant to date someone who didn't know her background. The men who did know about her past were often still connected to her old life. Matt had been the first man to tell her that her past didn't matter to him, and he'd made her believe it. Now she wondered if he'd realized that they were an impossibility and wasn't going to try. She told herself it was for the best. Falling for Matt was going to break her heart. Not that she wasn't already going to be emotionally battered by the events of the last few weeks, but sleeping with Matt would make it much worse.

Matt was doing them both a favour. So why did it sting so much? Gemma swallowed past the lump in her throat and tried to focus on the words on the page through the tears that were gathering in her eyes. She was not going to cry about this. She was *not*.

A tear dropped onto the page, blurring the words further. Gemma rubbed her eyes furtively, brushing away the tears and hoping Matt wouldn't notice. She wasn't that lucky.

"Hey, what's the matter?" Matt stuck a receipt in his book to hold his place and set it aside.

He reached for her hand, and the shock of his touch sent tingles from her fingers all through her body. How could a simple touch set her off like this? She resisted the urge to crawl into his lap. "I'm fine. Just the relief of it all being over, probably."

Matt's thumb rubbed circles over her palm, and Gemma tried not to think about where else she wanted his hands. She wanted to be more than casual friends, but it didn't feel realistic. They were from two totally different worlds. That didn't stop the ache in her chest. Finally, she found the courage to ask the question she needed the answer to. "What's going to happen when we go back home?"

CHAPTER 29

Matt gripped Gemma's hands tighter, apprehension making it hard to find the right words. Gemma was attracted to him, maybe as much as he was to her. At the same time, she was afraid to get involved with him, sure that any relationship between the two of them could never work. It looked like she was willing to take the next steps, but he wasn't looking for a casual hookup. He liked Gemma, admired how hard she'd worked for her nursing degree, her dedication to helping people who were going through what she had gone through. It was going to take all his negotiating skills to convince her that he wanted her for who she was, and that he wouldn't get hung up on her past. "What's going to happen depends on what you want. I want a relationship with you. I want to spend time with you, introduce you to my family, learn about your favourite things. I'm not looking for a fling. How does that sound to you?"

Gemma's eyes widened at his fervent declaration, before she ducked her head and let her long hair hide her expression. Matt waited. Gemma was skittish, and she had to want this as much as he did if they were going to have a chance. She was right about one thing: Dating someone with a criminal record, someone who was a known sex worker and recovering addict, would not go unnoticed among his colleagues. Matt could handle the blowback, but Gemma had to know it would be hard for her.

Gemma lifted her head up and met his gaze, smiling. Tears glistened in her eyes. "I'd like that. I'm not sure how to do this, though. I don't have a lot of experience with relationships."

Matt wanted to haul her into his arms, resisting the urge because he needed to be patient. Gemma was still hesitating, and she was so nervous she was trembling. "My last relationship ended a while ago. A cop's schedule can be a problem. Every relationship is different. We can make ours anything we want it to be." He laced his fingers through hers and pulled her closer until she was sitting up against him. He lowered his head and pressed a gentle kiss against her lips, ready to stop if she said no.

Gemma leaned into him and opened her mouth under his, her tongue flicking against his lips, wordlessly asking to be let in. With a groan, Matt let her take the lead, and as her tongue plunged into his mouth, she pulled her hands from his. She swung one leg over his thighs to straddle him. One of her hands gripped his hair while she ran the other over his beard. She surrounded him, devouring him, her breasts pressed against his chest and the heat from her core rocking against the full length of his erection.

Matt tried to focus on each sensation and the way she tasted as she kissed him, sweet like the hot chocolate she had been drinking. How her hands gripped him, tugging his hair to position his mouth exactly where she wanted it. The way her nipples had pebbled hard enough that he could feel them through the layers of both their clothes when she pressed into him. He rested his hands on her thighs, putting no pressure on her to do more than she wanted to.

Gemma grabbed one of his hands and pushed it under her sweater, her intention as clear as if she'd issued an order. Matt slid his palm over her ribs, gliding up until he reached the fabric of her bra. He cupped her breast in his palm, dragging his thumb over the point of her nipple, drawing a shuddering moan from Gemma. She arched into his palm, then reached down and tugged her sweater up over her head, leaving her wearing a plain T-shirt over a sports bra. Matt shoved the shirt and bra up, baring her breasts to him. He dipped his head and pulled one of her nipples into his mouth, dragging his tongue over the hard bud. Gemma held his head in place and bucked her hips against him.

"More."

The single word was all the encouragement Matt needed, and he continued laving his tongue over her nipples, alternating between them, nipping them gently before easing the sting again with his tongue. Gemma's fingers dug into his shoulders as she held on and rode him through his jeans, her breath coming in short gasps. His own need was raging, but he wanted this to be about her.

Matt slid one hand between them, tugging open the button of her jeans. He lifted his head and locked eyes with her, and Gemma took his hand and slid in into her jeans. "Touch me," she encouraged.

Her panties were soaked as he stroked his fingers over her mound. He sucked her nipple deep into his mouth as one finger worked its way into the wetness at Gemma's core. He dragged his finger along her opening until he reached the slippery nub that was his goal. He circled her clit, flicking the sensitive bundle of nerves, letting her grind against him exactly the way she needed. His cock throbbed in his jeans. Watching Gemma take her pleasure was the most erotic thing he'd ever experienced.

Gemma ground herself against his hand, her breaths increasing in tempo with her hips. In less time than Matt would have thought, her head tipped back and she let out a long, keening cry. Her thighs clenched around him, and slick moisture covered his hand. As she came down from her orgasm, Gemma slumped against him, her head resting on his shoulder.

"That was amazing." She nuzzled his neck before pushing herself up and tugging her bra and T-shirt back in place. She slid to her knees on the floor in front of him and reached for the button on his jeans. "Now let me pay you back."

Her words penetrated his lust-filled haze. Gemma looked like she was willing, but Matt needed her to understand that everything they did together was because they both wanted it. He reached down and pulled her back up until they were eye to eye. "You don't have to do anything to pay for your pleasure. You never have to do anything you don't want to with me. Am I hard as a rock from what we just did? Yes. Does the thought of your lips around my cock make me want to come in my pants? Also yes. But I'm a grown man who knows how to control myself, and if you don't want to, or are too tired, or simply aren't in the mood, that's fine too. Okay?"

"I understand. I want to do this," Gemma said earnestly, dropping back to her knees.

∼

GEMMA GLANCED towards the fireplace as she settled back between Matt's thighs. Winter was still sound asleep, although how he'd slept through her orgasm, she'd never know. It might turn out he wasn't a great guard dog after all. Right now she didn't care. She reached for the button on Matt's jeans, anxious to taste him. She was still buzzing from her own orgasm, and she wanted the opportunity to make Matt feel as good as she did. With the button and zipper undone, Matt shoved his jeans and boxers over his hips, and his cock sprang free.

Tall and proud, it stood straight up once released from the confines of his pants. Gemma had seen more than her share of male appendages, and she took a moment to admire Matt's before wrapping her hand around it and giving him a firm stroke. Matt's groan had her stroking him again, savouring the hot, smooth skin. She shifted until her mouth was positioned over him, then swirled her tongue over the head, tasting the salty droplet leaking from his slit, exploring each ridge and crevice excruciatingly slowly.

Matt's hands were fisted into the couch cushions, his head thrown back. A vein pulsed along his neck, and Gemma dragged the flat of her tongue along his entire length for the pleasure of watching it throb. Teasing him like this was something new for her, and knowing she was safe to explore him any way she wanted was the most liberating thing she'd ever done.

With one hand around the base of his cock, Gemma closed her lips around the tip and drew him into her mouth, taking as much of him as she could before she gagged. Squeezing and sucking, she teased and tortured until she sensed Matt getting close. She sped up her pace, her mouth moving up and down faster and faster. Matt gave a shout, and his hips jerked under her. His cock throbbed in her mouth. As he started coming, she pulled her mouth away and stroked him hard with her hand, and his ejaculate spilled across her hands and his stomach.

Gemma reached for the box of tissues on the corner table, wanting to clean up the sticky mess before it dried. Her days as a sex worker had left her with one big rule: She never swallowed.

Matt took the box from her. "Let me." He quickly wiped up the mess on himself and pulled up his jeans, while she cleaned up her hands.

Sated, Gemma rested her head against Matt's thigh, almost purring when his hand stroked her hair. "That was intense." Every part of her was loose and relaxed. She couldn't remember the last time she'd felt this good.

Matt pulled her up to sit next to him, wrapping an arm around her. "It was incredible. Still feel good about us?"

Gemma leaned into him, inhaling the perpetual scent of woodsmoke the fireplace left in his clothes. She'd never again be able to smell a campfire without thinking of Matt. Did she still feel good about them? There were a lot of hurdles they still needed to face, but today she felt like she was invincible. "I feel great about us."

CHAPTER 30

The first thing Gemma noticed when she woke was the quiet. The storm must have ended in the night, because the howl of the wind was curiously absent. Her next move was to bury deeper under the quilt on the bed, the temperature in the cabin much colder than she'd expected. It was *cold*. And where was Matt? She'd fallen asleep reading last night, waking only when Matt carried her to bed and tucked her in next to him. She'd drifted back to sleep snuggled in his arms. Now the bed was empty, and there was no fire burning in the fireplace. Before Gemma could poke her head out of the covers to search for him, the cabin door banged open, and the bright sunlight streaming in did nothing to take the edge off the cold air that came with it. Matt's huge frame filled the door, blocking the worst of the wind, and she noticed his arms were full of wood. Winter bounded in after him, covered in snow and practically grinning at her.

"Morning, sleepyhead," Matt greeted her, dumping the wood beside the fireplace. "Sorry about the chill in the cabin. We ran low on wood last night, and it was too dark and too windy to bring more in. I'll get a fire going."

Without waiting for Gemma to respond, he turned back to the fireplace and began laying in the wood. Gemma sat up and pulled the quilt around her shoulders, thankful she'd been wearing her wool socks before falling asleep last night.

"Since the storm is over, does that mean we can leave for Vancouver today?" Gemma hoped she didn't sound ungrateful, but she wanted to go home.

Matt shook his head without turning, slowly feeding kindling to the fire. "Probably not, unfortunately. The roads are almost impassible, even with four-wheel drive on my truck. I don't want to risk getting stuck halfway down the mountain with no way for help to reach us. As long as there's no more snow, the main road should be plowed by tomorrow at the latest, and we can head back." He turned to face her, his smile teasing. "Think you can handle one more day with me?"

One more day? How about a lifetime more days? Gemma smacked the thought down as soon as it formed. It was too soon for thoughts like that. This thing between them was brand new. Yesterday she had allowed herself to believe in the possibility of a future with Matt. She still wanted to believe, but she was also prepared for them to blow up. She already cared about Matt more than any other man she'd been with. Which only meant more pain for her if they crashed and burned. She could worry about that when they got back to Vancouver. Today she could enjoy being here with Matt, knowing that she was safe.

"One more day works for me. The last thing I want is to wind up stuck in a snowbank somewhere. Now how about I make us some breakfast?"

Gemma was putting away the last of the breakfast dishes when Matt's arms snaked around her waist, pulling her back against him. She twisted to face him, her hands roaming over his broad chest. Matt nuzzled her neck, sending shivers down her spine. "I was thinking." He peppered kisses between each word.

Gemma had a pretty good idea exactly what Matt was thinking, based on how hard he was against her belly. Not that she was complaining. "What about?" Her words came out as a whisper, all her attention focussed on the riot of sensations Matt was creating with his mouth.

"Let's go play in the snow." Matt stopped kissing her and tried to look innocent. "What? Were you thinking something else?"

Gemma smacked his shoulder lightly and tried to get her breathing under control. He wanted to play in the snow? She'd show him. "Last one outside has to cook dinner." She sprinted for the door. Stuffing her feet into her boots, she grabbed her coat and flung the cabin door open before she could pull it on. Winter raced out with her, eagerly bounding into the snow that covered the small clearing around the cabin. Gemma pulled on her coat against the cold, then turned to face Matt, who was still standing in the cabin doorway.

"You let me win," she accused with a laugh.

Matt grinned at her. "I'm a better cook than you. You knew I'd let you win." He zipped up his coat and followed her trail through the snow, handing her a hat and scarf to go with the mittens she'd pulled from her pocket. "You'll need these."

Gemma took them and put them on, then followed Matt as he broke a path through the freshly fallen snow. The storm had left everything stark white, and the way the sunlight hit the ice crystals made everything glitter. It was the literal definition of a winter wonderland. It was glorious. The air was cold and crisp, with none of the pollution or smog that she'd gotten used to in Vancouver.

The pristine snow was almost too perfect to ruin, but Gemma couldn't resist. She dropped backwards with her arms wide, then moved her arms and legs as far out as they would go. When she was satisfied, she carefully pushed up and turned to find an almost perfect snow angel. She had only ever made snow angels once before, after a freak snowstorm when she was little. She and her mother had made snow angels and a snowman in their yard before it melted away in the rain. The memory made her miss her mother, and she was surprised when the wave of grief she expected didn't come. Matt brushing snow from her jeans brought her back to the present.

"You'll be soaked if you let it melt."

"You want an excuse to grab my ass," Gemma teased. "It's your turn. We need matching angels."

Matt laughed, then obediently turned and looked for a clear patch of snow. He flung himself backwards with the abandon of a big kid, moving his arms and legs in unison before standing back up and surveying his handiwork.

Gemma took one look and burst out laughing. "Your wings are bigger than my entire angel, big guy." She began brushing the snow from Matt's backside, enjoying the way his jeans molded his cheeks. The man had a great ass.

"I'm going to bring that downed tree closer to the cabin in case we need more wood." Matt pointed at a fallen tree on the edge of the forest.

Gemma nodded and called to Winter, who ran over and dropped a ball at her feet. The dog was in his glory, playing in the snow as if he didn't feel the cold at all. She tossed the ball for him, turning when something thumped against her back and snow exploded around her.

Matt stood at the edge of the trees, grinning, a snowball in his hand. He cocked his arm back, and Gemma tore off in the other direction, dashing behind a pile of uncut wood before he could hit her with another snowball. It was temporary shelter, because if she stayed here, she would be a sitting duck. She peeked around the pile of wood and didn't see Matt. She needed a place to hide. If she ran for the cabin, Matt would see her every move. Finally, she crept out from behind the wood, staying close to the tree line and trying to make sure that every step she took was on top of footprints she and Matt had already left behind. Finally, she found a tall pine tree big enough to hide behind.

Gemma wiped the sweat out of her eyes with the back of her mittened hand, trying to stay hidden from Matt. Gemma squatted and started rolling snowballs, building up an arsenal as she watched for Matt. She found him studying the tracks, trying to figure out where she'd disappeared to.

"Gemma, you can't hide from me," Matt called, laughing. "I've been tracking people for years."

Gemma smiled as Matt moved closer to her hiding place. He might have been tracking people for years, but she'd dodged the cops for years too. Besides, he was almost exactly where she wanted him. One more step...

Matt took another step closer, and Gemma pelted him with snowballs in rapid-fire succession. With a roar, Matt charged towards where she hid, taking a snowball in the face before he wrapped his arms around her waist and slung her over his shoulder.

Gemma squealed and pummelled his shoulder. "No fair. Let me down!" She wriggled against him, trying to work herself loose without hurting him.

"You want down?" Matt dumped her into a snowbank, laughing as the powder puffed up around her. Gemma grabbed his ankle and yanked, and he tumbled into the snow beside her. When she tried to roll away, Matt gripped her wrist and pulled her tight against his chest. "You fight dirty."

Gemma stared up at him, the heat from his gaze chasing away the chill from the snow. The raw desire reflected in his eyes mirrored her own and left her weak. Wordlessly, she closed the distance between them and pressed her lips against his. His skin was chilled from the cold air, but his lips were warm and firm under hers. The snow in his beard was melting and leaving glistening droplets of water that soaked into her mitts as she cupped his face.

With a groan, Matt tore his lips away from hers. "I want you. Let's go inside." Matt pulled her up from the snow, brushing her off before looking down at her.

His words set off another surge of desire, and suddenly there was nothing Gemma wanted more than to be naked under that quilt with Matt. "Take me to bed or lose me forever."

Matt stopped short, then chuckled. *"Top Gun?* Really?"

"You're not the only one who knows their eighties movies," Gemma called over her shoulder as she ran for the cabin.

The cabin was cozy and warm after they'd been outside for so long. Their outdoor adventures had left Gemma chilled, and the melting snow had her clothing clinging to her. Excitement had her hands shaking as she stripped off her outerwear, taking the time to hang it up beside Matt's jacket. She wanted Matt, but this would change things. Before she could completely spiral, Matt emerged from the small addition that housed the bathroom, carrying a stack of towels.

"Let's get you out of those wet clothes," he said gruffly. He draped one of the towels across the back of the couch and moved to stand in front of her.

If Gemma had been cold, the desire in Matt's gaze was enough to warm her to her very core. With exquisite slowness, Matt grasped the hem of her sweater, edging it up over her abdomen, his long fingers brushing her skin as he exposed it. For a big man, his touch was gentle, every move designed to demonstrate how much he wanted her. Each touch stoked her desire. When the wet wool slid up over her breasts, he stopped long enough to brush a kiss against the skin exposed over the lacy cups of her bra. Gemma shuddered, aching to have him touch her everywhere.

Matt eased the sweater over her head, dropping it on the table and reaching for the towel. He wrapped it around Gemma before sliding his hands down to her hips. She glanced away from him, needing to avoid the look of tenderness Matt wore as he unbuttoned her jeans and slid them down her legs. He already had a grip on her emotions, leaving her open and vulnerable. She couldn't afford to give Matt more of her heart yet—it would destroy her if she had to walk away.

Once her jeans were gone, Matt stripped off his own wet clothes, leaving him in nothing except his boxer briefs. Gemma sucked in a breath. She'd known Matt was a good-looking man. Without clothes he was a god, radiating strength. Chiselled abs, heavily muscled thighs, broad shoulders. Heat burned in her belly, and moisture rushed to the apex of her thighs. She reached out and trailed her fingers over a puckered scar on his right shoulder. His skin was hot under her icy fingertips, and she wanted that heat to envelop her. "What happened here?"

Matt lifted her fingers to his lips, pressing kisses against them as he nudged her backwards towards the bed. "I was stabbed by a suspect a few years ago. Nothing serious, though I did get a nice scar out of it." The injury was a reminder that Matt was a cop. Now that had new meaning. Being a cop could put Matt in danger, even if he was being casual about it. Gemma pressed a kiss against the scar.

Matt trailed his lips from her fingers up her arm, making Gemma drop the towel that he'd wrapped around her earlier. Once her body was exposed, Matt stopped to admire her. "You are so beautiful." Gemma's cheeks heated at his praise. Her body had become a commodity, yet somehow this was different. With Matt, her emotions were involved, and hearing him say she was beautiful meant something. It felt real.

Gemma resisted her instinctive response to cover her flaws: the round cigarette burns left on one hip by a customer, her own knife scar under one rib. She'd gotten a couple of tattoos to cover the worst of the scars, but there were so many of them that she'd finally given up and accepted that her scars were part of her. Matt was looking at her like he couldn't see the scars, like her skin was perfect as it was. She could almost pretend her scars didn't exist. Right now she wanted to pretend. Pretend she was good enough for Matt. She reached for Matt's hand and tumbled back on the bed.

Gemma pulled Matt down to her, letting his weight press her into the mattress. His mouth captured hers in a hungry kiss, and she surrendered to the heat and desire flooding her body. His tongue stroked against her lip, coaxing it open. Once she let him inside, it danced around hers, teasing, taunting, and driving her wild. The need to have his mouth on her sex had her squirming under him, seeking release.

Matt's cock was heavy and hard against her belly. Gemma smoothed her hands over his shoulders, tracing every muscle, working her way down over his rib cage until she reached the boxers that were the last barrier between them. Matt raised himself up long enough for her to ease them over his straining cock, and she shoved them down, humming in appreciation. She wrapped her hand around him, eliciting a groan of pleasure. She ran her thumb over the tip, teasing his sensitive skin, working to drive him wild.

"Fuck, Gemma." He reached between them and moved her hand

off him. "If you keep touching me like that, I won't last five minutes. I want to take my time with you."

His words wiped away any faint sting of rejection she'd felt when he'd taken her hand away. Gemma stretched out on the bed, and he hovered above her, pressing kisses over her body. Her nipples were hard peaks, begging for his touch. The heat of his mouth closed around one while his big hand pinched and rolled the other, making Gemma gasp. The pleasure-pain combination almost short-circuited her brain, and it distracted her from what Matt was doing with his other hand. His hand dipped between them, he slipped one finger into the wetness at her core. She arched up, seeking friction against her clit, desperate for relief. Instead, Matt's fingers danced away, tracing the line of her slit, circling her opening. Gemma smothered a whimper of frustration. She needed *more*.

Matt moved down her body, his eyes locked on hers as he slid first one finger inside her, then a second. When he withdrew them, they were slick with her moisture, and she smothered a groan as he slowly licked them. Gemma's breath was coming in short pants, and she was practically writhing under him. Gemma was used to pleasuring the men she was with, not having them pleasure her. Usually she got herself off alone, quickly and efficiently. This long, drawn-out foreplay was killing her. *"Matt."* She knew she was begging and she didn't care.

Matt nipped her hip, making her shriek. "What? Tell me what you want."

"If you don't quit teasing and put your mouth on me . . ." Gemma tried to look threatening.

Matt's grin bordered on evil as he whispered his reply: "As you wish."

The shock of his mouth on her clit had Gemma's hips bucking up, her back arching off the bed. Electricity hummed through her, every nerve ending feeling like it was on fire. His lips closed over her, sucking; then his tongue circled the tight bud and sent shock waves through her entire body.

She dug her nails deeper into the mattress, trying to resist grabbing his head and mashing his face against her pussy. He slid his tongue along the length of her slit, swirling through her wetness, and she saw stars. Then two of his fingers glided smoothly through her folds, probing deeper until they were buried inside her. Matt's mouth never stopped working on her clit as he finger-fucked her, each thrust, each lick, bringing her closer to oblivion.

Desperate for relief, Gemma laced her fingers through Matt's hair, holding his mouth against her where she needed it most. Then he crooked his fingers upward and hit her G-spot, and Gemma shattered, crying out.

CHAPTER 31

Matt felt the exact second Gemma fell apart, even if her moans hadn't made it perfectly clear. Her muscles went taut, her inner walls clamping around his fingers. Her thighs were trembling around his ears as he savoured the unique taste that was Gemma.

His cock throbbed insistently, seeking its own release. He ignored it, focussed on wringing every drop of pleasure out of Gemma. He wanted her to know that her pleasure mattered to him. This wasn't about him; it was about her, about them. He needed her to see how good they were together.

Her inner thigh quivered as he kissed it softly, and he trailed kisses up her abdomen and chest. Each time his lips touched her skin, she shivered, and her fingers still cupped his head as he moved back up her body. When he got to her mouth, he found it turned up in a blissed-out smile. "Liked that, eh?"

Gemma snickered. "If you ever want to give up being a cop, I could hook you up with a couple of high-end escort services. You could make a killing with that mouth."

Matt choked out a laugh. "That's good to know, if I ever need to change careers." He leaned over to kiss her, rolling onto his back and taking her with him so she wound up draped against the length of his body. His cock twitched under her, and a slow grin spread across her face.

She pushed herself off him and stood. "Condoms," she said in explanation. He was about to tell her that he'd picked up a box in town when she grabbed her purse and pulled out a couple of her own.

They were probably still in her purse from her last encounter with Russell, but Matt didn't care if the condom fairy had dropped them off, as long as it meant he would feel Gemma wrapped around him. He reached for the package, but she pulled it away, holding it out of reach. "I've got this." She tore the packet open and with infinite slowness rolled the condom down over his shaft, teasing and taunting him with her fingers. By the time he was fully sheathed, it took all his willpower not to roll Gemma over and thrust into her with all his strength.

Gemma straddled his hips and notched his cock against her opening. Heat radiated over him as she sank down on him, her body embracing him in her tight, wet warmth. Matt groaned and gripped her hips, holding her in place before he lost control too soon. He wanted her to enjoy this as much as he did, and going off like a teenager wasn't part of his plan. "Give me a minute," he gritted out.

Gemma folded her body down onto him, belly to belly, nipple to nipple. She scattered kisses across his neck and shoulders, taking time to gently outline the knife scar she'd asked about earlier.

Matt shifted and began to rock his hips against hers, each motion creating friction that set off his nerve endings. Gemma ground her pelvis into him, and he shifted so he could stimulate her clit with each rotation of his hips. With every move, Matt clung to his control, not wanting this to end, not wanting to come before Gemma had a chance to chase her second orgasm.

Her body quaked around him, and she bit down hard on his shoulder to stifle her screams. Gripping her ass, Matt thrust his hips faster, wallowing in her heat, the way her pussy was milking his cock. He lost control as Gemma blew softly into his ear. His body spasmed and throbbed with his release, and his fingers dug deeper into

Gemma's soft flesh as she collapsed against him. *This woman.* Matt stroked his hands over her skin, memorizing the feel of her against him. The trust they had built was still new, but something had shifted between them today. Gemma had let her guard down, had let him see her true self. It was a little humbling.

When the room stopped spinning, he rolled her off him and tucked the blankets around her before disposing of the condom and crawling back into bed beside her and spooning against her. It was only the middle of the afternoon, and spending the rest of the day in bed had never sounded so good.

A quiet woof came from the dog bed by the fireplace, and Gemma giggled. "I think he's confused."

Winter was staring at the bed, his head flat on his paws. "Sorry, buddy, you can't come up this time." *Great.* The dog was jealous. He was going to have to get over it, because Matt intended to keep Gemma here the rest of the day. Longer, he hoped.

He focussed on the woman curled up next to him. He traced a finger over some of the ink covering her body. She had tattoos all over, and he'd seen glimpses of them as they cohabitated, but this was his first chance to really see most of them. The one he was currently touching was a huge green-and-blue dragon that ran from her ribs all the way down one thigh to right above her knee. His mouth was open and breathed fire, and his claws dug into her flesh with little drops of blood dripping from under them. The scales were luminescent in the light coming in through the window. "This is beautiful. When did you get it?"

Gemma wiggled under his touch, and Matt hid a smile. She was ticklish? He'd have to remember that.

"I had it done when I hit my one-year-sober mark," Gemma said matter-of-factly. "A reminder that I have to fight the dragon every day if I want to stay sober. Plus it covered up a couple of nasty scars."

Matt could feel the puckered skin under his fingers. He'd already seen the round scars on her hip, clearly cigarette burns. He smoothed his hand over the marred skin, waiting to see whether Gemma would volunteer the source of the scars. Finally, she rolled onto her back and met his eyes, resignation and a little fear reflecting from hers.

"My body got pretty badly abused for a long time. Some of the scars are still visible—I'd be the tattooed woman if I tried to cover them all. The ones the dragon covers? When a pimp tried to force me to work for him, he fucking branded me so everyone would know who I belonged to. I had the brand marks cut off, but the scars they left behind were almost as bad as the brands. They were the second ones I covered."

Matt nodded, not wanting to say anything that might make Gemma stop sharing her life with him. He hated what she'd been through, and yet everything she told him increased his appreciation of how strong she was.

Gemma ran her hands down both arms, over the sleeves of tattoos covering them. "These were the first. I had to cover the track marks. It's weird, as ugly as those tracks were, seeing them made the cravings worse. When I couldn't see them anymore, it got better. Don't get me wrong, the cravings didn't disappear; they just weren't as bad."

Matt drew a single finger over the puckered white scar that ran along her rib cage, wincing inside. He knew what a knife scar looked like. Gemma sighed. "Knife fight. Another girl and I were fighting over who would work on a certain corner. I punched her, broke her nose. She came back up with a knife. I got lucky—the knife hit a rib and snapped. I barely felt it, I was so high when it happened. I got a bunch of stitches and this scar. She got six months for assault." Gemma smiled wryly. "And neither of us got the corner we were fighting over. Your turn. Have you ever been shot?"

Matt rolled with her changing the subject. She'd shared a huge amount about her past, trusting him with her truth. She could tell him the rest when she was ready. He grasped her hand and brought her fingers to his mouth, kissing each one. "Nope. I've never even had to fire my weapon. I've drawn it a few times, but luckily I've never needed to use it. Part of that is my assignment, though. Sex Crimes means I usually see people after the crime is over, often on the worst day of their lives. Words are much more powerful than weapons. Even when I was a patrol officer, I always tried to talk first. I took my de-escalation training to heart. At one point I thought about training for hostage negotiation. The problem is, there isn't a lot of demand for it here, and the current team is very good at what they do." Matt shrugged. In the end, his decision to apply for Sex Crimes had been more rewarding than he'd expected. Working for VPD was losing some of its appeal, but he did feel like he'd made a difference to a lot of people over the years.

"You're good at what you do too," Gemma observed. "Even when you were certain I was guilty of murder, you were polite, sympathetic, and kind. You treated me like a person, and a lot of cops would have looked at me and seen a junkie whore, guilty as charged. The fact I was in Russell's room? I must be using again. I might have traded sex for money with him, but I was not going to let him drag me back into my old life. I have too much to live for." Gemma frowned. "I don't want to talk about Russell." She trailed her fingers over the scar on his shoulder. "I know you got stabbed here." She traced a small scar on his abdomen. "What about this one?"

Matt laughed. "Appendix, when I was ten. Nothing exciting about that one." Matt pulled Gemma closer, fitting his body tight against his. He palmed her hair, threading the sleek, silky strands through his fingers and then gliding his hand over her skin. Gemma had given him the greatest gift, her trust. There had been none of her hard, streetwise shell between them, and Gemma allowing him to see her vulnerable was something he would treasure.

Gemma pulled her hand out of his grasp and traced her nail around his nipple, raising goose bumps on his skin. She scraped her nails down over his ribs and abdomen until she reached her goal. A simple tug was all it took for Matt to get hard all over again, and Gemma flashed him a satisfied smile. "Be a shame to let this go to waste..."

CHAPTER 32

Gemma woke abruptly, the dark of the cabin telling her it was still the middle of the night. She wasn't sure what had interrupted her sleep, but something had her senses on alert. Winter propped his chin on her leg, as if he felt her distress. Matt slumbered beside her, his arm draped possessively over her abdomen. Other than the newness of Matt's touch, nothing seemed out of place. The cabin was silent, she was with Matt and Winter, and no one knew where they were. Maybe it had been an animal prowling around outside that had woken her. Somehow Gemma didn't think so.

Knowing she wasn't going to be able to get back to sleep, she slipped out from under Matt's arm and padded to the bathroom, glad they had both pulled their pyjamas on before falling asleep. When she finished, she lit one of the oil lamps and curled up on the couch with a blanket. They were going home today. While Gemma was excited to go home, to get back to work, to school, to thank everyone who had helped her through this nightmare, the previous two days' activities had put a wrinkle in her return. Sleeping with Matt had been everything she'd hoped for and more: He was passionate yet considerate; gentle and fierce. Without saying a word, he'd shown her again and again that this was more than a physical thing for him. They had forged an emotional connection.

Which was why she worried about what would happen when they got back to Vancouver. Matt's belief that their relationship could be anything they wanted it to be was idealistic. His career wasn't the only reason they wouldn't work, but it *was* the biggest stumbling block. Would he get pressure from above to use her street connections? Or worse, would being with her hurt his career? Would he be passed over for promotions or plum assignments because he was with an ex–sex worker and addict? She couldn't allow that to happen. His job and her past would always come between them. If she was going to end it, it needed to be soon. She wasn't kidding herself; giving Matt up was going to hurt. She didn't want to name the emotion crushing her chest right now. She knew what it was. Better to do it now, before she had built her own dreams around their future. She didn't want the ride back home to be awkward, so a quick, clean break as soon as they arrived might be the best thing for both of them.

Winter's shoving his nose against her hands brought her back to the present. "It'll be okay, boy. I promise. You'll have a big yard to play in and a whole house to claim as your own. If you're lonely, maybe we can find you a buddy after a while. I'll be there for you, and we'll get through it together," Gemma whispered.

A low growl rumbled in Winter's throat, and his hackles rose slightly. Gemma strained to hear anything outside that might have set Winter off, but the night was as quiet as ever.

"What's the matter, puppy? Did you hear something?" Gemma moved towards the door, intent on figuring out what had Winter so upset. Instead, Winter stopped in front of her, blocking the door. A sudden gust of wind rattled the windows, and Gemma shivered, the noise reminding her how alone they truly were in this cabin. The wind seemed to calm the dog, and Winter nosed her back towards the bed. Stopping only long enough to blow out the lamp, Gemma crawled in next to Matt and resolved to enjoy the last of their time together.

∼

Matt turned the key in the ignition of his truck, frowning when nothing happened. While his truck was an older model, he kept it in great shape, and they had driven it to town only days ago. The storm had brought lower temperatures, but not so cold that it should cause engine trouble. Besides, a cold engine would have at least tried to turn over. His truck hadn't responded at all to the turn of the key. With any luck, it would be a simple dead battery. They could use the generator to charge it. It would only slow them down, not a real problem. If it was more serious, he would need to ask Murphy for help getting Gemma home.

Matt exited the cab and moved to lift the hood. Winter was hovering nearby, which was strange. Yesterday he had been out playing in the snow like it was his favourite game; today he had barely left Matt's side from the minute Matt stepped outside the cabin. Something had him spooked.

Right now Matt needed to focus on getting his truck running. He was no mechanic, but if it was something simple, he might be able to figure it out. He scanned the interior, and nothing seemed visibly out of place. When he dropped down to look under the truck, to check for leaking fluids, a chill ran through him that had nothing to do with the air temperature. The snow under the truck was packed down, and it was stained with pink fluid. The only way it would have been packed down was if someone or something had crawled under the truck. It might have been Winter when he was outside over the past day, except there was a person-shaped depression under the engine. Someone had found them. And that someone had purposely disabled his truck.

Matt's heart rate kicked up a notch as he stayed crouched behind the protection of his truck and did a quick visual sweep of the area around the cabin. He needed to get back to Gemma. He noted a few disturbances in the snow. Whoever had found them had been careful to stick to areas already tramped down by them yesterday. Matt finally detected a pattern that led from the woods behind the cabin to the rear of the truck, and then around the side of the rocky outcrop the cabin was built against. There was no way of knowing where the person was hiding now, and Matt wasn't going looking for them without a weapon.

He headed back to the cabin at a jog, Winter at his heels. Now he understood what had Winter so on edge. The dog must have picked up on the strange scents that were in the yard. Not that it mattered now. He needed to make sure Gemma was safe, then get on the sat phone and call Murphy for help. The distance between the truck and the cabin was less than a hundred yards, yet it had never felt so long. He was taking the porch stairs two at a time when a shot rang out. He ducked, and wood splinters rained down on him as the bullet embedded itself in the pillar next to his head.

Matt burst through the cabin door. He closed and locked it, then pushed the heavy bureau in front of it as extra security. He hated blocking their only exit, but they were too exposed here.

"What are you doing? Was that a gunshot?" Gemma grabbed Matt's arm.

"Yes, it was a shot. He missed me. Whoever is out there sabotaged my truck too." Matt moved around the cabin, securing the windows and pulling the curtains closed, staying out of sight as he did so. The interior of the cabin grew darker with every move, but he didn't want whoever was outside to have any easy targets. It might be hours before Murphy could get help out to them. The fact that no additional shots had followed the first was both good and bad. Good, because it probably meant there was only one person out there hunting them. Bad, because the person hunting them was patient enough not to take a shot unless there was a clear target. In other words, an experienced hunter.

Gemma's lips pressed together in a thin line, the only outward signal she gave of being worried by Matt's news. "What can I do?"

"Call Murphy and tell him we need help." Matt tossed her the phone as he looked for another piece of furniture to move in front of the largest window. The wooden shutters used to winterize the cabin were on the outside. The only way he could pull them closed was by going outside, and that was too risky. He flipped the kitchen table on its end and pushed it over to cover the window. Another scan of the room confirmed what he already knew: They were out of movable furniture. The rest of the windows were unprotected, and he and Gemma were trapped.

"Fuck!"

Gemma swore at the sat phone clutched in her hand. Creeping dread made his movements feel slow and shaky as he took it from her. He examined the phone long enough to confirm that there was no signal, then shoved it into his pocket.

"What happened? What did Murphy say?"

Gemma's cheeks were flushed red, and she was trembling. "Whoever is out there must be jamming the phone, because we'd barely connected before the call was cut off." She whirled away from Matt and swore again. "We can't count on Murphy figuring out we need him."

Gemma paced the small confines of the cabin, avoiding the windows.

Matt winced as Gemma paced. She was terrified, and he had promised to protect her. She was supposed to be safe at the cabin, yet still someone had found them. What he couldn't figure out was how. He couldn't worry about how, though; he'd solve that riddle later. Right now they needed to find a way out of here.

CHAPTER 33

Gemma continued pacing, trying to work off her fear and stress. Winter matched her step for step, picking up on her anxiety. Objectively, she knew this wasn't Matt's fault. Morin had had the entire power of the VPD at his fingertips before he was arrested, and they still didn't know who all might have been working with him. It was conceivable Morin had managed to ferret out Matt's link to the cabin via the genealogy site that Matt had found his grandfather on, or maybe someone from VPD had managed to get information from Matt's parents about his adoption. How they had found them didn't matter. What mattered was that someone was out there, and there was no way of knowing who, or how many people were with them. They had already taken one shot at Matt. Whoever was out there was here for one reason only: to kill them both.

Matt moved to the bed and lifted the rug that covered the floor beside it. Under the rug was a trapdoor that exposed a gun safe when he pulled it open. Opening it revealed several long guns, ammunition, and a few items Gemma couldn't identify. He pulled three of the guns out and checked them over carefully.

The cabin was darker with the curtains closed, but there was enough light still coming in that they wouldn't need to worry about the lamps or candles for hours yet. At least that was something. Lighting a lamp in the dark would be like painting a target right on them.

Carrying one of the guns, Matt moved to one of the front windows and edged the table over a couple of inches. He slid the window sideways, enough to poke the end of the rifle through, then peered around the curtain. Another shot rang out, thudding into the window frame beside where Matt's head had been, and Gemma sucked in a breath. Matt returned fire before pulling the rifle muzzle into the cabin and pushing the table back over the open window.

The guns made Gemma feel a tiny bit safer; they weren't completely defenceless. But the idea of being caught in a gunfight was still terrifying. "We need a plan," she said abruptly. Even armed, waiting to be rescued was not her style. Plus, in this situation, it was probably suicide. Murphy and Abel were hours away, and that was *if* they realized that she and Matt were in trouble.

"I know. I've got an idea, I just don't like it." Wrinkles creased Matt's forehead, and his scowl made him look scary and forbidding. This was not the calm, easygoing man she'd spent the last week with; this was a man capable of being dangerous when necessary. It was oddly comforting.

"Tell me your idea." Anything was better than waiting.

"Whoever is out there must have transportation of some kind. We need to get to it. The only way to do that is to disable them somehow. Confuse them, capture them, kill them if necessary. I have more than one hunting rifle here. Do you know how to shoot?"

Gemma shook her head. For the first time in her life, Gemma wished she'd taken an interest in the guns on the streets. Maybe if she knew how to shoot, this would be easier. "I've never even held a gun."

Matt handed her one of the rifles. "Rifles aren't as simple as handguns. This is a semiautomatic rifle. All you have to do is pull the trigger. Once it fires, it will load another round into the chamber for you. Unfortunately, it's not very sensitive, so you have to use a fair bit of pressure, and it has a vicious kick. If you need to fire it, try to brace yourself and be prepared to be knocked back. Hold it like this."

Matt stood behind Gemma and helped her hold the rifle in position, placing the stock against her shoulder. "Don't worry about aiming. If you're close, it won't matter. If you're far away, it's more of a scare tactic anyway. With any luck, you won't have to fire it at all."

Matt continued loading the two other guns he had pulled out of the safe. "You not being familiar with guns complicates things a little, but this might still work. I was going to distract the threat by taking a shot in his direction, giving you enough time to shimmy out of the cabin's back window. I can't do it; I'm too big to fit." Matt pointed at the window closest to the kitchen, one that looked out onto the woods surrounding the cabin.

Gemma sized it up. Matt was right—the window was far too small for him to squeeze through. "What am I supposed to do once I'm outside?"

"You take the rifle and circle around the cabin into the woods. I'm counting on him to return fire when I take a shot at him. That will let us know where he is. You could sneak up behind him and threaten to shoot him; then we could capture him. With you not knowing how to shoot, it's a huge risk."

Gemma played out the scenario Matt described in her mind, trying to put all the pieces together. The biggest risk she saw was that their adversary would go after her gun. With Matt coming from the other direction, it wasn't the worst idea. It might work. "Why does my not being able to shoot matter? If I'm behind him, pointing a gun at him, what difference does it make?"

Matt sighed. "If everything goes perfectly? None. What if he decides to fight? Or run? Or if he has a partner out there? You need to be prepared to pull the trigger if you're threatened. Not knowing how to shoot leaves you vulnerable. Too vulnerable." Matt shrugged. "I didn't like any of my ideas, but the cabin only has one door. There's no back way out. Which leaves us with three shitty options: stay and wait for Murphy, try to capture the gunman and use his transportation to get out of here, or make a run for it and hide in the woods. Which one do you hate least?"

Gemma resumed pacing. She couldn't bear the idea of doing nothing. What if whoever was out there stormed the cabin? Or tried setting it on fire? That eliminated option one. Running and hiding in the woods, in the snow and cold, with no way to get to town and a killer hunting them? No thanks. Which left them with only one option. She had to climb out a window and try to find whoever was out there, take them by surprise, and help Matt bring them into custody.

"Tell me more about how your plan would work. How will you draw their attention so I can get out the window?"

"First, I'd take a shot in the opposite direction of the window. That last shot told me where he is, and I doubt he'll go far. He's close to the driveway, behind a big stand of trees that provides perfect cover. It's where I'd have set up if it were me. The good news for us, this angle blocks the window you'll be going out through. My shot should draw his fire, giving you time to slip out the window and run for the woods. Get to the path that leads to the lake. You'll still be exposed as you run for the trees. That's when I'll fire at him, to keep his attention on the door and away from where you'll be. You take the trail out to where it forks, and instead of heading to the lake, go the other way. Come around behind him, take him by surprise. Yell for me, and I'll come out of the cabin and take him down." Matt gripped her shoulders. "You don't have to do this. We could try to hold him off until Murphy gets here."

Gemma swallowed hard. The entire plan was dangerous, but it wasn't impossible. Her ankle was mostly healed, so running on it was doable; she'd played hide-and-seek from pimps and cops hunting her more than once before to stay alive. Her biggest fear was mishandling the gun. That could get her killed. Gemma resisted the urge to lean into his strength and focussed on getting out of the cabin alive. "When do you want to do this?"

"Part of me wants to wait until twilight to give you more cover. The cold might affect whoever is out there, which is good. It would be easier for me to see muzzle flashes in the dark to locate him too. The risk is, the dark will make it harder for you to see, and I don't want you to injure yourself as you try to get behind him. He might get impatient, try to force us out of the cabin. That could ruin our plan entirely. We need to move soon."

Another jolt of adrenaline shot through Gemma, followed by a strange sense of calm. She wanted this over. Waiting would only make it harder, give her more time to think, to worry about the future. It was time to act.

Moving silently, they pushed the kitchen table under the window to make it easier for Gemma to climb out quickly. Winter watched them both, ears flat against his head and hackles raised.

"You'll keep him here so he's safe?" Gemma tucked her hair under a ball cap as she spoke.

"Of course." Matt made sure the gun was slung securely over Gemma's shoulder and helped her up on the table. Before she could ease the window open, he pulled her close and tipped her head up. "Do *not* do anything to put yourself at risk. If something goes wrong? You run. As far and as fast as you can." He shoved the satellite phone into her coat pocket. "Run until you get a signal, and call for help. But no heroics. Nothing is more important than you getting out of here alive." His lips crashed down on hers, his mouth devouring her like this was the last taste of her he would ever get.

Gemma lost herself in Matt's kiss, blocking out the emotions tearing her apart. She poured every ounce of love she had for him into her response, unable to speak the words and hoping he would get the message.

Matt tore his mouth away and pressed his forehead to hers, panting. "This is a stupid idea. We should try to think of something better."

Gemma cupped his cheeks and planted another quick kiss on his mouth. "There is no better idea. Let's do this."

CHAPTER 34

Matt took up a position by the cracked window. He relied on all his academy training to still his heart rate and focus on what he needed to do. He couldn't let his emotions distract him, no matter how worried he was. Matt needed their assailant to make a mistake, to expose himself long enough for Matt to get a shot at him, maybe even disable him, without Gemma having to do anything. He doubted things would be that easy, but it was the best possible outcome.

He locked eyes with Gemma, and once again he berated himself for even suggesting this plan. Fear for her safety had his guts cramping, and sweat soaked his shirt. He should be the one going out after their adversary.

As Gemma eased the window open to make her escape, Matt slid the gun barrel through the opening and took a shot at the stand of trees. He scanned the brush for any sign of movement and waited for return fire. In his peripheral vision, Gemma slid through the window and disappeared.

A bullet smashed through the window and slammed into the wall above the bed. *Shit.* That was closer than he wanted. Hopefully it would hold the attention of whoever was out there. Staying low, Matt returned fire and hoped it would give Gemma the time she needed.

Winter leaned against Matt's legs and whined, then paced restlessly between Matt and the open window Gemma had exited through. Matt whistled softly and Winter returned to his side, dropping down onto the floor. Taking a quick look out the now-shattered window, Matt noticed movement in a set of trees on the edge of where the shots were coming from. Hoping he could end this without Gemma being involved, he took careful aim and fired his rifle at the brush.

With no way to communicate with Gemma, all he could do was try to keep the gunman distracted. Matt shifted, trying to find a better line of sight while still remaining behind cover. He was a big man, and making a target of himself wouldn't help any of them. More unnatural movement in the trees to the west of the cabin's door had Matt taking another shot at them. Anything to give Gemma more time to circle around behind him. How long had she been gone? It felt like forever, but in reality Matt knew it had been only a few minutes. Barely enough time for Gemma to have made her way to the fork in the trail. She needed more time to get in position.

Matt poured another few rounds of gunfire out the window, angling them as far in the opposite direction of Gemma's escape as possible. The blast of a rifle filled the air, and a bullet missed his forearm by inches before he withdrew it into the cabin.

Dropping below the window, Matt shuffled over to the door and dragged the bureau away from it. He made sure both of his guns were fully loaded and slowly twisted the doorknob. He threw the door open and rolled out onto the porch, taking cover behind the thickest part of the railing as bullets sailed over his head into the open doorway. Even as gunfire rained down on him, Winter streaked out the door and across the yard, heading in the direction Gemma would have run after leaving the cabin. The gunfire continued to rain down on Matt's position on the porch.

Matt aimed in the direction of the gunman and let off a few shots before diving off the porch and racing for the cover of his truck.

Running or not, it would provide some cover. Every move he made was designed to give Gemma time. Pain exploded in his right leg as a bullet tore through his flesh, and he collapsed into the snow beside the truck.

∼

NO! Gemma bit her mitten to smother her scream as Matt fell to the ground and disappeared behind the truck. It looked like the bullet had hit his leg, and if it hit his femoral artery, he had minutes before he bled to death. As much as she wanted to race to save him, she needed to be smart. Showing herself now would give her assassin an easy way to accomplish his mission. She needed to disable him first, then go help Matt.

A furry body nudging her hand made her swallow another scream until she realized it was Winter. "I'm glad to see you, buddy. Now let's go help Matt." Gemma gripped the gun tighter, determined not to mess this up. She needed to be strong, to get to Matt to make sure they both survived this mess. His last directive, to save herself if things went wrong, echoed in her mind. But there was no way she was leaving him lying in the snow, bleeding.

She scanned the brush that the gunfire had come from. All was still now. He hadn't made any attempt to finish Matt off, but she couldn't tell if he was still in the same position as before.

Winter growled, and Gemma whirled around to find the black muzzle of a rifle pointed directly at her dog. Her gaze travelled up the length of the barrel until it met the hate-filled eyes of Claude Morin. The smile stretching his face radiated satisfaction. Nausea made her stomach cramp, replaced quickly by burning anger. She wasn't going to let this arrogant ass win.

"Move an inch and I'll shoot that mutt," he warned. "Now toss me that rifle."

Gemma gripped the rifle tighter, then looked at Winter and tossed the rifle over to Morin. She'd been in tough spots before and survived.

Now it was up to her to save both of them. "You're supposed to be in jail."

Morin's laugh sent chills through her entire body. "I have dirt on more VPD cops than you've got ex-johns. One of them conveniently forgot to handcuff me for transport last night. Now he's got a lump on the back of his head, and I'm free. Thanks to you, I'm a wanted man. I've lost my career, and that means I've lost some of my connections. All because you wouldn't die like you were supposed to." Morin shook his head. "I never should have left it up to that junkie to kill you and Russell, but I needed it to look like a murder suicide: a lover's quarrel that ended with you killing Russell and then overdosing after it was over. Neat, tidy, no loose ends. But no. First you leave the room and don't come back. Then you somehow get Foster and some fancy private security firm to protect you. I'd really like to know who you slept with to make that happen. Russell always did say you were a great fuck, but come on. Private security? That shit ain't cheap."

"Fuck you." Gemma spat the words at Morin. Anger burned through her, chasing away the fear that held her paralyzed. She had to keep him talking, find some way to distract him so she could run.

"If I had the time, you little whore. I wouldn't mind sampling what you've been giving out, but I've got a job to do. You've caused us no end of trouble, and it's time to make sure Russell's secrets die with him. You won't be able to blackmail anyone with the secrets he told you."

"He didn't tell me anything! We didn't have a relationship; we had a business arrangement. Nothing else. If your stupid cameras and microphones in my house had done their job, you would know that. You and everyone you work with are idiots." Gemma rolled her eyes, hoping her contempt would set Morin off on a rant, give her the chance to take him by surprise. If she could knock the gun out of his hands...

Morin's cheeks flushed red. "You're such a stupid bitch. You know what? I actually believe you. Which means that you didn't have to die. Now you know too much, so too bad for you. Once I take care of you,

I'll go finish off Foster for the fun of it. I hate that self-righteous prick."

"The feeling is mutual, asshole." Matt's voice made Morin swing around. Gemma lunged for the gun. She grabbed it as he was firing at Matt, pulling the muzzle down so the bullet buried itself in the ground. Matt fired at the same time, his muzzle jerking upwards to avoid hitting Gemma. The bullet from his rifle tore into Morin's forehead, sending blood and bone flying. Morin collapsed, bright red staining the white snow.

Gemma leaped back from Morin's body and wiped the worst of the bloody spray from her face before she raced towards the tree Matt was braced against. She reached him just in time to catch him as he slumped to the ground.

CHAPTER 35

"Shit, shit, shit!" Gemma frantically tore at the blood-soaked fabric of Matt's jeans, trying to get access to his wound. A strip of cloth ripped from the bottom of his shirt was tied around his leg, twisted tight with a stick. Even with that makeshift tourniquet in place, blood stained the snow around him, and there was a trail marking the path he'd followed through the trees to sneak up on Morin.

"Don't you dare die on me, you big jerk." She could not lose Matt. Not now, not when she'd realized that what they had was worth fighting for, and she hadn't even had a chance to tell him she loved him. Gemma fought down her panic and tried to remember all her training from nursing school. She located the pocketknife Matt always carried and used it to cut away a portion of his jeans, blinking back tears as she did so. She could fall apart later. For now she had to take care of Matt. A quick survey told her that he had done an excellent job applying his own tourniquet. It had slowed the bleeding, and with a quick twist of the stick, she was able to ensure it would hold for a while longer. Winter nosed Matt's face, lying down next to him when Matt stayed still. He was out cold as she worked on him. His pulse was steady, and the skin around the wound still had good colour. He was in no immediate danger of bleeding out, but she had to get him to safety.

Satisfied she had done everything she could for Matt until she could move him, she turned her attention to Morin. The minute Matt's bullet had struck Morin's head, it had been obvious he was dead. She still needed to find the phone jammer he'd used, and the keys to whatever transportation he had. Gemma reminded herself she'd seen both bad gunshot wounds and dead bodies throughout her practical training in Vancouver hospitals. She remained as clinical and detached as possible as she dug through his pockets, fishing out a key ring and stuffing it into her own pocket. He didn't have the phone jammer on him, and she didn't have time to look for it. Getting Matt to a town with proper medical care was more important. She could call Murphy for help once she was on the road.

Gemma hurried back to where Matt lay still in the snow, trying to decide whether she should take the time to drag him to the cabin and risk starting the bleeding again. Winter jumped up from where he'd been lying with Matt, his gaze inquisitive. Gemma didn't want to leave Matt out in the cold, but moving him would slow her down, and they needed Morin's vehicle. Making a quick decision, she commanded Winter to lie beside Matt again, then ran back to the cabin and grabbed the space blankets from the first aid kit. They would keep Matt warm enough while she worked to get them away from the cabin. She tucked the blankets around him and kissed him softly, thankful to find his skin was still warm and his breathing even. With a quick whistle to Winter, she set off to follow Morin's tracks.

Morin hadn't tried hard to hide his trail, so even an amateur like Gemma was able to follow his path through the snow. At the few points where she'd become confused because Morin had walked over his own prints while scoping out the cabin, Winter quickly nudged her back on track. It wasn't long before she located a nearly new Ford F-150 parked on the road that led to the cabin. Relief washed over her when Morin's key fob activated the truck.

In no time she'd started the truck and pulled it up the road to the cabin, driving it across the clearing to get as close to where Matt lay as possible. Gemma's panic was gone, replaced by her need to get help for Matt. She had to take him to a medical centre. The first step was to get Matt into the truck. Contacting Murphy was her second-most-important priority. She found Matt exactly where she'd left him, wrapped in the slippery silver foil blankets. He was still unconscious, which would make this harder, but she had to get him out of here.

Think, girl. He needs you. Gemma looked again at the slippery silver foil, then took one of the blankets and carefully rolled Matt onto it. She grasped the edges of one side and pulled. It slid across the ice-crusted snow with only a little resistance. Perfect. She dragged Matt across the snow, dodging branches and trying not to jostle his leg. When they reached the truck, she opened the passenger side and gauged the distance from where Matt lay on the ground to the back seat. She wanted to have him lying down for the ride, to reduce the risk of the tourniquet coming undone and his leg bleeding again. Nursing school had taught her how to move people a lot larger than her, and she put that training to work now, gripping Matt under his arms and pulling backwards until she could drag him into the truck. By the time he was wedged between the seats, she was panting and dripping with sweat, but filled with exhilaration. She'd done it. They could leave.

Stopping only long enough to grab her backpack with her wallet and identification, Gemma hit the road for Williams Lake. The director of the Northern Health District had done a presentation to her nursing class to recruit people to move to the region, and Williams Lake had been one of the medical centres promoted. Matt would get the care he needed there. She'd barely driven a mile down the road when the satellite phone Matt had given her began vibrating insistently. *Thank god.* Hands shaking, she pulled it out and put it on speakerphone so she could talk hands-free.

"Murphy? Is that you? Did you get my message?" The words spilled out in rapid succession. Gemma gripped the wheel of the truck as it skidded sideways on a small patch of black ice. She eased off the gas pedal and slowed the truck. The last thing she needed was to wind up in a ditch.

"I've been trying to call you all morning, ever since we got cut off. Abel and I are on our way up to the cabin now. We have a problem." Murphy's usual calm demeanour was still present, even though his voice held concern in every note.

"I'm guessing Claude Morin's escape is part of that problem? We know about that already. I have problems of my own. Matt's been shot."

"Shot? Is he okay? Was it Morin? Where is he now? Where are you?"

"Morin's dead. Matt's unconscious and he's lost a lot of blood. I'm on the highway headed for Williams Lake. They have a good hospital there, and since Matt took me there, I know how to find it." Gemma glanced into the back to see whether Matt's condition had changed at all. Satisfied his colour and breathing were still good, she focussed on driving as fast as she could while avoiding icy patches.

Murphy was barking orders in the background, then came back on the phone. "We're on a charter flight. I'm having them land in Williams Lake instead of our original destination. I called the local RCMP detachment and sent them out to pick up Morin's body. I'd rather have my team do it, but it needs to be an official police investigation. How did he die?"

"Matt shot him before he passed out. Killing him was self-defence. Morin fired at him, and Matt was defending himself and me." Gemma had been so focussed on getting them away from the cabin that she hadn't taken time to process the events of the morning. It felt wrong to be relieved that Morin was dead, but it was true. He'd terrorized her for the last time.

"Okay, so self-defence. That's good. We'll come straight to the hospital when we land." Murphy ended the call.

Gemma gripped the wheel so tight it hurt. All she cared about was getting to Williams Lake.

The closer she got to a populous area, the better the roads got, and it wasn't long before she was pulling the truck into the emergency area at the hospital. She raced through the doors and to the nurses' station. "I've got a male, mid-thirties, GSW to the right upper thigh.

Unconscious with significant blood loss. Can someone grab a stretcher and help me get him in here?"

Her announcement galvanized the ER team into action, and in short order Matt had been brought in, assessed, and immediately sent to the operating room. With doctors and nurses working on Matt, the adrenaline high that had been driving Gemma came crashing down, and she sagged into a chair in the waiting room. She'd done it. Matt was getting the care he needed.

Gemma waited until her breathing returned to normal, then stood to go move her truck and get Winter, who she had left in the front seat. A nurse stopped her as she was approaching the emergency room doors. "We need to take a look at you. You're covered in blood." The nurse pointed at the blood spatter coating Gemma's clothes.

When she had been focussed on getting Matt here, she had been able to block out the coppery scent of Morin's blood and ignore the way the blood had dried on her hair and face. Now, with the nurse staring at her, Gemma started to shake. The nurse led her to a gurney and made her sit on it. "It's not my blood. I need to move the truck and take care of my dog," Gemma protested.

"Is your dog friendly?" When Gemma nodded, the nurse continued: "I'll have an orderly move your truck. I can put your dog in one of our private meeting rooms for now, until we check you out. After we're sure you're not hurt, you can clean up while you wait for your friend to get out of surgery."

A shower sounded like heaven. Too bad she was a walking crime scene. "I want my dog with me. The RCMP should be here soon. They'll want to talk to me about the shooting."

After finally convincing the nurses that she wasn't hurt, they left her waiting in a room with Winter for the RCMP to show up. All Gemma could think about was Matt. Had she got him here fast enough? Would they be able to repair his leg so that he could return to his job? She would never forgive herself if he was permanently injured because of her.

Gemma wrapped her arms around her torso and rocked back and forth in her chair. Winter pressed against her legs, offering comfort.

The sound of a man clearing his throat brought her back to the present.

"Are you Gemma Milani? I'm Constable Carr of the Williams Lake RCMP. We got a call from a Mr. Murphy about what happened to you this morning."

Constable Carr looked to be in his early forties, with blond hair and kind eyes. He hovered in the doorway until she nodded. "I'm Gemma." He entered the room slowly, his body language nonconfrontational. Every move he made eased some of her tension.

The constable set a large box that looked like a fishing tackle box on the table next to Gemma. "I'm going to ask you some questions, and I also need to collect some samples of the blood you have on you. I need to take some pictures first." His voice was soft as he explained what he needed to do.

Gemma sat quietly as Constable Carr went through the evidence-collection process, too worried about Matt to pay much attention to what was being done. After what felt like hours, the constable handed her a large plastic bag and a pair of scrubs. "I need your clothes too. You can put the scrubs on until you have some of your own clothes brought to you. You can shower now too."

Relieved the evidence-collection process was almost over, Gemma followed Carr into the nurses' changeroom, Winter on her heels. Inside one of the shower cubicles, she removed her clothes and sealed them in the bag. Once she handed it to him, he left her alone to clean up.

Gemma stood under the hot shower spray as pink rivulets of bloody water swirled around the drain. Morin was dead. She could go home. She poured shampoo into her hand and worked it through her hair, the bright, citrus scent washing away the lingering smell of blood. If only she could wash away the last of her fear as easily as the blood. After towelling off, she pulled on the scrubs and headed back to the room she'd been waiting in.

The sight of Murphy and Abel in the waiting room was a balm on her tattered nerves. The tension drained from her body, and the adrenaline she'd been running on all day disappeared, leaving her exhausted. A peek at the wall clock told her it was barely noon. She felt like she'd been awake for days.

"You got here fast."

Murphy handed her a paper cup with steam rising from it. "Here. It's hospital coffee, and it's terrible, but you need it. Come sit, and you can fill me in on what happened."

Gemma sat down on the cracked vinyl seat beside Murphy and ran through the events of the morning. Anything to fill the time and keep her from thinking about Matt. What was taking so long? Gemma stared down at the floor before taking another swallow of the coffee.

"Ms. Milani?" Her head jerked up.

The doctor, an Indigenous woman with long dark hair pulled back in a knot, came over to where they sat. Her easy smile gave Gemma hope.

"Is Matt out of surgery? How is he?"

"Mr. Foster came through surgery with no trouble. The wound was clean except for one fragment that we had trouble getting out. It was too close to the artery, and we needed to get it out without nicking the artery. We succeeded, and he's in recovery now. If all goes well, we can discharge him in a few days."

Tears pooled, and Gemma swallowed past the lump in her throat as she realized this was finally all over, and she and Matt could go home. "Can I see him?"

The doctor smiled at her. "Of course. Follow me."

CHAPTER 36

The gentle pressure of his hand being squeezed made Matt aware of his surroundings. The white walls and bright lights would have been enough to tell him he was in a hospital, even if his leg hadn't throbbed. The only thing he cared about was Gemma's hand gripping his. She was alive. *They* were alive. As everything came back into focus, the sight of Murphy and Abel behind Gemma told him that Gemma was safe. That was all that mattered.

"Hey," he croaked. He squeezed her hand weakly.

Gemma's head snapped up, a broad smile spreading across her face. "Hey yourself. How do you feel?"

A crush of emotions threatened to overwhelm him: relief, gratitude, joy, and love. It took his breath away how much he loved this woman, but he didn't want to scare her with the intensity of his feelings. "Thirsty."

"We'll come back later," Murphy said as he and Abel left the room.

A cold nose poked his hand as Gemma held a straw to his lips for him to drink. Matt scratched Winter's ears as he slowly sipped, trying to gauge how Gemma was feeling. They'd been through a lot. "How are you?" He asked. "Were you injured?" The sight of Morin pointing a gun at Gemma had terrified him and given him the strength to push through the pain to get close enough to neutralize Morin. He remembered firing his weapon, then nothing after the gun went off. Was Morin in custody? How had they gotten away, and where were they?

Gemma gripped his hand again, shaking her head in response. "I'm not hurt. It was you we were all worried about." Gemma filled him in on what had happened while he was unconscious.

"You saved us," Matt said in awe as she finished. What Gemma had done was amazing.

"We saved each other," she corrected him, leaning over the bed to press a soft kiss on his cheek.

Tears glistened in her eyes as she pulled back. "Don't ever do that to me again. You scared the shit out of me. I thought you were going to die before I could tell you I love you," she finished, half laughing, half crying.

She loved him? Everything about her told him she meant what she said, and it took all his strength to resist pulling her onto the bed with him. Every part of him hurt, but her declaration made the pain irrelevant.

Matt tugged her closer. "I love you too. I promise to try to not die on you." He would happily spend the rest of his life proving it to her.

Raised voices in the hallway woke Matt, and he smiled as he felt Gemma pressed beside him on the bed. She had refused to leave his side ever since he woke up from surgery, and the night before had crawled onto the bed beside him when he'd wanted to hold her. The warm, furry body of Winter was curled up at his feet.

It had barely been twenty-four hours since they had tried to leave the cabin, yet a lifetime might as well have gone by. The walls Gemma had tried to throw up between them were gone, broken down by the risk of losing each other. She'd told him she loved him, and it was obvious in every word, every touch, every little gesture. There weren't words to describe how much he loved her in return. As soon as he was well and they were back home, he would spend the rest of his life showing her instead.

As his mind cleared from the drugs they were giving him to help him sleep, the voices outside his room became clear.

"He's my officer; you can't stop me from going in and seeing him." Michelle Chan's voice rang with the authority of her position.

"I don't care if you're the reincarnation of the queen, you're not going in there until he wakes up. It's family only outside of visiting hours." Matt suppressed a grin at the equally authoritarian response of the night nurse on duty. In her fifties, the nurse had introduced herself last night as Al, short for Alicia, and had made it crystal clear that she was in charge of the ward, and no one was going to bend the rules on her watch. Somehow Gemma had charmed her into letting both her and Winter stay overnight in Matt's room. From the sounds of things, Michelle wasn't going to win this one as easily.

"Al?" Matt whisper-shouted, not wanting to wake Gemma. "Al? You can let her in. I'm awake."

Al poked her head into Matt's room, took in the sight of Gemma and Winter both on Matt's bed, and rolled her eyes. "Fine. She can come in. Only because I like you, Matt Foster."

Matt raised the bed so he was in a sitting position as Michelle took a chair across from him. Then he waited. She wasn't wearing her dress uniform, although her navy suit gave her the same look of command authority she always wore in public. She projected confidence.

"The doctors say you'll come through this and be good as new in a few weeks. Your suspension has been lifted, and you can return to active duty as soon as you feel up to it."

Michelle broke eye contact, and a flush crawled up her cheeks when Matt said nothing, simply staring at her. She thought he could go back to work as if nothing had happened? "You mean after I'm cleared for killing Morin, don't you? After all, an officer-involved shooting doesn't just disappear."

Michelle shifted in her chair, looking ill at ease. "Yes, of course. The investigation has already started. The Williams Lake RCMP are handling it, and all the resources of the VPD are at their disposal as well. There are some items that the RCMP recovered we need to ask Gemma about, but it's a formality."

Matt resisted the urge to laugh. The resources of the VPD? A formality? What she really meant was she needed this all to disappear so that no one outside the force would ever know that Morin had escaped with assistance from within the VPD. That kind of reputational damage was hard to recover from.

"I'll answer questions anytime you want me to." Gemma shifted beside him, pushing herself up and sliding off the bed.

The loss of Gemma's heat left Matt aching to haul her back into his arms, to show her how much she meant to him. Something about this entire situation was bothering him, but he wasn't sure why. Michelle's visit was not that surprising, even if her arrival in the early morning hours was odd. The RCMP did need a statement from Gemma, sooner rather than later. Still, it felt wrong. All he knew was, he did not want to let Gemma out of his sight. Which was ridiculous. Morin was dead. Gemma was safe.

"Excellent. I can drive her down to the detachment myself later this morning. Once she's finished, she can come right back. It looks like you'll be discharged as early as tomorrow, according to the doctor I spoke to."

"Works for me. Let me clean up and grab some breakfast, and we can head out. I want to get this over with," Gemma said.

Matt wanted to object but couldn't think of any reason to. "What about Winter? He can't stay here with me."

Gemma scratched the husky behind his ears, and Winter thumped his tail against Matt's legs. "I'll take him with me. That won't be a problem, will it?"

Michelle was frowning at the dog. She finally shrugged. "I'm sure it will be fine. I'll meet you in the lobby in an hour."

MURPHY AND ABEL rushed into Matt's room, the grim look on their faces all Matt needed to see to know something was very wrong. He'd texted them earlier, hoping they would make it to the hospital before

Gemma left with Michelle. He had wanted one of them to escort her to the station with Michelle, but Michelle had been impatient, and she and Gemma had left while the doctor was examining his wound.

"Where's Gemma? And where's Michelle Chan?" Murphy was in full military-command mode this morning.

"Michelle left with Gemma, maybe ten minutes ago. Why? What's going on?" The unease that had been hovering below the surface all morning bloomed into full-blown dread.

"Jett called me. She decoded a bunch more of the files from the USB drive we found at Russell Molloy's. Morin had a huge network of underworld connections, and one email referenced someone higher up than Morin pulling the strings. Jett has been working all night to figure out who that was, in case you and Gemma might still be in danger. This morning she traced a payment from the same email address into Morin's bank account. The sender was a shell company, whose sole shareholder is Michelle Chan. It looks like Michelle was the mastermind behind the entire operation."

"Now she has Gemma," Abel said.

Murphy pulled out his phone and punched in a number. After a few words, he ended the call, looking grim. "That was Constable Carr. He's at the detachment. Michelle and Gemma haven't shown up."

"Fuck. We have to go find them."

Murphy held up his cell phone, which displayed a map with a blinking red dot. "Jett is tracking Gemma's cell phone. We had Gemma turn on location sharing after we found the cameras hidden in her house. When she was with you at the cabin, it was useless, but she turned her phone back on yesterday. We've been able to track her ever since. As long as Michelle doesn't toss it, we'll find her."

"Really? You have all these high-tech toys at your disposal, and you're using Google's location sharing to track her?" It couldn't possibly be that easy, could it?

"It's simple, and it works. I'm glad we didn't have her turn it off yesterday."

Matt grasped the bed rail and hauled himself to the edge, swinging his legs over.

"Whoa, you're not going anywhere." Murphy reached for Matt's arm, trying to get him back on the bed.

Matt's stomach flipped. His fear for Gemma had blocked out the fact that his boss, a woman he'd respected, was the dirtiest cop he'd ever seen. Morin had hinted that they'd discovered only the tip of the corruption iceberg. Michelle was not going to get away with this. He'd see her go down for murder if it was the last thing he did.

"I'm coming with you." Matt shook him off, then yanked at the IV tube and cables keeping him shackled to the equipment around him. The heart-rate monitor began to screech when he disconnected the leads, and the door banged open as Al rushed in.

"What do you think you're doing?" she demanded.

"Saving my girl. Now help me get this IV line out." Matt stuck his arm out towards her.

"I can't do that; you're not ready to be discharged," Al argued.

"If you don't do it, I will, and I'll mangle myself in the process. One way or another, I'm walking out that door in under five minutes. Your choice." Matt thrust his arm at her again.

Al threw her hands up in the air. "Fine. It's your life. You can explain it to the surgeon when you wind up back here with your wound torn open and she has to stitch you up again."

Matt gave her a nod of thanks. "I'll tell them I gave you no choice."

In less time than they'd been arguing, Al had the IV needle out and a bandage applied, and Matt scrounged up scrub pants to replace his ruined jeans. His heart was racing, and terror left a metallic taste in his mouth. He couldn't lose Gemma now, not after everything they'd been through.

CHAPTER 37

Gemma sat beside Winter in the back seat of the sedan Michelle drove, staring out the window, watching as the houses grew farther and farther apart. She didn't know where the police station was located, but they seemed to be heading away from the downtown area rather than towards it.

"Where are we going?" Gemma asked after they passed a sign for the station, pointing in the opposite direction.

"I've got a stop to make."

Gemma stroked the fur on Winter's neck, trying to soothe her ragged nerves. Matt had been with the doctors when she left the hospital with Michelle, and something had been bothering him. Her own instincts were telling her that something about this situation was wrong, but what? Michelle was Matt's boss; he trusted her. That implied that Gemma should trust her as well.

Now they were driving farther and farther into the wilderness that bordered Williams Lake, and Gemma's gut was screaming at her to run. Which was tough to do from a moving car that was picking up speed and flying down the icy highway. She needed help. Gemma gripped Winter closer and used his body to hide her movements as she reached for her cell phone. Michelle's attention was glued to the highway, trying to avoid patches of black ice. A quick tap of her password and she had it open, and she typed out a quick 9-1-1 text to Murphy. If he got it, he would track her down. She couldn't risk a voice call, so as a final bit of insurance, she turned the voice-recording feature on before sliding the phone into her pocket. If something happened to her, at least there might be enough evidence left to prove who was responsible.

"I'd really like to review that evidence and get back to the hospital. I need to make plans for getting Matt back to Vancouver."

Michelle turned the car into a gravel pullout filled with potholes that looked long abandoned and put it in park. "You really are a stupid bitch, aren't you?" Her tone was casual, as if she were discussing dinner plans.

Gemma froze in her seat. What the hell was happening? What was Michelle doing? "What?"

Michelle shook her head. "You can't really think Morin was the brains behind all of this? The man was an idiot. He was decent at following orders, and excellent at collecting dirt on people, so he had his uses. Then you had to ruin everything. If Russell hadn't gone and told Morin about you, making it seem like you were part of his trusted inner circle . . . I told Morin that there was no way Molloy would have told you anything. That he was bragging to make Morin jealous. It wasn't enough. Morin was obsessed with the idea that you could expose him. Plus he was still pissed that you refused to barter with him back when you were living on the street. Then you got clean, escaped the life? Yeah, you were the one who got away from him. That man had a long memory."

Was Michelle talking about the time she'd bit Morin? Was that worth trying to kill her for? "So he wanted payback because I *bit* him? How does that concern you?" Gemma played dumb, trying to keep Michelle talking. She needed to buy time for Murphy to get her message and track her down. All she could do was pray they would reach her fast enough.

Michelle released her seat belt and stepped out of the car without answering. When she opened the door to the back seat, she had her service weapon in her hand. "He wanted to punish you for the bite. It left a nasty scar. He wanted you dead because he believed Russell had told you they were working together. I can't believe you still haven't figured it out. He thought you were so smart." Michelle's laugh was slightly unhinged.

"What are you talking about? Who thought I was smart?" Right now, Gemma felt like the idiot Michelle believed her to be. It was obvious that Michelle was involved in all of this, but what was her role? How did all the threads tie together?

Michelle's eyes glittered dangerously. "They *all* thought you were smart. Russell, Morin, even Foster fell for your act. I couldn't believe it when I heard Matt Foster, Mr. Straight and Narrow, was working on clearing your name while he was suspended. Then he disappeared with you, to keep you safe. I never thought he had it in him." Michelle looked Gemma over from head to toe.

Gemma wasn't immune to Michelle's contempt, but she wouldn't give Michelle the satisfaction of seeing her angry. People like Michelle had been looking down on her for most of her life. Responding to the baiting only gave them what they wanted.

"Then I saw the videos Russell made. Men will do strange things for a great fuck. Now quit stalling and get out of the car, and leave the dog inside. I'll deal with him after I'm done with you." She pointed the gun at Gemma.

Gemma fought the fear that the gun triggered. She'd escaped Morin, and she wasn't going to let Michelle win. Winter was growling deep in his throat as Gemma slid out of the car. She closed the door, being careful not to latch it. She wanted to give Winter a fighting chance to escape from Michelle. "I still don't understand why you care about any of this. You knew Morin was dirty, so why didn't you stop him? Or were you trying to get to someone higher than him?" Gemma moved slowly, always keeping the gun in her sight. She couldn't believe Michelle planned to shoot her with her police-issued weapon.

Not when Gemma was unarmed and no threat. The investigation would ruin Michelle's career.

Michelle lashed out faster than Gemma expected. Her hand smacked Gemma's cheekbone. White light exploded behind one eye as pain radiated across her face. Gemma stumbled back, crashing into the car.

"*I'm* the one calling the shots! I've been building this organization for over three decades, since my rookie year on the force. I'd collect dirt on cops, force them to work for me. I'd make deals with criminals, get them to work with me. Anyone who refused? Well, let's assume Russell's death isn't the first one I authorized, and it won't be the last." Michelle's smile was feral, her pride in her accomplishments in every word.

Gemma fought her rising terror. Not only was Michelle Chan an immoral sociopath, but she was clearly slightly delusional, and jealous of Gemma. Her only hope was to unbalance Michelle enough that she became erratic and gave Gemma a chance to run. Fighting wasn't a good option, so running and hiding until Murphy came after her was the best possibility. "You've been hiding in plain sight the whole time. Impressive. Too bad no one appreciates how much you've achieved. Sounds like neither Russell nor Morin really respected you," Gemma said, poking at Michelle's ego. "A woman in a man's world. No respect, no appreciation for your intelligence or skills. It can't have been easy." Gemma shuffled sideways against the car, trying to get in position to release Winter from the back seat.

"Exactly right. Men either thought I was too stupid or too weak. When I did prove to them I was smart enough and tough enough? That made me too powerful and emasculating, so then I was no longer desirable. There was no way to win! I either had to be weak and dependent, or be alone. In the end, I couldn't give up the power. You're the last little wrinkle I need to take care of. You caused me all kinds of trouble, and you need to pay for it." Michelle's hand was trembling as she held the gun on Gemma, her other hand searching her pocket and coming out with a hypodermic needle filled with liquid. "Unfortunately, you're going to have a relapse today. And unlucky you, the drugs you bought were contaminated. You're going to become another victim of the terrible toxic-drug crisis. Now get down on your knees."

Gemma shook her head back and forth wildly. "No. Besides, how will you explain how I got out here? How did I get away from you between the hospital and the station? What made me relapse after more than five years clean?" She was babbling, trying to distract Michelle as she reached for the handle of the door to release Winter.

"I'll think of something. Besides, you're nothing but a junkie whore. Who do you think they'll believe? Me or you?"

Michelle advanced. Gemma yanked on the car door handle and screamed at Winter. "Run, boy!" She twisted away from Michelle and ran.

Winter leaped out of the car. A thud sounded behind Gemma, and she pivoted to see Michelle on the ground with Winter standing on her chest. Michelle was struggling to get Winter off her, and the gun had been knocked out of her hand. Gemma picked it up and pointed it at Michelle as Winter kept her pinned, growling in her face. "Don't move."

Gemma tried to hold the gun steady. The fear-fuelled adrenaline was making her shake. She couldn't believe Winter had tackled Michelle to protect her. There was no time to let her guard down; she had to make sure Michelle couldn't get away.

Tires screeched, and Gemma looked up to see a black SUV peel into the pullout, scattering gravel and snow everywhere as it skidded to a halt. Relief filled Gemma as Murphy and Abel jumped out, turning to shock when Matt limped out of the back and hobbled across the parking lot to where she stood.

Gemma called off Winter, and Murphy and Abel each took one of Michelle's arms. They zip-tied her hands behind her and pushed her into the back of the car she'd driven Gemma out here in.

Matt pulled Gemma into his arms. "I thought I'd lost you." His lips captured hers, hot and demanding. Every emotion she felt—fear, love, relief, joy—were all echoed back at her in that kiss.

"Never." Gemma laughed through the tears streaking down her face. "I love you too much to ever let that happen."

Matt crushed her to his chest, peppering kisses over her face and neck. "I love you too. But we really need to stop doing this."

Gemma laughed. "Deal. Now let's get out of here."

EPILOGUE

hree months later

MATT LOOKED up from the stove as Gemma opened the door and practically bounced inside. "Good day?"

Gemma dropped her bag on a chair, rubbed Winter behind the ears, and then wrapped her arms around Matt. "The best. The clinic made it official. I'm now a full-time, permanent employee." A wide grin covered her face, and she released him and did a happy dance around the kitchen.

Matt had moved into Gemma's house as soon as they'd returned to Vancouver, neither one of them wanting to waste another minute apart after all they'd gone through. He'd resigned from the force days later, unwilling to be part of an organization that was riddled with corruption. Murphy's offer to join True North had made the decision incredibly easy. The team at TNS had welcomed him with open arms, making him feel at home immediately. Even though the corporate offices were located in Edmonton, TNS had members posted all over the country, and several of the remote employees had helped Matt get used to working for a decentralized organization.

Gemma had graduated from nursing school a few weeks after their return and had been doing a work-experience practicum at a specialized drug-treatment clinic newly opened in the heart of the DTES. The news that her position had been made permanent was something they had both been waiting for.

Matt switched off the burner under the pot of stew he'd been making for their dinner and picked Gemma up, twirling her around the room. "That's fantastic. I knew they would; you graduated at the top of your class. They would have been foolish not to snap you up." He lowered his head and nipped at Gemma's lower lip, sucking its fullness into his mouth.

Gemma let out a soft moan and buried her fingers in his hair, refusing to let him go. Her legs wrapped around his waist, the heat of her core pressing against him and making him throb. When she finally released him and pulled back, they were both panting, and he was already halfway down the hall leading to their bedroom.

Gemma swatted his shoulder playfully. "Slow down. I want to hear about your day."

Matt carried her into the bedroom and kicked the door closed. He lowered Gemma onto her back on the bed and climbed over her, trailing kisses over her exposed skin. "You're wearing too many clothes," he muttered as he worked at the buttons on her shirt. "And my day was boring. More depositions for the Crown about Michelle Chan and the Morin shooting."

The work Murphy and his team had done, particularly the work done by Jett to decode the data on Russell's USB, had led to hundreds of charges being laid against dozens of people. Michelle Chan was facing kidnapping and attempted murder for what she had done to Gemma, but there were scores of other charges against her. Multiple other officers at VPD had been fired and charged, and some of the biggest organized crime figures in Vancouver were finally being held accountable for their crimes. Morin's obsession with Gemma, and his

FALLING FOR THE ACCUSED

belief that Russell had shared secrets with her, had led to the collapse of major criminal networks. Both Matt and Gemma had given multiple statements and would be required to testify at more than one trial, but it looked like these charges would stick and Michelle and her minions would serve many years behind bars.

Gemma moaned when Matt finally dragged the now-open shirt over her shoulders and traced the lacy edge of her bra with his tongue, stopping long enough to tease each nipple through the delicate fabric.

He paused in his exploration of her body to drop one more piece of news he knew she was waiting for. "Then I came home and worked on the second bedroom to get it ready."

"Wait, what?" Gemma sat up and stared at him. "Were we approved?"

Ever since arriving back in Vancouver, he and Gemma had talked about working with a dog rescue as a foster family. They had submitted applications to the same program his parents worked with, and their home inspection had taken place the week before. A new pit bull needing a foster family had come in on the weekend, and they had offered to take him. Matt grinned at her and nodded. "The call came when I was giving my deposition, and they left a voicemail. If we still want to foster him, we can pick him up tomorrow."

"Tell me you said yes," she demanded.

Matt kissed her again. "Of course I did. I know how much we both want this."

Gemma squealed and pulled him close. "That's definitely something to celebrate. Let me show you how happy I am . . ."

WANT to read about when Rebecca met Nate? Sign up here for my newsletter and receive a free novella! You'll also to be the first to learn about new releases, get exclusive content, sneak peeks, and more.

And coming soon: Murphy's story. When television personality

Monica Durant is in danger, Murphy can't turn down the opportunity to keep her safe. But will she be willing to give him a second chance after the mistakes that were made in the past?

Reviews help other readers find my books! If you loved this book, please let everyone know by leaving a review.

ALSO BY KRISTY MALLORY

Dirty Money

When investigative reporter Billy Cameron accuses Harbourview Casino of laundering money, communications director Sam Bennett must do everything in her power to contain the story and protect the casino. Falling in love with her adversary was never part of the plan.

Dirty Secrets

Lawyer Chase Jeffries has been in love with his best friend's older sister Leslie Carpenter since he was sixteen. Now she's a whistleblower in trouble with the law, and has turned to him for help. Can he defend Leslie and convince her to give him a second chance at the same time?

Dirty Lies

When a dangerous man from Meg Wallis's past threatens her safety, the last thing she wants to do is get involved with high ranking MC gang member Daniel McKnight. What she doesn't know is that Daniel is working undercover, and the man menacing Meg could ruin his operation. Can Daniel keep them both alive and still bring the MC to justice?

ACKNOWLEDGMENTS

I started this book in August 2022, and now, after multiple rewrites and revisions, and a few significant life changes, it's finally ready for you, the readers.

When I started this book, it was supposed to be book five in my Harbourview Casino series, but it quickly took a dark turn, and I was already thinking about writing a series about a security firm. This seemed like the perfect place to launch True North Security.

As always, I could not have done this without my support network:

My editors, Dawn and James. I really made them work with this book!

My writing community, who keep me motivated and inspired when I start thinking I should give up.

My husband, who continues to believe and encourage, even when he doesn't understand.

And to you, my readers, who asked me to give Matt his own HEA. I hope you love Gemma as much as I do.

Kristy
May 2025

ABOUT THE AUTHOR

Kristy Mallory is a Canadian author writing contemporary romance. She lives in the Vancouver, British Columbia area with her family and dogs, and most days can be found working on her next book or planning her next trip. This is the first book in Kristy's True North Security series.

Stay connected with Kristy by subscribing to her newsletter, to learn about new releases, see early cover reveals, and more!

Manufactured by Amazon.ca
Acheson, AB